West Is San Francisco

By Lauren Sapala

Also by Lauren Sapala

Nonfiction

The INFJ Writer:
Cracking the Creative Genius of the World's Rarest Type

Firefly Magic:
Heart Powered Marketing for Highly Sensitive Writers

Fiction

Between the Shadow and Lo
(Book One of the West Coast Trilogy)

For my Papa,
who taught me how to tell a good story.

If you're going to try, go all the way. Otherwise, don't even start. This could mean losing girlfriends, wives, relatives and maybe even your mind. It could mean not eating for three or four days. It could mean freezing on a park bench. It could mean jail. It could mean derision. It could mean mockery—isolation. Isolation is the gift. All the others are a test of your endurance, of how much you really want to do it. And, you'll do it, despite rejection and the worst odds. And it will be better than anything else you can imagine. If you're going to try, go all the way. There is no other feeling like that. You will be alone with the gods, and the nights will flame with fire. You will ride life straight to perfect laughter. It's the only good fight there is.

—Charles Bukowski

It's an odd thing, but anyone who disappears is said to be seen in San Francisco. It must be a delightful city and possess all the attractions of the next world.

—Oscar Wilde

East is East, and West is San Francisco.

—O. Henry

Prologue

Before I moved again, before I took off running from Seattle, I felt death beside me.

It wasn't the Grim Reaper; there was no long black robe, no grinning skull face, no scythe ready to cut me down. Death, instead, approached shyly. Padding up on four soft paws, like a cat, death waited for me to call to it, to give it invitation to jump in my lap. Death wanted me to put my hands on it, and to love it. Most of all though, death wanted me to listen.

But I didn't want to hear.

Like almost everyone else, I thought death was out to get me. I had been taught that death was a ruthless killer; a heartless assassin. I had been told that death showed no compassion and no mercy. I had been programmed to believe that death was The End, and not just an ending.

So, when I felt death steal up close beside me, when I heard death breathing next to me and felt it take my hand, I shrank away. I was terrified, and I ran.

From Seattle, I decided to go south, down to San Francisco. Because even though I was already on the West Coast, something told me that San Francisco was even further west, that San Francisco, in its own way, was the Land of the West, and that it was only there that

I would find something else that I needed to get where I was going.

The sun sets every evening in the west, its light dying slowly every day until black night overtakes it. And countless pioneers had made their way west—like everyone else, I learned that in school—a lot of them dying on the way there too. So, if death resolved to find me again, if it decided that I was worth waiting for, that someday I might have strength enough to listen, then it stood to reason that it would most likely be waiting for me in the west. It would probably kill time in San Francisco until I showed up there and it could kill me.

But still, something drew me on anyway.

1

I left Seattle in the autumn of 2004. I'd spent the last four years working in a bookstore by day and drinking myself to the edge and back in the city's seedier bars by night. I'd worked my way through different people and various strains of hard liquor until I hit the wall. Now, my prospects were thin. My new boyfriend James—who still somehow believed I was a halfway decent person—was willing to take a chance and move to San Francisco with me. Our plan was that I would get there first and then he would join me two months later, which would give him time to wrap up his life in Seattle. Having burned all my bridges, I had nothing left to wrap up.

I arrived in San Francisco early one chilly autumn morning. Before I left Seattle, I'd found a room in a house in the Mission District advertised on Craigslist. When I got there, I found that the room was on the second floor of a tall, faded Victorian. Red and gray paint flaked around the doorway and a steep dark staircase wound upward until it emptied out into a long dark hallway above. The hall was lined with doors that led into different rooms, and at the very end I found a big airy kitchen, painted a bright sunshine yellow and facing a yard choked with weeds in the back. A small balcony hung off the kitchen, the perfect place to stand and smoke cigarettes in the sun.

My room included hardwood floors and windows that stretched almost all the way to the high ceilings. As I stepped inside the room for the first time, I looked out those windows and saw two people sleeping at the foot of a mailbox on the corner, sharing the same sleeping bag. Matted hair frowsed out of the top. I couldn't tell if it was a man and woman or maybe two women. The people were one unit now, melded together, snoring in unison in the lemon-yellow morning sun. They looked warm.

I looked over and saw that one wall of my room was made up of a pair of French doors set with stained glass. Shadow shapes moved behind the glass as I stepped closer. It wasn't a trick of the light. I could see the silhouettes of two people moving around. As I watched them, I also realized I could hear them talking. It sounded like they were bickering in Spanish. I turned back to the window, letting my eyes rest on the couple in the sleeping bag on the sidewalk. Cars screeched by and a group of boys passed on foot, hollering at each other at the top of their lungs.

Over the next few weeks I explored the neighborhood. My room was on Utah Street, right down from 24th and near SF General Hospital. There was a bar on the corner called Jack's Place that I liked because of the name, and because they hosted bands that played mariachi music, which floated down the block and up into my window every night. The melody accompanied the bickering couple over in the next room nicely.

I quickly found out that in the Mission every sign was in English, and Spanish. Every bakery was a *panadería* and every butcher was a *carnicería*. 24th Street was long and shady, overhung with leafy trees that twisted their way to the upper floors of brightly painted Victorians, rooming houses like mine. Storefront churches folded back from the sidewalk, vibrating with the songs of performers on stages inside that I could see from the street. Murals—blue and purple, orange and green and gold—leapt off the walls of buildings and into my eyes. Young Latina women with kids in strollers walked by, murmuring in Spanish as they passed.

At the end of that October it seemed like it was always sunny and my room was a box that held the warm days. When no one else was around, I sometimes stepped out to the back balcony and sipped on a can of beer, looking out over the city. Jack Kerouac had been right—San Francisco was a city of white hills. *City of gold*, I thought to myself. City of sun.

In the evenings, when I was drunk enough, I left the house and went looking for new friends. I tried to start conversations in Spanish with the gangsters hanging around outside the bars but I didn't know anything beyond the basic few words. I couldn't string together a full sentence. The gangsters laughed at me but all of them were kind. I left them shaking their heads, still laughing, as I stumbled off toward someplace else.

The language barrier didn't stop me from getting to know a guy named Cuba who only spoke Spanish and lived just down the block. With furious intensity, he'd point at himself and repeat loudly, "Koo-BAH! Koo-BAH!" I was never sure if he was telling me that his *name* was Cuba or that he was *from* Cuba, but when I called him that he smiled and seemed satisfied. At least he stopped pointing to himself and yelling at me about it.

I stopped by Cuba's apartment most nights, a ground-floor room right across from Jack's Place with the mariachi music, and sat with him, watching the parade of people as they came and went from his apartment. Some sat down to play a hand of cards with Cuba, some only stayed long enough to swig from the bottle between us. I sat and listened as they went back and forth in Spanish and tried to pick some of it up. When I got tired of trying to follow the conversation I stared out the window, through the iron bars to the warm street beyond. The sidewalk was never empty.

When I got weary of the streets and Cuba wasn't home, I stayed inside, drinking six-packs in my room. I crushed the cans when I was done and hid them in a garbage bag in my closet.

That was at night. During the day I looked for a job.

I didn't really care what I ended up doing, but I had to do something. Something that paid money. I was fast running out. I had some resumes printed up at a copy center and put together three outfits that looked vaguely responsible and not so slutty. Then I rode the bus out of the Mission uptown to the Marina, where there were shops that hired girls who looked vaguely responsible and not so slutty.

Traveling the few miles between the Mission and the Marina was like traveling between different planets. Mornings in the Mission were bathed in a hot yellow haze. Jewel-shine blue skies twinkled outside my window and leafy green-gold shadows danced over the sidewalks. I walked through warm shaded streets, watching the warm dark eyes that passed me intently, as multi-colored sparkles of Spanish sifted over my head. At the bus stop I waited with women pulling grocery or laundry carts behind them with a powerful flexing of their small brown arms.

When I got off the bus at Union Street I walked down the hill until I got to the Marina. It was 10 to 15 degrees cooler on the northern side of the city, and as the sun argued with the fog the sky went from gray to white, back to gray again. Elegant shops decorated the main street, with display windows that retreated tastefully into the background. Even the mannequins looked haughty. The people I passed on the sidewalks didn't look at me.

I went from store to store, handing out resumes and asking if the manager was in, until I got a bite from a boutique that sold Armani. The woman at the counter took me into the back to meet the person in charge of hiring, a dapper little man who wore a perfectly ironed shirt and expensive cufflinks that winked condescendingly at me. He asked the standard questions about my retail experience, clean whiffs of soap and starch wafting toward me every time he leaned over the desk between us. I wondered if I smelled like beer and something else undetermined—a faint scent of unreliable, maybe. The dapper man told me that at least twenty percent of all employees' pay went toward the purchase of Armani clothes. Then he paused. Too late, I realized he was watching me, waiting for my expected burst of pleased surprise. Too late, I started in my chair, widening my eyes under his narrow gaze.

"What? Oh! Oh WOW! How...cool..." I tried, but then faltered. It was hard to argue with too late.

"Yes. Yes. Very cool. Yes. Well, we'll call you. Thanks." And suddenly the interview was over, snapped shut like a fan. The cufflinks flashed at me again as he stood. The cruel lines in his perfectly ironed collar pushed me politely out the door and, in a moment, I was out on the street again.

The next interview I snagged was at a boutique called Georgio. With its bright fluorescent lights and huge empty corners, it looked like a store that should be in a mall. The girls working there looked like they should be in a Britney Spears video. I sat and waited in a hot-pink plush chair near the door. The skinny salesgirl with cocker spaniel hair assured me the manager would be there soon and went back to cooing at the few customers I saw milling around. They all looked bored. I went back to watching the door.

45 minutes later a woman barreled past me and hustled up to the counter. I knew she was the manager from the way she bent over the salesgirl, like she was used to bossing her around. The salesgirl pointed at me and then I saw her hand over my resume. She took it from the girl without looking at her and headed back my way.

The manager had hair that had been brushed into a rigid updo and looked like it was held in place with a lot of gel. She was pudgy, wearing clothes that had probably fit her years ago, and her mouth was one hard line that seemed to be held in a permanent angry frown. When she sat down in front of me the short skirt on her canvas dress flapped up, showing me dimpled white thighs. Sad all of a sudden, I lifted my eyes back to her face. I could hear her breathing in hard little snorts.

"Hiiiii....Leah." She glanced down at my resume to get the name.

"Hi." I said, and held out my hand. She touched it briefly and then looked back down at the paper. Handshaking was done.

After the standard Q&A—*What would you say is your best quality? What's your worst?* I frowned, looking as if I were genuinely trying to come up with something shitty to say about myself—we chatted about the neighborhood.

"I'm sure you've noticed, but Union Street is *very* current." She pronounced it like a judgment. Like I should have been watching this latest development all along.

"Uh, yeah." I answered slowly. "It does seem pretty trendy."

"Trendy?" she snorted. "You do realize that some of the best-dressed women in the *world* walk down this street every single day?" She said 'world' like it had three syllables and leaned in toward me. I flicked my eyes out the window, catching sight of two more coat-hanger girls passing by. They looked almost identical to each other. And I couldn't tell them apart from the salesgirl I'd seen earlier. I looked back at the manager and her faded canvas dress. Once it had probably been a deep violet, now it was more of a washed lilac. And it really was too short for her, the flesh above her knees jiggled, the dimples on the side of each kneecap winking at me obscenely every time she moved.

"Wow. How cool." I said without feeling. I started to get up.

"Yes. Very cool. Very cool." she snapped. We were done.

"How will I know...?" I trailed off, limply raising a hand.

"I'll talk with Georgio *himself* and if he likes your qualifications we'll give you a call." Then she was gone, her ample ass wagging at me as she disappeared toward the back. I stood and pondered the idea that Georgio was actually a person, a man who designed all the ridiculous beaded clothes around me and then got all these surreal waifs to sell them to other people. I shuddered and walked out.

●●●

Sometimes when I drank at night I sat in my room and watched the tiny old TV I'd brought with me from Seattle. The antenna only got one or two channels. To make a bed for myself, I'd used all my boxes of books, packing them strategically in a big square shape and then throwing the old futon I used as a mattress over the whole thing. It was working out all right, except for the fact that it was bumpy on one side due to a couple boxes full of swollen, water-damaged paperbacks.

The state of the empties piling up in my closet, however, was not good at all.

When you're a full-time serious drunk, empties become a longstanding problem. They pile up fast, right under your nose, and you can't believe one person could use that much of anything. Empties aren't just garbage, they're evidence. Evidence of how much you use and so therefore evidence of what you are. Like corpses heaping up in exponential proportion, they force you into the business of digging mass graves.

I usually got mine out mid-morning. Most of the other people in the house were at work and so they weren't there to hear the clinking of the garbage bags as I dragged them down the back stairs. That's another thing about empties—they never shut up. Empties voice their accusations for all to hear the second you try to move them from Point A to Point B. You know that absolutely every single person on the block hears that *clank-clink-tink-tank* down the stairs and thinks to themselves: *alkie-alkie-alkie.*

In between dealing with the empties, I still kept up the job hunt in the Marina.

My third interview was at a store for runners and triathletes called 'MetroSpeed.' I stumbled across it one afternoon when I decided to take a detour down a side street to get away from the constant stream of yuppies up on the main drag. I saw a small 'Help Wanted' sign in the window and decided to go for it. I had nothing left to lose.

Hesitantly, I pushed the front door open. My eyes immediately struggled to adjust to the dimness inside and I thought for the millionth time just how fucking bright it was in California compared to Seattle. Once I got a paying job I'd need to buy some sunglasses for sure.

There was one old guy at the counter who looked like he could care less. Clean, crisp Nike shorts hung on one wall, and racks were filled with what looked like the same exact white sports top in different expensive brands. Shoes lined another wall, the pedestals they sat on jutted out like handholds at the rock-climbing barn. Faint music drifted from somewhere above. The old guy behind the counter continued studying his newspaper.

Except for him, the place was empty.

I cleared my throat. He didn't look up.

"Hello?" I said. I thought I saw an eyebrow lift, maybe, but he kept looking down at the paper. "Um...are you guys hiring?"

The old guy finally looked up. He squinted at me from behind a pair of glasses on a lanyard around his neck. I thought there was probably a whistle somewhere on it too. He looked like a PE teacher type. Disgustedly, he shook his head and then turned toward the back.

"Hernan! Girl here for you!"

Instantly, the person I could only assume was Hernan stepped out like he'd been waiting there all along for his cue to walk on stage. Tall and handsome, he had coffee-with-lots-of-cream skin and huge dark eyes. He walked out almost shyly and gave me a gentle smile, but his grace was offset by a hooked nose that looked dangerous, like maybe he had ancestors who'd disemboweled people with machetes in the jungle. His black hair waved back from his high forehead in proud dips and swells. I looked down at his neat khakis, ironed and spotless.

Hernan led me to the coffee shop next door and we settled into seats at a café table on the sidewalk. As I shaded my eyes from the sun he asked me where I was from, and where I was living now.

"Well, I moved here from Seattle. But I live in the Mission."

Hernan's eyes went up like a house on fire.

"Really!" he said. "Where?"

"24th and Utah." I answered, ducking around to the other side of the table to get away from the sun.

"What do you think of the neighborhood so far?"

"I love it." I said simply. Then I shut up. If he was looking for me to dog on the sketch side of the neighborhood he was going to be disappointed.

"Dude!" he said, jumping a little in his seat. "I live at 23rd and Capp!" I stopped ducking the sun for a moment, too surprised to do anything but stare. "Yeah," he laughed. "I grew up in the Mission. Lived there my whole life. I still live there, with my mom and my sister." He leaned back in his chair and laughed again, like we were old high school friends who'd just run into each other. Then he told me the best place to get a burrito and where to find the most delicious *pupusas*. Hernan's mom was from El Salvador and his dad was from Peru. He'd grown up in San Francisco, went to Sacred Heart Catholic School and spoke both Spanish and English fluently. Now, he was managing MetroSpeed while he studied to be a history professor.

After 20 minutes I decided to interrupt him. While Hernan had been telling me all about the Mission he hadn't asked me one interview question. I wondered if we should get the show going.

"Um, did you want to—?" I started.

"Oh! Jeez! Yeah—" He smacked himself on the forehead and laughed again. "I almost forgot." I took a deep breath. I hated interviews, even with nice guys.

"Let's get you started on the paperwork." he said, and pushed his chair back.

"Huh?" The sun had been in my eyes for almost half an hour now. I couldn't be sure I wasn't suffering from heatstroke. Had I missed something?

"You can start on Monday, right?" he asked.

I ducked around to his other side. The sun was finally out of my eyes and I could see again.

"Yes." I said, smiling. "Definitely."

2

I worked every shift Hernan could give me at MetroSpeed. In the early afternoon, I got off the bus in the Marina and walked along cold bright streets that formed a clean grid, eventually leading to the gray water of the Bay. At night, when I got off work and walked back to the bus stop, the thick white batting of fog enveloped me. I'd never encountered fog like this before. It wasn't a cloud low on the ground. It was a giant hand that grabbed and pushed at me, wanting more. Street signs swam in and out of the mist like otherworldly beacons. I had the feeling of going slowly blind and I finally understood the life-and-death importance of foghorns.

When I got off the bus an hour later in the Mission I stepped down into a different world. The air was clear and had an edge of warmth to it. Like leather seats in a car hold the heat imprint of the person who sat there last, the air in the Mission held onto some warm part of everyone who passed through it. People clustered outside bars, chattering fast in Spanish and English. Mariachi bands made up of Latino grandfathers in sombreros with sorrowful faces got off the bus with me, their instruments clanking as they made their way down the steps and onto the sidewalk. Guys in bandannas danced on street corners and rapped in Spanglish, one eyelid flickering toward me almost unseen, giving me the once-over as I passed. Frenetic charged particles hung over small crowds like lightning waiting to strike.

Every night I stopped into the little mom-and-pop party store down the block from my place to pick up a six-pack and a bottle. I came out squeezing the crinkly paper bag to my chest and then ducked into an alley to zip the cans and the bottle into my backpack. With a couple of t-shirts kept for this purpose, I padded the bottle and wove more fabric in between the cans. The woman who managed the house I lived in had made it clear that she didn't want partiers as tenants. So, I was careful to do the bag-to-backpack switch every night. No clinking allowed.

I'd gotten my routine with the empties down too, but getting them out of the house was still pretty unpleasant. Dealing with the huge garbage bag as I traipsed down the back steps was gross. It more often than not leaked, and one corner was always soft, almost obscene, like a tiny water balloon, where all the leftover liquid had drained. Even worse was the neck of the bag, clutched into a crushed bundle by my sweaty palm. If I let it go for half a second to adjust my grip I'd feel another grotesque tenderness—the feathery gentle fluttering of cockroach antennae as it quivered across the top of my hand. If I opened my palm completely they poured out of the bag.

●●●

The crew at MetroSpeed was made up of Hernan, who was the manager; Benito, a gentle soul from Guatemala; and Lou and Len, the two stringy old runners who worked the morning shift. Lou was the one I'd seen at my interview.

Benito was nicknamed 'Beet' and during our afternoon shift with Hernan he told us stories about Guatemala. He said he started drinking coffee at age five and that he'd been stabbed every day that he walked to school.

"Stabbed!" Hernan broke in. "What do you mean stabbed *puta*?" He elbowed Beet in the ribs and grinned.

"I deed, man." Beet looked at both of us and blinked slowly, as if only just now remembering where he was. Then his good-natured face broke into a wide smile. "I deed," he repeated. "Every day I got stabbed, man, six years old on the way to school. Every day. I deed." All three of us broke up laughing.

Hernan told us stories about the Mission. He said it used to be really bad, in the 1980s when he was just a kid. The neighborhood had been ruled by gangs. The *Norteños* and *Sureños* owned the streets, drive-bys happened every day. Hernan said he turned into a straight-A student and a bookworm because after the last bell rang, he ran home fast, dodging fists and bullets and flying saliva, and then spent the rest of the day reading.

Hernan had read almost everything. Hemingway and Jack London, and piles and piles of South American history. He started teaching me about Cuba, about Fidel Castro and Che Guevara, about what a revolution really was, what it meant and how it was organized. In between waiting on customers, I saw flashes in the jungle, shadow shapes crouched down in the brush, blobs that grew into Hernan and Benito, carrying rifles and packs on their backs. Whispering to each other and exchanging secret war looks, they wore black berets and military fatigues.

Some nights Hernan and Beet took me to their favorite spot, a bar in North Beach called the Cigarillo. Half the place was a patio and the other half a dance floor. The Cigarillo hosted live bands that played salsa and Latin jazz. Because of the heat generated from sweaty bodies dancing to the constant *thrump* of the drums, every door was always wide open, sucking in the fog, trapping the cold air in pockets around the large open rooms. I was always either sweating my ass off or freezing, at the Cigarillo there was no in-between.

By the time I got to San Francisco I'd been drinking hard for seven straight years. It's impossible not to let a thing like that spill over the edges of your life and onto other people. After our nights at the Cigarillo, I started calling in sick to work. If I didn't call in sick I came to work sick. Hernan and Beet just thought I drank a lot. I didn't plan on spelling it out for them. If I didn't have a steady source of income I wasn't going to be able to find a place to live for me and James. So, I needed that job. But I was fucking it up already.

●●●

When I met my boyfriend James I had been coming off a rough four years. I'd had my heart broken by the guy I'd moved to Seattle for, and then systematically worked my way through a long list of random men, taking my pound of flesh from each of them in what I felt was rightful payment for the way the first guy had annihilated me. When I met James, I'd been more lost than ever, down-to-the-bone weary, and almost out of hope.

But James was different. He was a person like me. Scarred and cynical, but a survivor. He drank just as much as I did but handled it better, mostly. He frequently blacked out, but somehow managed to stay out of trouble and out of jail. Looking back over the past year before I'd left Seattle, I couldn't say the same for myself.

James was also honest. When he gave his word, he meant it. Before I'd left Seattle, we'd sat one morning at a run-down casino on the side of Highway 99 drinking whisky and James had pulled out his wallet and then pulled two locks of hair from one of the inner folds. When I asked him to explain, he told me about how he had taken care of both his grandparents when they were dying. He'd made a promise to himself to be there for them, and so when they'd needed someone to change diapers and administer medication around the clock, James had unhesitatingly volunteered.

I thought about how terrible it had been at the end for my mom when she was dying of cancer. I knew firsthand that death was never easy on anyone involved. It was messy, and terrifying. And it could wipe out every emotional resource you'd ever counted on in two seconds flat. I looked back at James sitting across the table from me, one hand fisted around his tumbler of whisky, the other delicately balancing the two locks of hair.

I knew this was the man for me.

●●●

When James showed up in December I was finally able to move out of the rooming house in the Mission. I'd held out long enough at MetroSpeed to keep a steady paycheck and use Hernan's help as a reference in finding an apartment for just the two of us. I located a flat on the top floor of a Victorian near Divisadero Street. The house was three stories high and the color of beach-faded gray clapboard. Our flat was so dim and tunnel-like that it felt to me like someone had plunked down one long train car on top of the building. A tiny cramped hall functioned as the entryway and all the windows were mostly on one side and faced the building next door. The buildings were so close together that if I leaned an arm out I could touch the dirty scaly sides of our neighbor's house. At the end was the kitchen and—just like at my old place—it was the only room that got any sun. The light oozed in, red and bleak, when it sank down into the west every evening.

The place was dingy and the steps to the third floor were steep, old and wooden and creaky. Once I got up them I didn't want to deal with them again so fast. It was easy to trip going down, like the steps had it in for me sometimes.

When James got into town we started drinking more than ever. I blacked out almost every night. Drunk and lonely, I called Bret, Cassady, and Sadie, my old friends from Seattle. Bret was carrying on without me, Cassady was still partying every night herself, and Sadie had moved to Chicago and now sat huddled in her own cold apartment. She'd never been to the Midwest before, the snow in Chicago baffled and scared her.

I felt the same way about the fog.

But talking to them wasn't the same. Sadie was the only one who somewhat understood, because it was happening to her too. For Bret and Cassady, nothing had changed. But I was out of Seattle now. I was enveloped in fog in San Francisco. I was trapped in a train car on top of a house.

My blackouts came on like a mob of angry black flies now, and after only a few drinks. I got sloppy. I dropped things and fell, a lot. My motor skills turned into lumpy gray sludge whenever I tried to hold onto objects or follow anything with my eyes. I couldn't keep track of one sentence to the next, mine or anyone else's. Blood vessels broke daily, one spread into a pool of raw red spiderweb under my left eye, little ones burst open on my cheeks, and one or two marked the bridge of my nose, like tiny crosses made out of capillaries.

For Christmas, James and I got a bottle. When we woke up that morning the San Francisco sun poured into the kitchen, its bright chilled edges spilling over all the windowsills, and we looked out and saw the empty streets, the way they always are on Christmas.

I spent the rest of the day on the couch, drinking off the fifth until I blacked out.

3

In the spring of 2005—St. Patrick's Day to be exact—I quit drinking.

Quit is a funny word. Kicked is more like it. Like kicking heroin, I kicked drinking. I fell down, and at first it looked like I was dead. At first, I thought I *was* dead. But then I kicked.

My first stop that morning was an Irish pub downtown. When I got there, I scanned the crowd quick and then sat at one end of the bar. Two guys in suits immediately flanked me. Their ties were beige, soft and bland, their ring fingers marked with gold wedding bands. They had hands like bankers, and boyish hard faces like cops. Finance guys on lunch who'd stopped in for a green beer before they got back to the office to kick polished loafers up on desks and cut smooth deals over the phone. I convinced them to stay. Then I got us all a round.

At 2:00pm the suits called their boss to beg the day off. He gave it to them and then came down to the bar himself. Now he swayed over me drunk, smiling and almost sinister, black shadows leaking from his eyes.

Day passed and then paused, hesitating to go on. Day blushed and tripped over itself, then looped back around. Suddenly it was late afternoon and we were outside, at a block party, crushed between what felt like thousands of bodies and hemmed in by that yellow tape city officials always put up to contain the crowd. I was still with the two suits and one of them held a paper cup of beer.

"So I sez, fucking Christ I know I fucked the stripper night before m'wedding, but for fucking Chrissakes I wasn't married yet...God, I mean what a fucking bitch, yeah?"

The suit burped and sloshed toward me. He winked, gross and in slow motion.

Time, tired of me altogether, gave up. Day moved on without me.

Then it was night. I was in an alley, a fun dream alley. I saw little colored lanterns strung up and down between two cozy brick buildings. Neat black tables and chairs dotted the skinny sidewalk in between. There sure were a lot of people around. Everyone was laughing, having a good time. Two bobbly shamrocks sprung from my head and I was covered in green glitter, like a St. Patrick's Day alien. I also had two friends with me, one fat and one small, two happy guys with friendly bald heads and shiny drunk faces. I told a joke and they laughed hysterically. At some point I must have been transported onto this plane, into a different dimension. As with all inter-dimensional transport, I had no memory of the *before*, of the getting-there-logistics, and no idea or expectations concerning the future. For all I knew there was no future in this dimension.

Then dark night, late night. Party over. I started the walk home. It was me and the street. The fog was back. There were no stars. I had to get home. I was close to the end. My body was like a cell phone that was going to die any time now. And I was on the phone myself, on this long walk home, talking to someone. I didn't know who, I couldn't hear them.

Then I died.

In all that night with no stars, through the fog and all that lost time, between dimensions—somewhere in there—I died.

And then I woke up.

Inventory of pain: My head throbbed, my stomach was tied up in angry knots. But my arm—my ARM—was SCREAMING. I couldn't move it—ah, there—I could. Barely. I risked looking down at the maybe (dead) broken arm. My palm hanging at the end looked like dried out hamburger meat.

It appeared there had been a fall.

I rolled over, keeping my arm stiff and straight. It hurt to breathe.

Shafts of pale sunlight filtered in through our murky bedroom window. James was lying in bed beside me, on his back and wide awake. He stared up at the ceiling, his face blank and unbreakable like a cold tile floor.

"Hey..." The voice that came out of me was a mangled (maybe dead) croak. I cleared my throat and swallowed rust. "I must have...eh, hum...must have grabbed a cab..."

Gingerly I lifted myself off the bed and swung my legs to the floor. I cradled my arm like it was an infant's corpse. It was still warm.

James didn't move.

I let my eyes rest on the bedroom door and tried again.

"Uh...did I? Do you know? I mean—about the cab..." I turned halfway toward him before my arm stopped me.

"A woman brought you home. She found you on the street." He paused and then:

"The cops were here."

I winced, more out of habit than anything else, a habit long ago formed out of vague obligation. I knew I was supposed to wince. Wincing, I didn't feel anything. Not even the contraction of my face.

"You were yelling—screaming—throwing things," James continued. "They thought I was beating you, the neighbors did." I heard the almost imperceptible shake in his voice. And then he sighed, like he was beyond tired. Like maybe he was dead too.

"I tried to put you to bed, tried giving you water...you were in bed when the cops came...and then...I talked to them, explained—sort of about you—and then..." He paused again and I smelled gunpowder in the silence. "Then you were all of sudden *there* goddamnit, really fast before I knew it, you busted out of the bedroom. You kicked open the fucking door and there you were, in your panties and totally gone, fucking wasted. You fucking shook your ass in the cop's face and you laughed and laughed. Like you were so fucking proud of yourself and you were. You really were."

He stopped suddenly, all the air going out of him. But I knew he wasn't finished. I knew myself too well for that. I turned and looked at him. I saw his eyes, still open but locked up now. Fortressed against me.

"And?" I had to know.

"You asked him to spank you. You laughed and laughed like an insane person and you asked the cop to spank you." Like a slot machine, James's eyes rolled back up to the ceiling. I was dismissed, maybe forever.

"Fucking stop, Leah. Fucking stop or I'm out. For good."

And of all the times to be reminded, I remembered why James was the first man I'd loved in a long, long time.

Because he always meant what he said.

●●●

I couldn't call in sick to work, not again. I'd bailed on Hernan too many times to count. I wanted to kill myself but I still had to go. So, I pushed on, not pushing death off of me, but moving forward underneath it.

I puked on myself in the shower and then collapsed on the floor and watched the clotted slimy ropes of bright yellow phlegm weave their way down the drain like lazy worms. I walked to work and puked in the bushes on the way there. Almost every big fancy house I passed in Pacific Heights had a big fancy hedge, and I left almost every one with a sliver of radioactive worm on it.

When I got to work things got shitty.

The moment I got in the door Hernan bolted. His mind already off to the place he had to be, he barely noticed the half dead way I dragged myself to the counter. He didn't notice at all that I was actually half dead.

It was almost noon. Lou—who was, as it turned out, a track coach—had agreed to stay for the early part of the afternoon to cover for Hernan. Beet was supposed to be in at 4:00pm to relieve him. Until then it was just me and Lou.

Hernan might have missed the way I looked—and smelled—but Lou didn't. He squinted at me hard, like Clint Eastwood in an old Western, and then took a long sniff. I saw his nostrils flare and heard the sniff, long and dry, sounding like judgment. I couldn't look at him. I ran for the bathroom.

I was all out of puke, my ribcage aching like I'd been gashed in both sides and the back of my throat raw, but I sat huddled in front of the toilet anyway, taking comfort in the cold floor and the temporary silence all around me. I leaned my head forward slowly and let it rest on the seat. I was so tired that I didn't even care whose ass imprint my forehead was resting on at the moment.

Then I passed out, I think. There was no going. Only a coming awake again, a *coming to* inside of a new reality. It fit so perfectly with the rest of my life I accepted it completely. No exit, only more doors.

When I woke up I was lying flat on the floor of the MetroSpeed bathroom, the toilet looming above me. I lifted my good hand and ran it down my forehead, my nose and cheeks, like my face belonged to someone else. Someone who had just died in a makeshift hospital in the jungle. Someone who was cold and slimy, and smelled like sour rotting whisky.

I had no idea how long I'd been out. I was pretty sure that Lou hadn't come to check on me, and he probably wouldn't even if I stayed back here for the rest of the day. I'd seen the look in his eyes and felt the sniff. Lou had already decided not to waste any more time on me.

After last night, James was seriously thinking about leaving. Other than Hernan and Beet, I didn't know anyone else in San Francisco. My threadbare connections in the City were mere cobwebs. They would dissolve like sugar in hot water the minute I threw any heat on them.

But I couldn't go back to Seattle either.

I still had good friends there, yeah, but they were tired of me too. And what would it be—a few days of couch surfing and then what? *Yeah, then what Leah?* chirped a gleeful wicked voice at the back of my mind. *Then what? Then what? Then what?* If I went back to Seattle I already knew there was a decent chance I'd end up like my friend Tom, a good guy who had turned into a meth head, falling so far into addiction and despair that he couldn't pull himself out again. As far as I knew, Tom was probably still wandering the rainy streets of Seattle, a pain-wracked howling ghost of his former self.

I stared at the ceiling, too numb to care anymore, and closed my eyes. I felt the soft petals of violets flutter down from somewhere above. They ate through my flesh as they landed on my skin. My face upturned, I remained quiet and still, surrendering to the downiest of shrouds, waiting for it to be over.

But then, a memory.

I remembered being eight years old, surrounded by people slowly dissolving into despair. No one would tell me anything, not really. I had no idea what was happening, only that things were bad, very bad. And everyone was in pain. I felt like how I imagined an animal in a steel trap must feel, stoically considering the option of gnawing off its own leg. I had to get away. The pain and the despair would kill me. But I was only eight years old and there was nowhere to go.

I dreamed at that time of being an escape artist. I dreamed of being a magic man like Houdini, who could be trussed up with ropes and chains and padlocks, hands tied and eyes covered to make him helpless and blind, locked up in caskets and trunks and immersed in water behind glass walls, who could go through all of that and always, *always* work himself free again.

Since that time, I'd found many more prisons. I broke in and then broke out again. I built traps, pushed myself into them, and then broke free. I broke through things, so many things, just to feel them break. All my life I'd played at escape artist.

The memory of this knowledge dragged me up, off the floor. Wilted petals sloughed off me like flakes of dead skin, dandruff with the weight of salt. I pulled myself all the way up to a sitting position and shook off the remaining bits of flower that clung to my hair.

I knew I had two options now. Up or down.

If I went down, it was going to be for real this time. If I wanted the gutter, that would be easy. I'd been on my way there for seven years now. It was only in the past couple that I'd hired a driver to get me there all the faster.

But I couldn't go up either. Up meant I had to quit drinking. Forever. That meant the rest of my life. That could be 30 years, but what if it was 50? What if I turned out to be one of those crazy little senior citizens who against all odds makes it to 95 or 100? It could possibly be more than 50 years, and I'd have to live every single one of those days dry.

I felt like I might faint.

Forever was out of the question. But I had to give up something. I knew how these kinds of traps worked. I had to gnaw *something* off to get free again. So, I would give something, yes. I would agree. Not to forever, but to a very long time.

One year.

I would quit drinking for one year. It would put a little distance between James and this latest debacle, but most importantly, it would convince everyone that I *could* quit. That I could do it if I wanted to. Someone who goes a whole year without drinking is very definitely not an alcoholic. Not with that long healthy year, swollen and wholesome, swinging from under her belt. Alcoholics do not carry years on their skinny (or bloated) frames, not whole ones. Nothing alcoholics carry is intact.

If I made it a year I would have irrefutable proof. I was no alcoholic.

Only, I *was* an alcoholic. And I knew that. Sitting in that bathroom, it was actually the only thing I was completely sure of. But I didn't need to prove to myself that I wasn't an alcoholic, it was everyone else—most especially James—that I had to get around.

All right, one year, I said, and was surprised that I'd said it out loud.

One year.

Escape I would, the outcome was on its way. But just like when I was a kid, dreaming of being Houdini, I had to be patient. I had to go deep inside myself and wait for the opportunity to break out of my imagined cage. And when the time came, like Houdini, I wouldn't burst so much as blossom forth from my chains, a magic vanquisher of water and steel.

●●●

Beet was the first person I told, since he was the first person I ran into after leaving the bathroom. Lou had gone home. He listened carefully as I explained my plan and then pooched out his lower lip and stared past me, thinking.

"Wow." he said.

"Yeah," I said. "Wow."

Then I told everyone else. I went home and told James and I called Bret and Cassady in Seattle and Sadie in Chicago. I didn't call anyone from my family. Being alcoholics themselves, I already knew they wouldn't get it.

Other than Benito, no one believed me.

Of course, no one said it. But everyone's voice had that weird empty sound in it, like when you thump on a hollowed-out book. Everyone kept their words short and changed the subject fast. No one tried to revisit the topic after it was closed.

4

The next few weeks were torture. I moved through April like a person in deep mourning. Not only was my lover gone but I'd triggered the event that had killed him. I'd stamped him out in a moment of passion, lopping off his head before I even knew what I was doing.

The headaches came every evening, right around five or six. Just a slow throb at first, like when I skipped coffee in the morning, but they grew until they were as loud as a train driving right through the middle of my head. Also, I couldn't sleep. Plagued by nightmares—bars and bottles, drink after drink until I drowned, breathing in gin, choking on vodka—I woke up every hour bathed in sour sweat. I moved from the bed to the couch to the floor.

At the 3:00am hour, when the rest of the city was asleep except for the time-constant homeless who rattled shopping carts under shuttered windows all night long, I sat wide awake and watched the Weather Channel. The revolving collection of maps soothed me. I liked to see where I was. I wanted to remind myself of the exact patch of land I stood on (or sat on, wide awake in the dark). I had the most bizarre off-balance, tilting feeling. Like I was hanging on to a globe, about to fall off, gravity the only thing keeping me glued down. But who could trust an outside force for that long anyway? I knew it was just a matter of time before I started falling again.

Sometimes I switched to the late-night cable music channels. I watched three and four-hour blocks of music videos, Butt Rock or New Wave hits from the '80s. Slick women in brightly-colored suits with purple eyeshadow gazed out at me from 1982. Pretty men with teased hair wearing tight animal-print pants crooned to me, casting a glance at the set behind them rooted firmly in 1986. All of them lived forever in MTV land.

But I knew that behind the illusion was the truth. The bejeweled and feathered '80s rock stars I watched all night, every night—in between the maps—were made up of people who were mostly dead, done in by car crashes or drug addiction. Or maybe they were slowly dying now, sallow-skinned skeletons with a paunch in forgotten places like Fresno or Pensacola or Pierre. As they sang their hearts out to me on the screen, I never forgot they could be dead or dying somewhere else.

Looking into the past like that was a comfort, because when I looked into my future I saw nothing. I couldn't imagine where I'd be next month or next year. I didn't know why I was where I was right now. I had no idea if there was any point to this, if there was any point to me. Sober and disoriented, I had no idea how to get myself back. I had no idea if I'd ever even had a self to begin with.

In the mornings, I ran. After six weeks with no liquor I was running 35 miles a week. I ran until my lungs felt like they were going to collapse and my heart felt like it was going to give out. I ran until my legs wept like someone was shredding their meat with a fork. I ran until my bones were pounded into dust.

And in this way, the days moved on.

●●●

In the middle of May, I got a new job.

An old college friend who lived in San Francisco had heard I was in town and emailed me to say that the secretary at her office was just about to get fired and they'd be looking for someone. When I read that the position started at $16.00 an hour I knew I'd do anything to get it. Hernan was still only able to give me part-time work at the store and James's bartending work had been running thin. We were almost out of money. I called her at the number she'd listed in the email and asked where she worked.

"Pagliarani Investigations. It's a PI firm."

Behind the cash register at MetroSpeed, I gently replaced the phone in its cradle. I scanned the slick shiny credit card of a skinny woman who grinned at me like a botoxed scarecrow and thought about that name—Palli-what Investigations? I bagged up the woman's Nike shorts—just as slippery as her credit card—and absently watched her leave as I tried to repeat the name again.

Pall—what was it? Palironi. No, it was Pallilloni or...Pagliarani? I could hear my old college friend saying it, but my tongue couldn't wrap itself around the word. The name slipped past me before it could leave my mouth full and intact.

Pallirini? It was useless. I couldn't say it.

Pronouncing the name correctly didn't matter though. I knew how to answer a phone and I could type pretty fast, even if I did only use two fingers in a rapid but precise hunt-and-peck method. I could *get* myself the job—that I knew.

I just hoped I could keep it.

●●●

I got lost on the way to the interview. And of course, I wore the wrong shoes and got blisters because I was lost and then late and had to run in the horrible heels I'd so stupidly chosen. When I arrived, I was sweating and red-faced, with sticky pieces of hair in my eyes and dark swampy circles pooling under my armpits. After I rang the wrong doorbell and was then shown into the correct office by the next-door neighbor, I found the girl I was to replace cheerfully typing out an official-looking letter with the carefree air of one who has secured solid employment for the near future.

The owner, who was also the CEO, and his wife, who did the books, took me to the restaurant across the street with my old college friend who, it turned out, was the operations manager. The girl's name was Margaret. I'd lived with her during our junior year of college in Ann Arbor in a huge house that overflowed with addicts and horticulturalists, drunks and hippie vegans and astrophysicists. We hadn't really talked since then. Now, out of the blue, she was practically saving my life. I tried to give her a quick little smile to show my gratitude, but I was nervous and pretty sure my feet were bleeding under the table.

The four of us sat and made small talk as the waitress deposited our plates in front of us. The restaurant had a ceiling made out of glass and the sun poured down on us from what seemed like thousands of skylights. After we'd exchanged the usual pleasantries the owner and his wife looked at me expectantly as if they were prepared for me to tell a really great joke everyone had heard about. I felt my smile getting bigger and faker by the second. I just wanted it to be over.

Salvatore Pagliarani, the owner, leaned into me around a mouth of fettuccine alfredo.

"Well, you can type and you've had experience with customer service." His florid cheeks and forehead seemed to grow a film of sweat as he chewed, like the pasta was fighting him but he was courteously hiding his exertion. I eyed his plate and moved an invisible increment away from the soupy pile. I locked eyes with him and forced myself not to look at it.

"And you can answer a phone I'm sure. Margaret says you went to college with her." He pointed his fork at me, jabbing it slightly forward for emphasis. "U of M. Damn good school."

The fork leaked white sauce on the table in front of us. It could have been snot, or the viscous slime of a mutant worm. I dragged my eyes back up to his and smiled harder.

"That it is, sir. A very good school." I cleared my throat politely.

"And you seem normal." Sal went back to attacking his plate of fettuccine.

"Aah," I interjected. "*Seem*. That's the operative word. I *seem* normal." Without being able to help myself I gave him a small grin, a real one. *I am more than I seem sir.*

"Ah—" Sal hesitated, his mouth hanging open. I saw half-chewed white noodle scurrying back in fear from the wily pink beast of his tongue.

"—HA!" Sal spluttered the noodle into his napkin, which he now fluttered violently around his face, like a drag queen caught without her makeup on. "Seem!" he coughed. "Seem!" He gave up and resigned himself to choking and gasping, laughing into his napkin. His face was almost purple. I thought it very likely that his neck would explode, leaving a shredded stump jutting out of his white-collared starched shirt. I already suspected the shirt left deep embedded rings in his skin, like carefully spaced noose marks, when he took it off at night. That neck was just fighting to get out, even before I'd egged him on.

"I like that! You see that Gemma?" He turned suddenly on his wife, who'd been sitting there, mute and indifferent and impossible to read behind square-shaped glasses and burgundy red lipstick.

"You see," Sal said to Gemma as if she hadn't been sitting there the entire time. "I said 'you seem normal' and right away she picked up on that—that one word! Detail. That's what I like—that's what Pagliarani needs!" His fork clanked as he threw it down, glinting with the million sparkles of sunlight washing down over our little table. Sal raised his arms and threw back his head.

"Detail! You're hired! Gemma! Start the paperwork!"

Gemma didn't move. Sal bowed over just as quickly as he'd bent back. I saw the fork once again captured in one beefy red palm. He chuckled to himself as he forked in another mouthful of fettuccine.

"Seem! That's the fucking best...seem." Looking at me out of the corner of one eye, he chuckled again.

None of the rest of us had touched our food.

●●●

So, I got the job. Sitting down at my new desk the next day, I noticed all trace of the girl I'd replaced was gone. No leftover piece of candy rattling around in the desk drawers, no personalized paperclips with cutesy designs hiding under the phone. It was like she'd been erased. I had the feeling she hadn't been there long. One of my very first phone calls confirmed it.

"Palla—Pal-lee-ah-rah-ni Investigations," I spelled out, eyes glued to the scrap of paper Sal had taped onto my desk with the phonetic spelling. I still couldn't say it without trying once and then starting over again.

"Well heeeey!" A deep friendly voice boomed out of the phone. "Eddie Chavez here, also known as Second Dog PI—Guy's first of course—and you must be the new secretary girl. Glad to hear you're onboard. Sal give you much shit yet?" Without waiting for an answer, he barreled on. "He'll be nice 'cuz you're new. Hope you end up staying. The way things been goin' Sal can't *keep* anyone answerin' that phone. Say, can you run a plate?" He delivered it all in one baritone locomotive of words. *Run a plate? A license plate?* I had no idea what he was talking about. But he'd already kept going.

"Ready? Cool. Henry John Adam 5-6-4. Wifey's been out with the kiddies so far, no dice on the claimant. Get me that plate and then I'll do a contact. Thanks." The phone clicked in my ear. I hadn't written down any of the names he'd given me. I looked around for a pen but the phone was already ringing again. This time when I answered I was greeted by a sophisticated voice with a thin nasal edge to it, the voice of someone who was a cross between a gentleman and a hipster kid.

"Hey are you Leah? You must be Margaret's friend." The voice paused, waiting for me to respond. Startled, I realized he actually wanted an answer. I'd sort of assumed this one would just plow through like Chavez had. I confirmed that yes, I was Margaret's friend.

"Cool shit yo." The voice was silent again. Chavez had sounded like he was calling from out in the middle of the street—car horns, kids' screams, and traffic noise accompanied him like a chaotic music score—but this voice sounded like the person it belonged to was sitting in a dark room with padded walls.

"I'm Guy," the voice went on. "Margaret's cool beans, give her mad props, she's the best yo." I said I would and he continued.

"Yeah, this address is bunk. No for sale, but empty. No furniture, no newspapers, nothin'. Number goes nowhere. Margaret's gotta run it again under the AKA. Let me know." And then the voice hung up.

The rest of the morning was like that. Pagliarani Investigations specialized in tracking people who were faking injuries for workers' compensation claims, and so a lot of insurance adjusters called, sounding cranky and tired and like they wished they had another job. Lawyers called too, brassy and big-voiced, trying to sound important. And every single one of the detectives called, every 15 minutes it felt like.

During lunch I took a walk around the neighborhood. Since I'd started that morning my panic had only mounted. Now I thought I might throw up.

I still couldn't say the fucking name, that was one thing. Marching around the block I repeated the syllables just as I'd seen them on the sheet of paper taped to my desk. *Pal-lee-ah-rah-ni, Pal-lee-ah-rah-ni, Pal-lee-ah-rah-ni.* If I spit the word out in five chunky little blocks I could get it all out. It was when I tried to say it fast—like I had to when I answered the phone—that I chewed it into a garbled mess.

For another thing, it didn't appear anyone was going to train me. Sal had shown up around 9:00am, but

38

after he thundered up the stairs and blustered into the place, he'd shut himself up in his office and then all I'd heard was his voice, muffled through the door for the rest of the morning. The little red light on my phone blinked on and off every few minutes as he made call after call after call. And Margaret was nearly chained to her desk, running plates, background checks, and claimant profiles. When she wasn't knee-deep in writing reports she was busy talking to different clients on the phone, just like Sal.

Sal's wife, Gemma, had come in briefly, but she hadn't said anything—to me or anyone else—and then when I checked her office a little while later she was gone.

I was on my own. I sighed and decided to take another lap around the block, seeing if I could count how many times I could say *Pal-lee-ah-rah-ni* until my lunch break was over.

5

Over the next few weeks I got to know the three main detectives: Guy, Chavez, and Dave. I quickly learned why Chavez had introduced himself as 'Second Dog.' As a PI, he was good, but nowhere near as good as Guy. When it came to down-and-dirty sleuthing, Guy was the best. He found people when we had no picture and no description. He zeroed in on one solid address out of a dozen dead ends. He had a preternatural instinct for when an address was bad and he never wasted precious morning hours waiting for clues to pan out. Most of the time, almost all of the time, it was like he just knew.

When I met him in the flesh I wasn't at all surprised that the reedy, refined voice I'd met over the phone issued forth from the dark-eyed, hawk-nosed Guy standing before me. He seemed like a retired junkie from a wealthy European family with old money. He looked like he'd been through the wringer, but he reeked of class.

Guy also had a habit of hissing out the ends of his sentences. He held his arms bent woodenly at the elbows, and rocked slowly back and forth, from his heels to the tips of his toes, whenever he talked. His dark eyes pierced whomever he spoke to, his gaze slicing out from under knitted black brows.

Chavez was Guy's exact opposite. A robust man who could probably turn fat if he didn't watch it, Chavez was always smiling, his brown eyes always twinkling. He laughed big and raw, clapping his chubby hands together, hands that looked too small and hopeful to be on his body, like they should really be paired with a fast-growing eight-year-old. Chavez's innocent-looking hands branched into two brown meaty arms, each covered with a full sleeve of tattoos. Almost as a joke, he wore wife-beaters every day as part of his cover.

"Heeey, no one's goin' to notice the tatted up *vato* in the wife-beater sittin' out on the street, right?" he chuckled, and winked. "They think I'm just sittin' there waitin' on drugs anyhow, huh?" He let loose a huge vibrant laugh. "And what if I am? Two birds and one stone baby," he said, winking at me again. "Two birds and one stone."

Our third detective was Dave, and he was completely forgettable. He had the kind of face you have a hard time remembering half an hour after seeing it, the kind of voice that could belong to anybody. After I got to know the business a little better I came to see this was probably the reason Sal had hired him. No one wants a PI who stands out.

In addition to our three guys, we also had Grove, who worked for us sometimes, but was also still an independent agent. Grove had his own one-man-show PI business, and sometimes he needed hours to supplement his case roster. He was an enormous bear of a man who dressed only in tie-dye, smoked a pack of Pall Malls a day, had a handlebar mustache, and had been friends with Sal since they were 11 years old. Sal and Grove claimed they'd lugged equipment for Jefferson Airplane and Janis Joplin in 1967, and they'd stayed friends in all the years that had passed since those long-ago foggy summers when they'd chummed around the City together, watching the remnants of the Summer of Love and the seeds it had left behind sprout up, wide-eyed adolescents waiting for the rest of the country to catch fire.

Now, Sal was a fat cat PI boss with slicked back hair, dark glasses and black suits to match, with a black Mercedes to finish off the effect. Grove was still a hippie. He grew weed in his backyard and wasn't shy about his homegrown enjoyment of it. He worked surveillance out of his van, which was a legend around the office, not only because of the amenities it contained but also because of the record-breaking length of time Grove was able to camp out in it. It was big and gray, the nondescript neutral tone of crumbling warehouses on a rainy day. Inside Grove had a portable generator, a mini-fridge, a microwave, and a sleeping bag. Instead of bottles like the other guys kept to piss in, Grove had a one-gallon jar. Rumor was, he only emptied it when it was full.

●●●

The number one rule to being an excellent PI is easy: *don't waste time*. But as easy as it is to get that rule, it's just as hard to keep to it. Obstacles are thrown into a PI's path second by second and each one of these little monsters devours time. In everyday life, we don't notice it much. In fact, most people unwittingly collaborate with the evil forces in the universe that would kill time forever if they could. But being a PI is like suddenly waking up in the middle of the night and the house is on fire. All at once, you see. You get what's important. Time is important. In a house on fire, and in the life of a PI, there isn't any to waste.

With good PI's their cases went one of two ways, either they were done by 9:00am or they worked it all day. And even the best PI's sometimes blew it because they weren't efficient in the morning. They didn't nail down the right address soon enough or definitively identify the claimant before the claimant took off and they lost him. A few minutes squandered in the morning could trash an entire day.

Don't waste time was rule number one. On the heels of that came rule number two: *don't lose your head.* Also known as *don't panic* or *don't think like a fuckwad.* Rule number one was applied in the beginning, when the PI had just shown up at the house at 5:00 or 6:00am, bleary-eyed and ready to wait. But rule number two—*don't think like a fuckwad*—came later, when the case got moving. When, for the first time after long stretches of the PI patiently watching and waiting, the rabbit poked its head out of the hole.

It's a test to wait for the rabbit, but it's also extremely difficult sometimes not to lose the rabbit once he has appeared. Most people don't realize how often PI's deal with escaped quarry. You think running after a rabbit in an unfamiliar forest is confusing? Try hunting a human being in the middle of San Francisco. Tailing someone on the freeway isn't so bad, but when gobs of crowds and cars are set up every 10 feet, almost as if the entire world plays along against the PI, chasing after one little person can be like fighting a one-man war. That's why any good PI is an underdog at heart. He's used to getting what he needs from a world determined not to give it to him.

If a PI loses his head when he loses someone, he's done. Game over. If he allows panic to rest for one second in his mind, his options dry up like they were never even there to begin with. He'll look in all the wrong places, turn down every wrong street, see so many faces that look like the one he's looking for that he'll completely forget the one he truly does seek. Then he's really fucked. He can't envision where the rabbit would go next because he can't even remember the most basic patterns and habits it's already displayed.

Fucking up as a PI is pretty much the same as fucking up in everyday life. It doesn't matter if you get lost, lose the scent, lose your sense, lose the thread. The only thing that matters is if you can pick it back up again.

●●●

I ravenously chewed my way through reports at Pagliarani. Every morning Margaret gave me a stack of folders containing profiles and all the past surveillance reports from the detectives. I scanned the info in each file, wrote up a cover letter, and then edited the most recent report from the detective working the case. I quickly found that the tone of each report matched the detective it came from. Guy's reports were precise and detailed. He didn't waste time, and he didn't waste words either. Reading his reports was like riding along with a highly trained professional killer—no mistakes. Chavez's reports matched his personality too. He slipped in funny stuff, a jab at the claimant's appearance or hilarious suppositions of what they might be doing inside the residence. And when it came to Dave, the information delivered couldn't get more boring. Plus, it was usually inaccurate or missing the really important stuff.

As fast as Margaret piled on the reports, I cranked them out. On Sal's way through the door for a client lunch downtown, he brushed past me in his black suit, the fabric whispering between his massive thighs like silk on sandpaper. He hiked his black shades up and looked down at me.

"That's what I like to see!" he bellowed, laying a meaty pink hand on the stack of finished reports on my desk. "Keep crankin'! Keep crankin'! After this meeting I'll have 20 more cases this week alone—80 more for the month! Keep crankin'!" He leaned down conspiratorially, lowering his voice a notch from his usual shout to just plain loud, and winked at me.

"This client's a bird dog—a real azzhole if you know what I mean—but he'll throw us some cases. Goddamnit yes! Keep crankin'!" And then he lurched forward and I heard him pounding his way down the stairs. The entire second floor of our office shook with his departure.

I was surprised the suit could hold him in.

The neighborhood was just as loud as Sal. Our office was in a roomy Victorian smack dab in the middle of the Castro. Poised on 18th Street, we were just a few blocks away from Market, and only two blocks from Castro Street itself. Rainbow flags dotted every street lamp. Big burly men walked with each other's hands in their back pockets or strolled along with their arms around each other, like truckers impersonating teenagers in love. Down the street were the Leather Depot and the sex shop, intermingled with gourmet organic grocery stores and fashionable boutiques for dogs. The pizza joint around the corner hung a whiteboard in its window that twinkled with catty new comments every day, sometimes on Britney Spears, sometimes on the latest fad in the neighborhood. Every single bar was a gay one.

All sorts of men, cowboys and bikers and slender boys who looked no more than 16 and prettier than I was, brimmed over the edges of every street I passed. Guys with long gray beards and leather chaps stood arm in arm, clinking bottles at the Bare Steel bar across the street. Skinny femboys swirled fizzy pink drinks at the hipster bar with rainbow neon in the windows down the block. Everywhere I looked there were men and I couldn't stop looking.

As a biological woman I walked among them unnoticed, they paid more attention to the tiny dogs the queens carried in their purses. I was invisible. In this new life in San Francisco it seemed I was only made up of what I was not.

6

When my dad called in July I ignored the call at first. His name popped up on my phone and I watched the letters shivering like a wet dog, and let it go to voicemail. But when I checked the message I knew something was wrong, really wrong. My dad sounded broken.

My stepmother had left him.

They had been married for 18 years, but for the past three years he had lived in New York City while she had stayed in Michigan. He was still there now, working at least 12 hours a day, rarely taking a day off, and drinking three martinis or more every night. I wasn't surprised they had split up, only that it had taken this long.

I called my dad back and told him I'd come out to New York to see him. We'd talk and hang out, I said. I couldn't imagine that we would actually do either. Neither of us understood leisure activities. We didn't relax like other people did. We worked or we drank. That was what we did and that was all we did. And I didn't drink anymore. All I did now was work and there was hardly any life in it. I wondered if I was being sent to New York to watch it die in my father.

When I arrived there a few weeks later my dad's appearance shocked me. He looked like he'd dropped about 20 pounds and his hair was now entirely gray. But his face looked the worst. It had folded in. His eyes seemed to have shrunk down to slits, forcing him into extremely limited vision. But for once, since I wasn't drinking anymore, I could see clearly. My dad had been blown apart.

As soon as I got to his place, my dad mixed a martini and I poured myself a glass of water from the tap. We pulled the blinds and trapped ourselves in the hot room, the sun and the sounds of Greenwich Village poking in around the cracks. I knew we were pretending we were dead. We'd locked ourselves up until the game was over. I was already familiar with the rules. Since I'd quit drinking, I played it all the time now.

My dad talked to me in lists that whole afternoon. This was also familiar to me. I had my own lists, and so I wasn't at all surprised to see him going back through his, mapping his way out of the emotional avalanche that had almost killed him. Rules are: When you feel weird or insecure, make a list. When depression's sucking at you like fish biting underwater and you feel the pull getting stronger, make another list. Feel like blowing your head off? Make a fucking list. If that doesn't work, better get to making a list of all your lists. Cataloguing emotions makes it easier to find them and isolate them later. When an emotion's alone in a corner it's not nearly as difficult to step on its head and kill it. Then, check it off on the list.

For the rest of the day I sat with my dad and drank warm water, wishing it was gin, as he drank martini after martini and I listened to him detail his lists. When he got tired we watched *Casablanca*. When it got dark we restarted the movie again and my dad made a fresh pitcher of martinis. He cried silently the whole time. I only knew he was crying because the glare from the TV reflected off the wet tracks running down his cheeks in the dark. It looked like silver paint on his face and the paint was all I could see. The rest of his face was lost in the darkness.

The next day we went out. Perversely, my dad seemed set on taking me on a tour of New York. He was adamant we get out to see the sites even though I said I wasn't interested. We'd gone out as tourists last time I'd visited but now he acted like he didn't remember any of that. I wondered if maybe he really didn't remember anything from before a few weeks ago. Like maybe the shock of my stepmother leaving him was so great it had knocked loose the archives he kept in his head. Maybe now all his files were scattered, and he couldn't find what he was looking for. I could see him inside his head, crawling around on the dark floor of his mind, tears dropping onto his trembling hands as he desperately hunted for his lost memories.

Maybe that was why we were repeating past events now, so he could replace some of the lost files. Because without memories, who would he be? Even if he started over and accrued new ones, he would forever be at a disadvantage, working with files defined almost wholly by what they lacked. If he ever wanted to find himself again then he had no choice but to reassemble the files that had been scattered, to locate what had been lost. He had to put the archives back in order. I understood that urgency. Like I said, I made lists too.

I had my own files.

Our first stop of the day was Trump Tower. We walked to the edge of the building and then leaned back and looked up. It felt a bit like being a little kid at a wedding, balancing on a grown-up's feet to dance. I'd done this before with skyscrapers and it always made me want to rest my head against the building's warm flank and sleep for a while. Like dancing, I wanted to let go into it.

But my dad and I never let go. We just stood and stared. Finally, my dad moved off and I started snapping pictures. When I turned around again he was sitting on a bench nearby. Stooped over, he held his head in his hands and cried. Tears dropped onto the pavement off the end of his nose. I wondered if I were small, as small as a bug maybe, and found myself underneath my father's great shaking, weeping head, if it would be just like a forest when it's raining in the middle of summer. I wondered—if I was underneath all my dad's sorrow— would I be able to hear him crying then? Maybe I was just too big to hear him now. Or maybe it would be the same no matter what size I was and still I wouldn't hear anything at all.

Maybe, still, he would appear only as a giant, silent, trembling cloud.

●●●

That summer—my first summer in the City—I spent most of my time at Pagliarani listening to the radio and editing reports. I followed along with each detective's case, just as if I were right there riding in the car with them. I saw middle-aged men with sprained backs roll garbage cans out to the curb in Marin County—a place that sounded luxuriously green to me, filled with rich people wearing expensive sunglasses and cropped khakis that creased up like the spidery lines around their eyes. I vicariously watched lithe young black men play basketball in Vallejo—when one of them had a knee injury and wasn't supposed to be playing anything at all. From inside dark cars getting cooked during the hottest part of the day I spied on field workers down in Watsonville or over in Los Banos, people who had migrated to California for a better life, and now broke their backs under a broiling sun.

I sat inside Guy as he camped out at the Marina in San Francisco, tracking down a claimant who lived on a boat, no physical address to go on. Then I hid with him when he ducked into a twisted alleyway after the claimant's husband saw him filming their sloop and came after him with a baseball bat.

I crouched down in the backseat when Chavez made it up north into meth country, the home of people who lived in places like Hayfork and Junction City and used to be in prison or the Angels or both. People who didn't take kindly to strangers in those parts. I was with him when he got chased down a road that was really no more than a mountain trail by a couple of true-blue California outlaws. Breathless, I hunched behind the driver's seat and let the car beat every bump and rut of the road into me, jouncing up so high at times my head went clear through the roof of the car. I saw the outlaws tearing after us, grinning through the dust clouds kicked up by our terrified retreat.

Imagining myself inside of each different detective, I saw California through their eyes. I flew over fields that glowed a rich sunshine yellow, the glimmer washing over everything for miles around, like waves of pollen or fairy dust. Everything glittered, everything was gold. The sun never set.

Back in San Francisco, where my physical body sat and typed and answered the phone at Pagliarani, I fought off the summer chill. Cold, foggy, and capped with a bone-dissolving drizzle, June, July, and August in San Francisco held me down like three heavy iron prison bars. I felt like I was living in London, in November. I went to work in wool sweaters every day and kicked on the space heater at home every night. The old Victorian that was the Pagliarani office was drafty, and the old Victorian that was my apartment seemed to be made out of nothing but clapboard and planted on a beach off the coast of Greenland. At night, I huddled in fur blankets as I watched the weather and old music videos. I swore I heard the wind rattling in the eaves.

Around 3:00 or 4:00am, James got home from his shift at the bar and sometimes joined me on the couch to watch the music videos. He had always suffered from insomnia and the bar schedule didn't help, so it wasn't unusual for him to go to bed at 7:00 or 8:00 in the morning. When I got home in the evening around 6:00pm, he'd be getting ready to go back to work at the bar. So, the only time we ever spent together was in the middle of the night. James usually lit up a joint and we passed it back and forth as we watched old '80s rock stars burst through walls, jump onto cars, and skid on their knees across stages, wrestling golden riffs out of their guitars the whole time, and James reminisced about shows he'd gone to as a metalhead kid in the early '90s.

At those times I remembered everything: I remembered meeting James in Seattle and falling in love with him. I remembered sitting in bars and all-night diners and talking for hours and *knowing* he was my other half. I remembered the feeling I'd had when we first met, that he was the same as me, he could see inside people, he could see beyond the surface.

In those bleak early morning hours, as we sat and smoked and talked and were prisoners together, in the train car on top of a house, I remembered everything.

But then I got up and went to work and forgot it all over again. I trudged down the creaky stairs of our apartment house every morning, made my way through the gray streets and waited for the train. I forgot the golden fairy dust land of California that lay outside the City, and all that I had seen in James before we came to San Francisco to start over. Instead, I felt myself a fading gray ghost of a person, bleeding into the background of the fog, my blood now only clear drops of water.

●●●

James and I didn't talk very much about how I wasn't drinking. Obviously, there was a difference both of us could see. I wasn't at the bar four or five nights a week now. I wasn't charging up all our credit cards due to bar tabs. I wasn't puking every morning in the bathroom. And, maybe the best thing: I didn't seem to regularly turn into a raging crazy bitch anymore.

Lo was the name of the demon that had lived inside me for the entire four years I'd lived in Seattle. She only came out when I was drinking. She'd largely fallen silent at the end of 2004, right before I moved to San Francisco, during the same time I met James, only making spotty appearances up until the time I quit the booze. Now, it was the summer of 2005 and I was sober. It felt like I hadn't seen her in forever.

Sometimes Lo had looked like a spider and sometimes like a beautiful woman—like a better me. Someone with my face, but taller, stronger, and paler. She had started out as a voice in my head but then she became part of me. Now that it seemed like she was possibly gone for good, I was worried and relieved at the same time. In Seattle, Lo used to do horrible things.

Some of them to complete strangers and some of them to men I knew well. Some of the horrible things seemed funny later and some of them I felt really shitty about. All of them, funny or not, were shitty at the bottom of it.

But that was Lo. She was a real bitch.

It's easy to see why I felt relieved.

But, to be honest, I also missed her.

Lo might have been a demon, but I couldn't argue with her strength. And I had never felt very strong. In fact, I'd always felt like life wasn't much different from a dripping jungle laced with land mines. Insects as big as panthers perched breathless above, and then the hidden bombs waited below, ready to blow off both my legs. Until Lo, I'd made my way through the jungle alone.

But when Lo arrived she built a fort in the trees and installed insect zappers right outside the front door, made to take down bugs the size of dinosaurs. She drew me a map, showing me where the land mines were. She taught me how to step around them without tripping the wires. She made me learn the patterns, memorize the design, and then she tore the map up and threw it into the wind like confetti. She made me build my own bomb and then she swallowed it to see if it worked. When she exploded all over the place—chunks of white skin and snow-blonde hair mixed with teeth sticking all over the walls of the tree fort—I stood back and watched as she put herself back together again. All her particles spun into a blur, sparkling as they solidified back into her frame. She patted a single sleek white-blonde hair back into place and smiled at me.

"See?" she said, and shrugged her shoulders. "No big deal."

Lo did a lot of stuff like that.

Letting Lo in had been more than easy, it had been fun. My new unexpected life as a sober person, and all the questions that came with it, was not easy, and it definitely wasn't fun. I'd been sure that after my year off alcohol I'd go back to drinking. But now I wasn't so certain. Because somehow, I knew that Lo wasn't gone forever. Somehow, I knew she had been caged, that she now lived in a prison cell deep inside of me, that her cell was comfortable, and that I'd employed servants to keep her alive. And somehow, I knew that only the slim hope of ever fully inhabiting me again gave her the determination to go on.

7

At the end of that summer I felt strong enough to go back to the bar, *without* drinking. I went out one night with Beet and Hernan to the Cigarillo and Beet and I camped out at a small table while we watched Hernan making the rounds of the room. Beet sipped his rum and I twirled the swizzle stick in my virgin drink. I'd spent the last half hour detailing to him how much James hated San Francisco. Even though we'd been in the City almost a year already, he still felt out of place and like it wasn't his home. During our 3:00am talks he'd told me over and over again that he couldn't stop thinking about going back to Seattle.

Throughout my monologue Beet glanced at me quick and watchful every few seconds before dropping his head to take another thoughtful sip of rum. In the background Hernan worked assiduously on the blonde sitting up at the bar, every now and again laughing softly when he caught one of Beet's secret grins.

"Things are just different now, that's all," I said. "When James and I first moved here, he wanted to be here. He wanted to be with me. I know he still does, but...I honestly never expected he'd hate it here so much. I thought he knew what he was getting into."

"But Lee-ah, maybe his mind will change, no? Right now, he is scared, but that might change too." Beet smiled gently at me and patted my shoulder.

"I know..." I sighed and swizzled my drink violently. "But what am I gonna do? If he goes back to Seattle...that's it."

Beet nodded but didn't say anything. We both went back to indifferently tracking Hernan around the bar. After the blonde, he'd burned through a brunette and was now onto a redhead.

I sighed again, feeling the wet ropes of self-pity twine slowly around my ankles, leaving watermarks, dragging me under. Beet raised a small grin along with his eyebrows and took another sip of rum. He waited cheerfully for me to continue my lamentations.

"It just wouldn't be so bad if I were drinking," I said. I set my glass on the table and pushed it away from me. Sliding along the stone exterior it sounded like a coffin being dragged backwards. I looked over at the warm amber waves splashing up to the halfway mark in Beet's tumbler, the finger and lip prints all around the rim looking like the rumpled damp reflection that greets you in the mirror after you spend all night making out with someone. If I leaned in just a hair closer I knew I'd be able to smell the rum on the air between us. I sniffed like I didn't care and looked away.

"If I were drinking it'd be so simple...but now...now if I went back to Seattle it'd be weird...because I couldn't go back...to my old bars, I mean. But that wouldn't be for long—only until next spring...until March..." Beet's puckering eyebrows and lips tried to keep up with me as I thought out loud.

"You still going to drink again? After the year?" Beet asked.

"Well...we'll see what happens," I answered evasively. "But yeah, maybe I will. Who knows? A lot could change by next year." I flashed an invisible blow of red-eyed rage at my nonalcoholic drink sitting abandoned in the middle of the table. I imagined it was a warm golden shot of tequila instead. Being so near Beet's rum had put me in the mood for heat, sun and sand and sex—all in one powerful little ounce of liquid. That was something I could get behind. My jaw twinged. All of a sudden I was salivating so much I was practically drooling. At the same time, I realized Beet was still watching me.

"But—of course—I'll be careful. Very careful." I patted Beet reassuringly on the shoulder. "And who knows?" I threw up both hands and offered him my best *don't-lose-hope-anything-might-happen* smile. "I'll probably kick it for good."

Beet stared at me. He didn't appear entirely convinced.

"What? C'mon...let's go dance." I tugged on his shirtsleeve, hoping the worried thoughts I saw in his eyes would slide to the back of his mind. Like runny sludge, those same thoughts were bogging me down too.

Beet knocked back the rest of his rum and scooted out of his chair. He let me lead him out from behind the table and onto the dance floor, but I could tell he was still worried. I could tell he wanted to look away.

●●●

October came and with it the warm weather. The fog finally lifted. At Pagliarani Investigations we had the windows open, enjoying the balmy air, but our tranquility was broken by Sal one morning, cursing a blue streak outside below in the driveway.

"You FUCKER! Get the FUCK out of my driveway! You Goddamn COCKSUCKER!!!"

Margaret and I ran over to look down onto the street and driveway below. She gingerly pushed the creaky window high enough for both of us to squeeze through and get the full view. Sal's black Mercedes was half in the driveway, half in the street. Parked at a crazy angle with the driver's side door hanging open, it resembled an obstinate mechanical donkey that refused to go any further.

Although we hadn't seen this particular drama unfold from the very beginning, we'd seen it all before. I pictured Sal barreling at breakneck speed down 18th Street, slamming to a stop with a silent, almost animal grace. I saw him angle the car at that crosswise slant like he was pulling a schooner around, craning his neck to get a better look at the downright stupid driver who'd parked in Pagliarani's slim driveway. The second Sal finished evaluating the situation—*cased the fucker* as he'd say—he'd probably leapt out of the car at the same breakneck speed at which he'd dashed down the street just a few moments before. Like a panther, he was on his victim before the hapless driver could even look around. I always felt sorry for the people who hadn't made it out of the car yet after parking in Sal's driveway. A car with no driver left Sal screaming in the middle of the street with no one to take it out on. Then we called the tow company. Knowing Sal like I did, I would have picked having my car impounded any day.

But this driver hadn't made it out of the car. Margaret and I were just in time to see him frantically roll up his window as Sal jabbed one meaty finger through it and into the guy's face.

"Oh no you don't you son of a BITCH. Don't you roll up that fucking window on me. I will FUCKING KILL YOU."

The guy was already backing out, completely ignoring any threat of the traffic moving in both directions on the street. I think he understood that getting creamed by a semi-truck could very well be preferable to dealing with Sal when he was mad. The only object the driver did seem to notice was the black Mercedes and the bubble of space that surrounded it. I wondered if, underneath his immediate fear, the driver somehow instinctively realized this was Sal's lair, the cage the panther had sprung from. I wondered if the driver probably assumed that if he bumped the car—jostled the cage so to speak—an entire ferocious pack of big cats might stream forth.

Margaret and I looked at each other and chuckled. Then we heard the front door and Sal's characteristic *rattle*-SLAM as he battled his way through it. We raced back to our desks.

"Goddamn motherfucking cocksucking cocksucker. I'll give you a fucking knuckle sandwich you fuck—goddamn it..." he muttered to himself up the staircase and down the hall into his office, and then I heard that door slam shut too.

I watched the clock. After 10 minutes had passed I swept my reports together and headed down the hall. 10 minutes was all it ever took for Sal to cool off.

Without hesitation, I knocked short and solid, three times.

"Yes!" Sal barked and then smiled when he saw me. "Leeeeah, hellooo! Got your cheaters on today, lookin' sharp." He grinned and snapped his fingers, already starting to wiggle around in his chair like he wanted to get up and dance.

"My—? Ooooh...these." I raised one hand to my face and fingered the stem of my glasses. In Sal language glasses were known as "cheaters." Cigarettes were "turds" and guys who went after other men's wives were "bird dogs." I had the language down pretty well by now, but sometimes Sal still threw me for a loop.

"Just need to give you the morning's run down for Margaret. Guy's chasing someone in Vallejo and she can't get off the phone."

Sal smiled wider and waved a hand for me to go on. He swung his black wingtip shoes up on his desk and leaned back in his chair. I marveled again how a man of his size and stature could move so much like a gymnast.

"Ok, well here it is. We'll go from good to bad." Sal's smile drooped and he started forward. I pressed on with the good before he could start grilling me about the bad.

"Guy's in Vallejo like I said. The claimant's driving fast but he's not hot, just drives like a bat outta hell. He got video this morning—an *hour*—and of the guy fixing his car." I continued on, encouraged by the greedy smile spreading across Sal's face.

"And not only with the car, but carrying around some kid too, looks like a grandkid. Whatever the kid is, he looks to be *at least* 40 pounds. He's like, five or something, and Guy says he's a big kid. Claimant carried him around the front yard for almost 20 minutes, so it seems that back injury can't be paining him that much. All on tape." I snapped the file shut and quickly flipped to the next one, eager now to get to the bad while Sal still had the good fresh in his mind.

"Then we got Chavez. Put him on that woman in San Rafael again this morning, but it definitely doesn't look like she lives there, either that or she's morbidly obese and never leaves the house." I held the top of the file open with my thumb and quickly scanned down the claimant's profile.

"Hmmm...nope. 5'4" and 130 pounds. Supposed to be 'attractive' as well. She's only 25, and she's a blonde. So no way she's a recluse. Chavez did a phone contact and got no answer. The plate we've got down for her is there, car's parked in the driveway. But it hasn't moved in three days and when Chavez went to the door and did a personal some guy who could be the boyfriend just said she 'wasn't available' and he didn't know when she would be. But—" I overrode Sal before he could interrupt. "The dude said he'd sign for any packages for her so the address doesn't look totally bunk."

"Hmmm..." Sal pursed his lips together and held his hand out for the file. I handed it over and he flipped through it, pausing at the list of previous addresses we'd found and Chavez's short report from the day before. He shut the file and sailed it back to me.

"See if we can get an appointment. This chick could have lots of boyfriends. We need to get film of her at the doctor's office." I nodded once, making a mental note.

"And uh..." I paused but knew I couldn't delay the wrath any longer. I plunged. "Dave fucked his case. The guy got hot when Dave was on him on the freeway. Kept checking his rearview, driving weird and then crazy to shake Dave...and, well...Dave burned the guy."

Sal hovered in his chair, still as a statue.

"And—?" He cocked an eyebrow at me.

"The guy called his lawyer and they called our in-house counsel. She's fucking pissed. She wants to talk to you."

"FUCK!" Sal shot up and out of his chair like he'd just had a red-hot poker shoved up his ass. "What the FUCK! That Goddamn ROOKIE!"

I didn't take the opportunity to point out that Dave had actually been working for Sal for over four years.

"He can't just fucking BURN 'em, he has to SCORCH them beyond recognition. What an IDIOT, whatta FUCKING IDIOT." Sal paced around his office like a raging bear. He picked up the phone and then bludgeoned it back down into the handset. I heard the slight but audible crack that signified the phone could only take another two or three blows from Sal before it splintered into pieces. I sighed. It would be the third phone Sal had gone through since I'd gotten there.

He picked up the receiver again, this time punching the buttons. With every punch the phone scooted closer to the edge of the desk. When half of it hung suspended in midair and the other half started to lean precariously close, I backed out of the office as silently as I could and crept off down the hall.

"FUCK!!!" I heard the crash of the phone as it hit the floor and dove back into my seat.

At noon, Sal took us out for lunch.

For kicks, we rode up to Twin Peaks before we hit the restaurant. Sal had lived in the City all his life. He knew every curve and dip of every street in San Francisco like it was the well-tread carpet in his own living room. He drove the black Mercedes like it was an extension of himself, flooring the gas and ripping it around tight curves like he was flexing his own outstretched hand and feeling the tendons work.

As always, whenever Sal drove us anywhere, he talked nonstop the whole way.

"Man's a bastard that's for sure, but he's damn smart." From where I sat in the backseat I saw him tilt his head toward Margaret on the passenger side and crack her a wink. Sal jabbered on while Margaret gave brief but solidly intelligent answers to the questions she picked out of his relentless monologue.

"And I tell you something else—no matter what, no matter who it is or what a fuck they are, no matter what kind of idiot, you take something from everybody. Every single person you run across in this life gives you something, and if you're smart enough you'll take what they're giving up. Learn something from everybody they say, yeah, but this is different from learning. It's *taking*. You put in your dues with someone, you take what they give you, you take what you can. And every single one 'em has something for you. Even the bastards."

Sal fell silent. I could hear his heavy breathing and thought he sounded tired, like a guy coming up on 50 who wasn't in the shape he used to be, who had two grown daughters, and who felt the cold stirrings of death in the middle of the night. Probably right around 3:00am. I looked out the car window, watching the streets run by, and wondered if 3:00am was treating Sal the same way it was treating me these days.

●●●

As that fall wound down into winter, James went to Seattle for a few days, to see if he really did want to be "there instead of here," as he put it. When he came back he said he wanted to stay in San Francisco and so we decided to move out of the train car on top of a house. We found an apartment down by Ocean Beach, two blocks away from the Pacific Ocean and at the end of the light rail line for the N Judah train. I thought a change of scenery might do us both good and James was just glad to live somewhere with more windows.

I had now been sober for almost nine months, and I was growing more certain every day that I wouldn't go back to drinking. I still *wanted* to drink, of course, but I also had to admit that everything was way better. I wasn't constantly broke, I had an interesting job, and I wasn't systematically alienating all the people I knew by committing heinous and unforgivable acts every single time I came into contact with any single one of them. Plus, I didn't feel like I was dying anymore. Not that I felt what I'd call "good," but I definitely didn't want to kill myself these days, and I figured that was a big step in the right direction.

In fact, the only thing that hadn't seemed to improve as markedly as the rest of my life was my relationship with James. He now worked at a nightclub in the SoMa and so he worked even later hours these days, sometimes not getting home until 5:00 or 6:00am, and still the most we ever saw each other was maybe one hour out of the day. On the weekends I spent my days walking around the city by myself and on James's days off he drew the curtains and cloistered himself in our dark apartment, glued to the computer and barely speaking.

I knew he still missed Seattle, even if he had decided not to go back there. I also knew that he still hadn't found his place in San Francisco, but neither had I. Other than my job at Pagliarani, I had no life, and no friends. I hardly saw Hernan and Beet anymore since all

I did now was work and sleep and endlessly walk from one end of the city to the other, trying to untangle the knots in my head.

Alcohol had always been my one great passion. It had been my lover, my best friend, and my entire social life back in Seattle. It was what I always came back to in the end, the way a womanizer fucks around but always comes back to his one great true love. Booze was my one great true love. Now that it was over, I was still getting over it. I had zero interest in anyone new, preferring instead to pine for the one I'd lost.

I fought the truth of my continued state of sobriety daily. Deep inside, a black storm thrashed, lashing the underside of my heart, making me bleed steadily. I still felt like I couldn't walk by a certain kind of bar without the energy of that bar grasping its wormy phantom skeleton fingers after me, catching my long hair or pricking my cheek and leaving scratches. I couldn't pass by without the smell of it pressing on my chest, suffocating me even as it drew me in. That's what being sober felt like. Something like not enough oxygen.

Sometimes, passing those certain kind of bars, I got heady from the fumes, as if someone had poured gasoline all over me. I knew how dangerous it was, how flammable, and with fire on all sides of me, edging into my small circle of space, how vulnerable I could become. But the silky thinness of the fluid on my skin entranced and trapped me. The smell was so sweet, so chemical and strange, as powdery soft as evil. I knew I was playing with fire, but I wanted to lick it off my fingers anyway.

I still remembered how to saunter into those dark bars, how to pick the guy, how to get him alone. I remembered the way to go to work on him. Walking my

66

beaten track around the city, I pondered the reasons behind my compulsions. My intuition, my preternatural ability to read people, had always been almost like a psychic advantage I carried my entire life. I couldn't stop doing it if I tried. But somewhere along the way I had been wounded, damaged by events beyond my control, and consequently my ability became deformed. Then, instead of using my intuition to help, I used it to manipulate. My ability to read people from the inside out became a handy tool used to control them, and to isolate myself even more.

It seemed my alcoholism was merely a symptom. It was a characteristic of a more pervasive illness from which I suffered: the sickness of being not-like-other-people. I couldn't stop thinking. I couldn't stop feeling. I couldn't hold the world back. It crashed into my soul every second of every day, with full intensity and without any mercy. I felt too much, and I knew more about other people than I wanted to know.

Now, I saw, the alcohol had provided a convenient bulwark between me and the rest of the world. Without it, I felt like I was walking around with no skin. And in that state, anything could get in.

Out of everyone I had ever met in my life, James was the only other person who seemed to be not-like-other-people in the same way that I was not-like-other people. So, even though we didn't have common interests in things like books or movies or music, we shared something deeper. Because of the way we were, feeling too much inside our own skins and knowing too much about others out in the world, both of us suffered from an all-consuming anxiety that drove us through addiction, insomnia, paranoia, and various obsessions. We steadfastly agreed on rules regarding the strangest of things. Like: not eating in public, or in front of strangers. Or: not touching each other without warning first. And: not trusting people, not for a good long while. That last one was the most important.

Like me, James had grown up in a situation that swung back and forth between weird and downright shitty. He'd had a few stepfathers, and one of them had been murdered. He'd taken care of his grandparents when they were dying, waking up every two hours night after night to put morphine drops on his grandmother's tongue. He'd dropped out of school and moved to Seattle entirely on his own the day he turned 18.

Both of us were quiet types, and neither of us minded spending whole days alone. "Alone" was something we knew and knew well. It was our refuge, our touchstone, and our strength. As kids, we'd survived our childhoods by dealing with adults who were too busy, too sick, too stressed, and too drunk, and we did that by embracing what it means to be truly alone. Making it through and then making it work.

Neither one of us was afraid of being alone.

But both of us were terrified of being together.

8

When Aleksia first walked into Pagliarani Investigations I had no idea why she was there. Sal hadn't mentioned he was interviewing, but I also hadn't been paying much attention to anything Sal had said lately.

Margaret had announced her first pregnancy a few months before and by the end of February she was as big as a house. When she gave her notice and told Sal she wasn't coming back after maternity leave, he gave me her job. Now I had the office next to Sal's, and I was the one overseeing surveillance.

It was me every morning on the phone with the guys now, not only running the plates but calling the next move based on the reports that came back. It was me who decided if Chavez or Dave sat planted at the house they had originally been assigned to, or drove onto the next address that surfaced in the profile. I managed all the other PI's we worked with too: the detectives who interviewed claimants and witnesses and wrote up 30-page injury reports based on what they found for the insurance companies.

One of these guys was an older PI by the name of Mack Reaver. All I knew of him was his weary, sometimes caustic voice. He never came into the City so I never met him in person. Over the phone he explained to me that he'd worked surveillance for 20 years. He quit when his back gave out, and then shortly after that his compassion, both from cramping himself into a ball for hours on end in the back of a van, and from spying on everyday scam artists for years. People were shit, he sighed. He'd seen it all.

Then we lost Guy, our best surveillance man.

When he gave his notice, Sal cried. He begged and pleaded with him to stay. But Guy waited him out, sitting as still as a crow on a telephone wire, watching Sal clutch his head in both hands and bang it on the desk. Sal looked up quick and sly from under his performance like a little girl checking on the progress made by her crocodile tears. Then he lunged across the desk at Guy, straining his hands out toward him, a drowning man in need of desperate rescue. Guy didn't blink.

In the end Sal gave in and wrote him a reference. Guy's departure was inevitable after all. He was in his late 30s and didn't want to be doing surveillance forever. Old men don't do well sitting for hours on end in a hot car with a full bladder, which is understandable. Most people don't do well in that kind of situation, regardless of their age.

So, we were down a surveillance man. Our best man at that.

And then Aleksia showed up.

I'd just opened the office that morning, running into Sal as he came galloping down the stairs.

"Jesus—the parade—Columbus Day—FUCK—be back—" he spluttered and gasped, almost falling down the steps past me. He tore his way down to the street below, and like a tornado he picked up bits of trash and scattered debris as he went. A cigarette butt stuck to one of his gleaming black shoes and tiny flecks of lint dotted the front of his black suit. In one fluid swirl he kicked the butt off his foot and ran one beefy hand across his slicked back hair. With the other he brushed off the front of his jacket, restoring himself to crisp black-suited grandeur again, like a king on his way to a funeral in a hurry. As the black Mercedes roared out of the garage and down the street—the horse not expecting the depth of violence in that first kick from its master—Sal's hasty departure echoed in my ears.

The front door hung open, swinging slightly as if it were dazed. I sighed and pulled it shut. I was a little dazed myself.

Relieved to have the promise of an entire morning in which to work relatively undisturbed, I set about editing the stack of surveillance reports in my inbox. From Sal's out-of-breath garbled explanation on his way out the door, I'd translated that something had gone wrong with the Italian Heritage Parade, which happened on Columbus Day each year. Sal was the main organizer. Even though the parade was months away any little crisis could upset the balance of everything. If the Grand Marshal suddenly canceled, Sal would be stuck trying to find another Italian celebrity willing to come to San Francisco to be in his North Beach parade. It was likely he wouldn't be back until early afternoon. Hours of blessed peace, I thought to myself, opening the first file in the stack.

Then the doorbell rang and ruined everything.

Apparently, Sal had made an appointment with this strange-looking girl now standing in the office doorway, and then forgotten all about it in light of the Italian Heritage Parade crisis. Now she stared at me calmly and waited to be taken to her interview. I didn't know what to do with her, so I invited her in. She followed me up the stairway.

"I'm Leah. I kind of...well, I run the office. Uh, what are you here for—I mean, which role did Salvatore go over with you...?" I faltered and gave up. I had no idea who she was or what Sal planned on doing with her.

"Surveillance," she said, so low I barely heard it. I turned around and looked at her but her face remained blank.

"Oh...okay." I didn't know what else to say. She made me nervous but I didn't know why. Something about her made me want to talk more, and that same something made me feel like I wanted whatever came out of my mouth to be good. But suddenly, I didn't feel like I had one good thing in the entire world to say.

"Uh...well...um..." Did I have to sound like such an idiot? "Here! Let's put you in here!" I seized on the empty chair in the corner of my office. PI's are notoriously suspicious and Sal was no exception. I knew he'd be livid if I didn't keep an eye on her. The trouble was, it was also fast dawning on me that I never should have invited her in to begin with.

I sat down at the old typewriter we kept in my office for typing up file labels and glanced down at the list of files that needed a name. I could hardly concentrate. It was like this Aleksia girl was staring a hole into the back of my head. My hands shook and I dropped the paper I was holding. Trying to catch it before Aleksia noticed, I spun too far in my chair and overbalanced. The paper flew away from me and the chair almost tipped over.

"Whoa!" I huffed. I looked behind me. Aleksia was still seated in the corner. Like Guy, she seemed to be good at staying completely frozen in space for long periods of time. I turned back to the typewriter, but not before sneaking another look at what she was wearing.

Of course, I'd taken it in when I first answered the door. But with me being caught off-guard, and then flustered by her almost spooky silence, it was like my brain had just finally caught up with my eyes. After sitting down, I found that now I couldn't push the image out of my mind. What the hell *was* she wearing anyway?

From neck to ankle Aleksia was covered by a long coat that looked at times as if it were an old-fashioned duster—like ladies wore back in the day when they were driving—and at other moments like a cape. Whatever it was, it appeared to be made entirely out of thick, supple, deep red leather. The collar was fringed with pinkish tattered fur that was gray at the edges and complemented Aleksia's hair, which was a rich black and styled in a way that parts of it looked like a thorny dark halo.

I grabbed the paper off the floor and turned back around.

"So...um...how long have you lived in the City?" I asked.

"Two years." She was so fast with her answer that it was like she'd seen the question form in my mind before I'd even asked it.

"Where did you work? I mean, uh...where do you work now?"

Aleksia chuckled and I turned around again. Her green eyes were laughing at me and suddenly I saw the memory of her pale face reflected in water, one morning a long time ago. That pale freckled face...was there an Irish lilt to her whispering voice? I saw her kneeling in the warm, damp grass next to a clean pool of water. She looked around as if she were hunted and pulled a wrapped handkerchief from her bosom. She wore a black and white robe, something like a medieval surcoat. Glancing furtively around again, like someone was after her, she opened the parcel. Before I saw the twinkling steel of the blade, I saw the blood. Deep red, it clung to the linen in sticky mucous strands. She held it for a moment more, loving the blade. Not for what it could do, but for what it had done, for her.

She dumped the knife. Straight into the water after looking around for a third and final time, just like I knew she would. Then there was a rustle as she disappeared into the bushes again and was gone.

I came back to myself, to the Aleksia sitting in front of me now.

She was still staring at me, and smiling now. No more than two seconds had passed.

"Do you really want to know?"

"Yes!" There was no question, I knew she was about to tell me something terribly important.

"I work at Rickenbacker's." she said.

"Where is—what's—?" I wasn't sure if she'd just pronounced the name of a company or the name of an obscure disease.

"Eddie Rickenbacker's. It's down on Second. It's a bar. I work for Delbert. He owns the place." The sentences were delivered with sterile efficiency. I had no doubt she'd been the one to use that blade.

"Delbert? He owns it? Is he your boss?"

But Aleksia only laughed softly like before, like Delbert was a ghost or an alien, someone it would be hilarious and ridiculous to work for, but like no one else would ever get the joke.

74

"Owner? Yeah, he's the owner. The boss." And now she sounded almost cruel. "But he lives there too. In the bar. We take care of him."

"Who's we?"

"The girls. Us. Me and the other bartenders. Delbert pretty much lives on the couch in the front window. With his TV and his cat, Higgins. Higgins has one eye and three legs. He loves that damn cat." Aleksia paused and chuckled again. "I mean, really loves him." There was something in her voice, but like before I didn't get the joke.

"And what do you mean you take care of him? Is Delbert old?"

"Well, he is and he isn't." She stopped smiling and stared at me seriously now. "Delbert's only 72, but he's not in the best health. He's obese and can hardly walk. He sits and lays on that couch day in and day out and so he gets bedsores. But we turn him," she said, then she winked at me.

I kept quiet, not wanting to risk her not going on with the story. Stories were my Achilles' heel. I was hooked.

"There's also an attic space he lives in, right up above the bar. Kind of like a loft." I nodded. This was getting interesting. "Well, he gets depressed and then he takes the elevator up there and just festers in that loft space, and he won't come down. Not when he gets like that. He refuses. But he has to use the bathroom, you know? So, there's a bucket."

I widened my eyes.

"To shit and piss in," she added.

"Wow..." I managed.

"Yeah." Aleksia smiled and leaned back in her chair, satisfied that I understood. "Of course, we—the girls and me—help Delbert with other things too. Like shaving. We shave him when he needs it," she said, pointing to herself. I waited.

"Naked."

I knew it. Home run.

"What?" I was fully engrossed now.

"Delbert prefers to be in the nude when he's being shaved. We obey his preferences."

"But you aren't naked?" I asked.

"Oh no." Aleksia laughed as if I'd suggested something crazy. "Never. Delbert doesn't want to see that."

I got caught up on her last words. *Delbert doesn't want to see that.* Why wouldn't a disgusting 72-year-old guy who was almost totally immobile and lived in a bar, who was obese and had bedsores, and demanded to be shaved in the nude by young beautiful women (for Aleksia was very beautiful, as I had no doubt the others were as well), why wouldn't this same skeezy guy want to see those young chicks naked? Something didn't add up.

Something didn't smell right, as Sal would say.

"So, how often do you guys shave him?" I asked.

"Oh, maybe once a week. His beard's not what it used to be, no more than patches of stubble, really."

"Have you shaved him yourself?"

"Of course! We all have. I'm one of his favorites, so I've probably done it the most, actually." I marked pride shadowing her voice.

"Wow," I breathed. "You're so lucky."

Aleksia looked up and locked her eyes with mine. Something dark and definite, like the ghost of a missile, passed between us.

"I know." she said.

"Tell me some more about Delbert."

Aleksia leaned forward and clasped her hands on her knees.

"Delbert's a racist."

I nodded for her to go on.

"He hates black people. And he's got a son—not his real son, but like a real son. The bar manager, Key. That's his adopted son. Key keeps the bar for him, keeps the books—down to every cent—and keeps Delbert alive. He's the only one Delbert doesn't abuse. The only one he doesn't scream at, and call names, and harangue, day in, day out..." For a split second I saw Aleksia at Delbert's bar, slaving away and shaving Delbert naked, and I knew what a tyrant Delbert truly was.

"Key's the only one who's okay in Delbert's book, the only one he trusts. And it's always been like that. In his eyes Key can do no wrong." She threw up her hands and they trembled in the air, at either side of her temples, exasperated.

"So what's the deal? I don't get it."

"But don't you?" Aleksia smiled at me and folded her hands neatly on top of her knees again. "Key's black."

"What? But what about Delbert saying...the racial slurs?"

"It's like Key doesn't hear them." Aleksia shook her head. "Of course, they're never directed specifically at *him*. But they are directed at someone. Other black people. But it's like Key's immune to Delbert's nastiness. Not like he ignores him, but like he actually doesn't hear it. It's remarkable, really."

I sat back, pondering this.

"Well, what about Ricker...Ricano's—the bar? What's Delbert's bar like?" I asked.

"Delbert is...responsible...for Rickenbacker's décor." Aleksia coughed and looked down. She was going to come out with something repulsive again, I just knew it. "It's mostly furnished with antique motorcycles. Everywhere. Floor, ceiling, motorcycle parts hanging off the walls."

Avidly, I scanned her words. Nothing. This was the intro. There would be more.

"It's got a lot of antiques, that place does. But the...ah, I guess you could say, the most interesting ones, are the World War II relics. Helmets, guns, belts. From the Nazis. Picked off the dead Nazis." There it was. Impatient, I wanted the whole story at once now. I wanted to glut myself on Aleksia and her life. I wanted to eat her until I made myself sick.

Instead, I let her talk. I didn't move.

"But that's the thing, too—that you've got to know, about Delbert. He's a liar. And he'll tell you that upfront. He lies about everything. Or at least, he says he does. But that could be a lie too. So, you never know, when you're dealing with Delbert. You never know. He says he's the one who traipsed over those fields and picked over those corpses, he says he's the one who robbed the dead Nazis and that's how he got all the stuff hanging up in the bar. But who knows? Who really knows? Delbert's a liar."

All traces of the dusty residue of exasperation were gone from her voice. I saw Aleksia again behind the bar, waiting on Delbert, who I pictured as a cross between Jabba the Hutt and Rodney Dangerfield. Sitting in front of me now, her eyes sparkled, her lips parted mischievously at me, and she smiled. I saw her lit up from the inside out and it was like gazing up at a full moon with my ankles deep in the black sucking mud of a swamp.

Aleksia was still sitting in my office when Sal came back. He took her into his office and after a little while they came out again and Sal told me she was hired. He introduced her to me all smiley and big-voiced, like she'd just gotten there and he already knew her, instead of her being a stranger who had just shown up that morning and then spent three hours with me in my office and Sal not even there, the whole time her telling me stories, embedded in the center of each a cold secret like a metal stud buried in the soft flesh of an earlobe. But Sal acted like he'd been the first to meet her, so I went along with it. Even though I knew I could sneak a closed knowing look at Aleksia and she would understand, because it was like that between us now.

When she came back the next morning I set her up with all her equipment: her phone, her camera, and a few props we kept at the office for personal contacts, wigs and sunglasses for the guys to use when they pretended to take voter surveys or carried a bogus delivery for the wrong address. Aleksia laughed when she saw some of the wigs. I broke in with my serious face to pull her back down to the nuts and bolts.

"So, you know there are no lunch breaks, right?" Rookies were usually shocked.

"I know," Aleksia answered softly and pushed her tongue up inside her top lip, making the lip swell out toward me. It gave her expression a sober defiant edge that vanished entirely whenever she smiled or laughed. Working with her at Pagliarani, I grew to know that look well. It meant she was absorbing. Not just listening, not just taking the information in, but letting each new fact come to her, allowing the data to poke around inside her and get comfortable. I knew that when Aleksia pushed her tongue up inside her top lip she was getting ready for anything.

"And you know you don't really get breaks. Like...at all...right?" But somehow, I already knew that she did know. I trusted her. Absolutely. My girl Aleksia knew exactly what she was getting into, and if she really didn't she'd think it so much the better. The harder it was going to be for her, the better she'd enjoy it. And I already knew that too.

"I know," she said again, but then suddenly she brightened. "Not even to use the bathroom! I know. But I've got these. You have to check them out, they're amazing." She tossed me a small package.

"Travel johns?" I read off the label. Clear plastic encased the front of the box, through which I could see a lump of latex that resembled a balled-up rubber glove. On the back were instructions on how to use the travel john and stick figures in various postures as examples. I got it. It was like a shrunk-down litter box for human use, the head fitted snug right over your crotch and emptied into a bag filled with odor-absorbing crystals. Then it sealed up to keep everything in the bag. I'd never seen these before and I was impressed. Our guys usually used empty soda bottles.

"Well, tomorrow you'll work with Grove and you can show him these things then too." I gently waved the box in front of her. "But Grove's got a travel john of his own," I warned. Aleksia looked at me and tipped her head to one side, quizzical.

"He does? But I thought—?" I put a hand up to stop her.

"It's called a big pickle jar in the back of his old van." We stared at each other for a second and then we burst out laughing.

"Let me guess? Sometimes Grove drops a pickle?" Aleksia asked, and we exploded into giggles again.

9

Sal put Aleksia on one of our toughest cases with Grove for her first day. By the time I got in at 8:00am that morning, they'd already been at the residence for three hours, sitting in the dark slowly pinking its way into cold dawn and chatting over the phone out of boredom. The house was in the middle of Northern Nowhere California. Sitting outside of a tiny little town holding only about 500 people, both Grove and Aleksia said they couldn't even see the residence. It was cloistered in a forest of trees, with a long and narrow, winding drive up to the house that seemed specifically designed to thwart PI's. Sitting on the street was impossible, there was no street. Only dirt roads. Our usual set-up for difficult residences—propping open the hood, the PI using the guise of any average broken-down-car owner, while all the time surreptitiously running the camera with it pointed at the house—wouldn't work. Staying undercover almost didn't matter if we couldn't even see the residence for the trees. I asked Grove about the back of the place.

"Are you kidding?" he said. "We can't even get to the front. Fuck. The back's probably just as crazy. Trees, vines, tons of brambles and shit. Anyone who crawls through that mess is going to make so much of a ruckus the claimant'll hear them coming a mile off."

Shit. If we wasted this day the insurance company would strangle us. It was 250 miles just driving to the place and back, and we charged for the hours and the mileage. If we sent the client a bill for eight hours of work, two ops on the case, and no footage to show for it, we'd really be fucked. I pictured the veins straining out of Sal's neck and the way those couple seconds of dead quiet just hung in the air right before he really lost it.

Shit. Shit. Shit. I cursed to myself but drew a blank. Not even a description of the claimant, much less a past sighting by one of our guys. No way around it, this was a shitty case.

"All right, Grove," I said. "What about sending Aleksia on foot instead of you?" Privately, I'd do anything I could to keep Grove in the car. At almost 300 pounds and dressed in his usual tie-dye, Grove would stick out like a sore thumb. City surveillance was his specialty, and for that, especially in San Francisco, he blended in seamlessly. In NorCal BFE the game was changed. I'd send Aleksia.

Grove's voice brought me back to the situation at hand.

"Send Aleksia?" he said hesitantly. "Well...I mean she's pretty good so far. Keeps her head down and seems to have a lot of smarts...but...well, isn't this only her first case?"

"Yeah..." I sighed. How could I explain to Grove that I already knew Aleksia would come through for us? I just did. I just knew. And I couldn't explain it.

"But Sal's not here and we need film. She can check it out. It'll be good." I hung up before Grove could respond and dialed Aleksia before I could change my mind.

I told her to keep it fast, just a short run around the back. *Get in and get out,* I told her. Just take a quick look and then get back to the car. Just to see if there's even a yard, or if it really was all forest. She called back 15 minutes later.

"I found a way in! There's a backyard! There's a way in *and* a spot to set up my camera!" She sounded like a breathless little girl. I grinned to myself.

"Really? Grove was pretty sure it'd be all forest, too much junk to get past—"

Aleksia cut me off.

"Oh it is, it is. But there's a moat!"

"A what—?" What was that last word?

"A moat!" she cheerfully repeated.

"Like a castle moat?"

"Exactly. Exactly! Like a castle moat."

"Aleksia—"

"I'm going to swim it."

"Wha—wait, what? No, Aleksia, what—?"

She interrupted me again. "Ok, listen. I've got some rope in my car. I'm going to tie my camera to my head and swim over to the other side. If I don't call back in 30 minutes, call Grove."

"Aleksia wait—" But she was gone. The phone was dead in my hand.

For the next 30 minutes I paced the office. Nervously looking over the Castro from two stories above the street, I couldn't imagine being farther away from Aleksia than I was right now. Below me I caught sight of a pink and black Mohawk on a man that matched the pink and black diamond collar of the Chihuahua attached to him. Taxis roared past and sucked dirty sheets of newspaper littering the sidewalk into traffic. A horn honked as another car drove through the whirlwind and a flock of pigeons scattered at the sound, one almost flying right into the pink and black Mohawk. The man hurriedly bent to his Chihuahua and smoothed its tiny haunches before disappearing into a gourmet chocolatier's shop on the corner.

I released a trembling breath. Where was Aleksia and why didn't she call?

I left the Castro city scene for a moment and flew to her in my mind.

Swimming in a strange river, the current pulled at me, a cloud of gnats buzzing above my head. The forest creaked and twittered all around. When a roaring wind came through it sucked a rush of dead leaves off the branches. A little brown sparrow hopped away from its perch and back again as the wind passed, smoothing its feathers as it groomed itself back to order. I watched the leaves settle on the water's surface and kept swimming.

My breath caught and I came back to the Castro. Worlds away from each other.

The phone buzzed to life.

"Aleksia!"

"Yup. Back. Water was great!" I heard the smile in her voice and the steel cords binding my chest loosened all at once.

"Aah...you made it. Jesus. I was fucking worried." I heard her familiar chuckle and breathed deeply again. "Get any film?"

"No." And now I heard serious Aleksia. I could see her pushing her tongue up under her top lip from here. "I didn't see anyone and I didn't figure it'd be smart to stick around any longer than it takes to get a lay of the land so I wiggled just as close as I could and filmed the scenery. At least we'll know what we're going into the next time, right?"

"Right." I didn't have the heart to tell her that Sal would never let any of his guys do what she did—a goddamn moat. I inwardly groaned and did cartwheels at the same time. She fucking swam across a goddamn moat, and all to get the "lay of the land" as she put it. Christ.

What Aleksia really didn't understand either, was that not only would Sal never let one of his guys do what she did, but none of them would ever volunteer to do it either. It was her first day on the job, and already she'd blown the balls off every man on our team.

Except for Sal, I corrected myself. I could kind of see Sal swimming across a moat. Definitely if he was pissed.

I sighed to myself and walked over to Sal's office. I wanted to see what he had on the roster for Aleksia tomorrow.

●●●

Over the next few months Aleksia became Sal's golden girl. He snatched up the phone jealously when she was due to call. He stayed in the office longer so he wouldn't miss it. Like it was between weird old Delbert and his adopted son Key, in Sal's eyes, Aleksia could do no wrong. And now, when I buzzed through any other call to Sal, he practically snarled into my ear when he picked up.

"Aleksia finally?"

"No, Sal. Chavez again. His claimant's hot."

"FUCK—" I jabbed the transfer button and let Chavez receive the rest of it.

I stared at the lifeless telephone. Sal was worse than a high school girl waiting for her crush to call. But damn it, I knew how he felt. Aleksia was harder to hold onto than water. She was the very definition of elusive. I was addicted to people who were more like definitions than actual people. And the person who went beyond a definition to the summit of being wholly an idea...well, that person was irresistible.

Then, finally, one day Aleksia asked me to hang out with her.

It came in the form of an email, and attached to the email was a story. The story was about a frog jumping contest: *The Celebrated Jumping Frog of Calaveras County* by Mark Twain. I skimmed the story and then clicked it shut and focused on the email.

L,

If you're not previously engaged this coming Saturday afternoon I'd be much honored if you'd consider attending the famous Frog Jumping Contest of Calaveras County with me (see story attached). It's in Angel's Camp and I'll drive. If you're going, let me know what time to pick you up. We'll need to get on the road early.

—A

Well. I blew my hair off my forehead and hit reply. 8:00am I typed, and then I hit send.

Three days later we were on our way to Angel's Camp and I was looking forward to the long drive. I felt sure I could talk to Aleksia the way I wanted to always talk to people. With direct and interesting questions, and no small talk getting in the way.

First, I asked her how she ended up at Pagliarani. She said Craigslist and I swatted a hand at her. "That's not what I mean," I said. "And you know it. I mean, why did you want to become a PI?"

Aleksia stared straight ahead at the road in silence, and then a slow grin broke across her face. When it did I saw how the delicate skin at the corners of her eyes was seamed with strain, hidden there until her smile exposed it. Her delight cinched tight onto her suffering, like two hands shaking and then trying to crush each other.

"The real answer to that question is how I came to be in San Francisco." She shot a look at me when I tried to interrupt. "You can't have all the answers you want by skipping the maze at the beginning. Nobody gets to the core first, right off the bat. You should know that. Of all people." She rolled her eyes at me.

I flopped back against my seat. She was right, but if anyone else had said it in any other way, I wouldn't have bought it. I had to give it to Aleksia. She had me.

"Fine," I gave in. "Why did you come to San Francisco?"

She'd been bumming around Lake Tahoe, she said, waitressing, doing odd jobs, trying to figure out her life. And then she knew—all in one moment—it was time to go. She saw suddenly that things had become unbearable where she was in the present and it was unacceptable to stay frozen there. She didn't know anything else and she had no plan, but she knew she had to move.

I understood completely.

But she didn't know where to go, she said.

I understood that too.

She couldn't go back home, she explained. That was a non-option. And she'd gone to college on the East Coast, but she couldn't go back there either.

"Really?" I interrupted her. "Where'd you go to school?"

"Harvard." She paused for a second to look back at the road and I pushed my eyeballs toward the window at my side so she couldn't see the impression left there. It wasn't the school, it was the way she had said it. Like I'd asked what she'd had for breakfast in the middle of life-and-death surgery and she'd snapped, "Cereal," before ordering me to hand her the scalpel. Like Harvard was just another bowl of flakes, just another morning. A past event, absolutely non-essential now.

And again, I understood.

The immediate future, she continued, loomed bright and menacing and huge in front of her, waiting to be filled with meals to be eaten and sleeps to be slept. Tapping its fingers impatiently, that future leered down at her, daring her to step into it.

But instead of stepping, Aleksia flew. Away.

Something in San Francisco had called her. A voice had cried out to her and seemed to resonate with the darkness she'd always felt inside her, the constant shadow that dragged down her very blood. She came because she had to. Something had beckoned her.

"So did you finish?" I interrupted again.

"Hmmm? Finish?" She looked over at me, bewildered. "Finish what?"

"Harvard!" I almost yelled. Aleksia was maddening sometimes.

"Oh, that." she said. "Well, I finished all my course work if that's what you mean. But I never got my degree—not the actual paper." She rapped on the steering wheel, like she was knocking on wood. "I didn't get to walk."

"Why not?" I asked.

Aleksia groaned and then looked at me and laughed.

"I ruined three library books and refused to pay for them."

I kept quiet, letting the seconds spin out.

"See, I like to sleep in water," she finally continued. "So, I usually sleep in the bathtub. But at Harvard I lived in the dorm. And I couldn't have a bathtub. There was one bathroom to a hall and we all shared it. So, I had to make my own."

Quite the opposite of what I felt with most people, I couldn't possibly imagine what she would say next.

"Well, what I did was steal a recycling bin from the cafeteria. I cleaned it out with Pine Sol and ran a hose into it from the sink in our room. When I went to bed I'd fill it halfway with warm water and fall asleep in it. When I woke up a few hours later and the water was cold, I'd know it was time to fill it the rest of the way. This time with hot, to make the cold water warm, see?"

I nodded.

"Uh, so..." Her eyes flickered toward me and then she glued them back on the road again.

"So, one night I fell asleep in my tub, like I always did, but I fell asleep studying and the book I was reading was the first to go in. The other two I bumped with my arm, I guess. They weren't balanced the best anyway." She paused and seemed to consider something. "A recycling bin just isn't a bathtub," she said finally, and sighed like we were in a Victorian drawing room, having tea. *Good servants are sooo hard to find*, I imagined her drawling.

A recycling bin just isn't a bathtub. Her words rang in my ears. She talked about the recycling bin's unwillingness to be a bathtub as if it were exactly that—unwilling. Not that it was impossible, unchangeable, or strictly non-transferable. Just plain unwilling to be what she wanted it to be.

And again, I totally understood.

●●●

When we got to the frog jumping contest I wasn't disappointed. It was like a fair, but out in the middle of nowhere and all about frogs. Peddlers in booths lined a path that led to a stage set up in the distance, presumably where the frog jumping took place. One booth sold wooden boxes with frogs carved on top, another displayed neon green frog-catching nets, and still another offered huge blow-up frog dolls. Mixed in were shacks frying up vegetables, funnel cake, and corn dogs, and the same snow cone tents that are at every county fair. It was the perfect place to be on a beautiful day in the middle of June.

Aleksia grabbed my hand and pulled me into the center of it all.

We got paper cones full of hot peanuts and then decided to duck out of the crowd. We wove our way to a nearby grassy hill, sat down, and started picking the peanuts out of the paper as we talked. Licking the salt off my fingers, I asked Aleksia more questions.

"So, you still haven't told me...why did you become a PI?"

Aleksia didn't say anything and went on eating her peanuts. For a moment I thought she would refuse to respond, would go on staring dreamily over all the people blurring together now like watercolors down at the fair, and I'd never know her reasons.

But running underneath that fear was the strange feeling I had that Aleksia had already let me in. If a person's mind was like a house, then Aleksia had left her front door unlocked—on purpose—inviting me not only to take a look around but also to take anything I felt like stealing. It was like everything inside her—even the dark secret parts, the parts everybody else thought of as their skeletons in the closet—all of it was up for grabs with Aleksia. You just had to be brave enough to enter and put your hands on it.

"I used to feel ugly, when I was younger," she finally said. "I was nerdy. I wore glasses. I didn't know how to act. Ironically enough, I was a cheerleader in high school, even though I was on the chubby side. And I was good at it. But then I went to Harvard and got to be a hermit. A bookworm. When I moved back home I got depressed. Real depressed. All the baths I could take didn't help," she said. "All the water in the world didn't matter."

She stopped and stared past me again, this time at the California hills in the distance, looking a little like big swollen green frogs themselves.

"You already know what happened after that. I told you. I came to the City because I had to move and the City called to me and took me in. But after I got there, I changed. I lost weight. I started cheerleading again. Just for fun." She laughed and I started at the sound. "I'd forgotten how much I loved it. Completely forgotten. Like amnesia. But when I started doing it again it all came back. Like I had forgotten, but my body remembered for me, you know what I mean?"

I nodded. I did know what she meant.

"So of course, I lost even more weight. And then I started buying clothes. New clothes. That fit me and looked good on me. Clothes I never would have worn before. And I felt different too, really different. Like a different person..."

I nodded again. I knew.

"Then I started working for Delbert, and that was when I knew. When I knew I was *changed*—from what I was before—changed into this different being. And when men looked at me it was different than before too...it was like they couldn't look anywhere else."

I didn't need to nod my agreement anymore. It was like she was reading me from the inside out.

"So, I struck on the idea of becoming a PI. Because I knew as this different person, this *changed being*, that people would let me in. Men would be the easiest targets of course, but I'd have some power over almost everyone, and the ones I didn't, I wouldn't care about. So in the end, I guess that's why I did it. Because I knew they'd let me in."

"But wait—" I stopped her. "I know sometimes claimants let you in—when you're doing fake deliveries and shit. I know some of them actually open the door and invite you in for a cup of coffee or whatever." And it was true, they had and they did. Aleksia charmed people, even the ones she was stalking. "But most of the time you're just doing surveillance. Most of the time you don't have any direct contact. Most of them definitely don't 'invite you in' as you put it." I curved my fingers into hooks and made quotation marks in the air.

"But they do," Aleksia continued as if she were half-asleep, or hypnotized. Still, she gazed out at the hills beyond. "Whether they know it or not, they do. When you're working someone, when you're spying and they don't know it, they know all the same. Everyone feels it. Everyone. That's why I'm the best at surveillance you've ever seen. Because I get it." And now she looked back at me.

"Never look directly at them," she said. "Not even through the camera. Line up your shot, glance back every few seconds, but never stare, because they'll feel it and some part of them will know and then they won't be what they really are anymore. They won't be themselves. Because when you watch someone like that, when you observe them against their will and without their knowledge, they're letting you in...whether they want to or not."

We sat quietly together then, watching the afternoon turn to evening and the vibrant green hills fade to a dusky purple. After a while we went down and watched the contest and *oohed* and *aahed* over the frogs, how big they were and how far they could jump, but the whole time there was something dancing in the back of my mind. One more thing I wanted to ask Aleksia.

When everything was over we headed back to her truck. On the way there, the question I wanted to ask jumped out of my mouth.

"Aleksia." She turned the key in the ignition and then inclined toward me, her eyes a dark glassy green, like waves in a storm, and waited.

"Will you take me to meet Delbert?"

She nodded once and then, in silence and under swell of the storm, we drove home.

10

The next Saturday night Aleksia called and told me to meet her down at Rickenbacker's, the bar where she still worked part-time and Delbert lived. When I got there, I spotted Aleksia as soon as I walked in. She was sitting up at the bar, laughing and flirting with a handsome bartender, the guy who could only be Key, Delbert's adopted son. Wearing a short skirt, with her long black hair hanging sleek and dangerous down her back, she was stunning. I pushed my way through to her.

I hoisted myself up on a bar stool as she swiveled toward me. Aleksia being Aleksia, she'd probably picked up my scent when I was still halfway down the block.

"He's over there. On his couch in the window," she said, barely moving her lips. Her head tilted almost imperceptibly in Delbert's direction.

From where I sat I could observe Delbert pretty well. He was a fat old man with a gigantic body and a little head. A baseball cap was tilted jauntily back on his white hair and he wore overalls that bagged loosely at his chest. Thick glasses smeared with fingerprints covered his eyes, which he held in a concrete squint. He might have looked like a cute old-folks kind of man if it hadn't been for the snarl carved across the lower part of his face, and the tubing that snaked out of his nose and down over the front of the overalls. His swollen hands curled possessively over the ball of the cane he leaned his upper body on, the lower bloated half of him settled immovably into his couch.

His corner was actually in the front window of the bar, so anyone passing by outside could see him on display. It was a space that appeared to function as living room, kitchen, and bedroom. I wondered if the bucket was concealed somewhere. An old TV set sat planted atop an ancient cabinet, right across from where Delbert sat, and a scuffed coffee table squatted in between. Covered with prescription bottles, inhalers, old tissues, and plates of half-eaten food, it was like a toadstool blossoming with the entrails of a decaying medicine cabinet. An oxygen tank stood next to Delbert, and I saw two or three more behind him.

The rest of the bar looked like a typical Saturday night scene—couples with wine and hot chicks on hot dates, guys doing shots and clapping each other on the back—but in the window Delbert sat alone. An old man in a forgotten room. No one else in the bar even glanced his way. It was like they didn't—like they *couldn't*—see him.

I turned back to Aleksia.

"Well?" I asked, cocking my head toward the corner. "What's the deal?"

"I told you he lives here...that's where he lives. In that corner. Sometimes he gets depressed and takes the elevator up to the loft, goes into his hole. But most of the time he's down here."

I shook my head impatiently. "No, I mean, why's it like everyone else in here ignores him? He's in plain sight."

Aleksia shot me a small crafty grin. It made her look like a fox. She pushed her tongue up under her top lip.

"For them...there's nothing to see."

●●●

After that I stopped at Rickenbacker's occasionally to see if Aleksia was in, but really to see Delbert.

One Sunday afternoon we sat at the almost totally empty bar. Aleksia sipped a beer and chatted lazily with Key. I watched the ice melt in my club soda and kept an eye on Delbert. Now I understood the wariness Aleksia had displayed on that first night I'd met her here. Delbert made me jumpy. I'd seen him lash out suddenly and viciously at the waitresses more times than I could count. The fact that Delbert was completely immobile had no effect on his presence, which seemed everywhere in the room at once, or rather, concentrated in the center of the bar, up near the ceiling, like a frozen and monstrous black spider that crouched upside down over all of us, pulsing and waiting. The moment anybody fucked up it spooled down scary and fast, catching and devouring "the stupid," Delbert's name for nearly everyone who incurred his disfavor.

Because of this power Delbert had, he fascinated me. But I still hadn't ever spoken to him. Not yet. I was too scared.

"Who was that senator's wife you said you fucked, Delbert?" Aleksia called over to him, laughing. "Key can't remember."

"Not Key can't remember, it isn't. It's you, you stupid bitch," Delbert snapped. "Stupid, stupid," he muttered under his breath, loud enough for us to hear.

"Well?" Aleksia's sunny smile hadn't flagged for a second.

"Feinstein! All right!" he shouted, and then went back to watching his TV. "And she wasn't no

97

goddamned stupid senator's wife ya dumb cunt. She was the fucking *senator*. Dianne Feinstein. You hear that, stupid? You know that name? Eh, stupid? The— goddamn—senator—Dianne—Feinstein."

Aleksia giggled as she shot a look at Key, and a smile broke across his face, the color of warm honey. I thought to myself again how handsome he was, and how friendly. How odd that he worked here, and that he was Delbert's adopted son.

Suddenly the cordless phone lying on the bar buzzed and Key snatched it up.

"Rickenbacker's," he answered. And then, "Um hm. Um hm." He nodded and then said, "hold on," and cradled the phone to his chest. "Hey Delbert!" he yelled. Delbert gave no sign of hearing him. "Delbert!" Key yelled again. "There's a girl on the phone—says she wants a job!" Delbert stared at the TV as if he hadn't heard a thing.

"DELBERT! Girl on the phone for you!" Key walked toward him now, shouting as he got closer.

"Eh?" Finally, he turned, slowly, as if he'd just caught the last part of what Key said. From what Aleksia had told me, Delbert was half deaf when he wanted to be. At other times it appeared he could pick up the sound of a dog whistle.

Key leaned over the couch and placed the phone in Delbert's bloated clamshell hand. I could see from where I sat that the nails on that hand were long and starting to curve over.

"Who the fuck is this?" Delbert spat into the phone, never taking his eyes off the TV. "Who am I? You fuckin' stupid bitch, I'm the fuckin' owner! I repeat—who the fuck are you?"

Aleksia elbowed me as she tipped her beer up and took a swig. Watching him, she used two fingers to fish the lemon out of her Corona and began munching on it. I could see the rind being mashed to a pulp between her white even teeth. She spit it out into a napkin and then pushed her tongue up under her upper lip. She nudged me again.

"I told you Delbert only asks girls four questions when he interviews them," she said in a low voice. I nodded and shrugged at her. *So?*

"The interview has begun," she said simply, and then went back to watching.

"What the fuck you say your name was?" Delbert ranted into the phone. "Kathy? Damn stupid name," he growled. I winced for the poor girl on the other end of the line.

"Fine. You wanna work here? Lemme ask you some things stupid." Aleksia's elbow was in my side again. *Here we go.*

"Where'dja go to school?" Delbert paused, actually listening now. "Northwestern? Where the fuck's that? Fuckin' vague general name—could be anywhere. Northwest of fuckin' what? Chicago you say? Fuckin' shithole town."

Aleksia turned back to me and shook her head. She made a slitting motion across her throat. But I already knew the girl was out. As Delbert put it, he only hired stupid bitches from Ivy League schools. He'd probably go on with the interview though, just because he enjoyed it.

"Are you a homosexual?" he asked abruptly, and then paused again, apparently listening. "A *homo-sex-shul* stupid. Do ya eat pussy? A woman who eats pussy is known as a homosexual here in San Francisco. Are you one? Eh, stupid? Well, are you?" He paused again while the girl made what I could only imagine was her stammering reply.

"Will you consent to a lie-detector test?" he asked, switching angles abruptly again. "On what?" he cried. "On fuckin' well anything I ask you stupid, that's what!" He kept his eyes trained on the TV. "All right, now answer this stupid." Fourth and final question. "Do you steal?" Another silence. "Do you fuckin' steal? Are you a thief? Do you *take things*? No? Really? You've never taken one thing that didn't belong to you? Not one thing in your goddamned life? Think back. Think hard. Do you steal? Are you a thief?"

Delbert's question made me think. I wasn't a thief and I didn't steal...and yet...I had taken things in my life. Things that didn't belong to me: books from a store, secrets from the odds and ends of the people I collected. But I didn't do it on a regular basis. I wasn't a thief...but now...it looked different now. The truth was I had taken things.

Yes, I was a thief.

Thinking I'd known why Aleksia orbited Delbert before, I saw now I didn't know anything, not really. After that last question, there were others that opened up inside me. Being around Delbert, I wondered how many he could answer.

●●●

"What are you doing this Saturday?" Aleksia asked one afternoon when she called for the plate on her latest case.

"Nothing. Why?"

"Delbert. We're taking him to the state fair in Sacramento. If you really want to observe him at his finest you won't want to miss this. We're hitting the 4-H booths," she said in her smoky monotone, the hush of silk rope twining around my wrist.

"4-H? What? What do you mean?" I kept one eye on the screen in front of me, and one hand typing at the keyboard. I was editing her latest report. She'd posed as a prospective renter to a guy illegally subletting his apartment in the Marina. During the walk-through, the guy had given her a pair of panties he'd said were sewn by an underground sweatshop he had going on in Hunter's Point. I was only half listening to the latest I was getting on Delbert over the phone. It seemed not even Aleksia could distract me from Aleksia.

"Delbert's into mapling but he—"

"Wait. What? Mapling? What the hell's that?" I asked.

"*Mapling.* Like maple as in 'maple syrup.' But a verb. As in, 'Delbert usually maples his cat but he'd prefer to maple a more substantial animal—like a calf.'"

"But what is it? What does it mean?" I asked again. I cradled the phone between my ear and shoulder to peck at the keyboard faster.

"To bite and or suckle the flesh of an animal in a sexual manner," she repeated dutifully, as if explaining things to a very small child.

"What?" My hands froze over the keys. I swiveled away from the screen. "So, Delbert...is he going at it with these animals? Does he fuck them or what?"

"No, he doesn't have sex with them." Aleksia chuckled. "It's really only a matter of the mouth. He says he grew up alone and friendless, and on some sort of farm in Singapore, and that his only source of comfort were the calves. He says he used to lay down with them in the fields and maple them. These are his 'golden memories' of childhood, I guess. But I don't really know much more. Like I said, Delbert lies. What I do know is that the only animal he maples now is his cat, Higgins. That three-legged, one-eyed cat you've seen at Rickenbacker's. Higgins is all he's got and so Higgins will do. But he says what he really wants is a calf. So, me and one of the other waitresses, Lynette, are going to get him one. That's where Sacramento comes in. Where else are you gonna find your pick of the calves but at the state fair?"

The possibilities bloomed like fireworks in my mind. I pictured obese, obscene Delbert in the middle of a barn packed with innocent bright-eyed youngsters showing their best pig or calf. I saw Aleksia distracting one of them, turning Delbert loose on their animal before they had time to realize that old people can still be evil and powerful and crazy even if they can barely move and are ensconced in 400 pounds of rotting flab. Never again would anything like that—anything so Delbert—happen to any of those people the rest of their whole lives. This was something that would burn a guaranteed memory, and I'd get to watch the burning as it happened.

"Yeah?" Aleksia laughed low and throaty.

"Fuck yeah," I said. "I'm in."

11

I knew that Saturday morning when I showed up at Rickenbacker's there would be no way for me to avoid talking to Delbert. With only three of us, and the long car ride there and back, I wouldn't be able to get around it. I screwed up my courage and made the leap as soon as I walked in the door. Aleksia and the other girl, Lynette, were over in Delbert's corner helping him up and out of the couch. I walked right over, smiling at Aleksia and giving Lynette a small nod.

"Hi Delbert," I said.

"Eh?" He peered up at me from where he was half standing, leaning between Aleksia on one side and Lynette on the other. "Who're you?" he demanded. The girls froze.

"I'm Leah."

"Who?" he barked.

"Leah." I pushed my voice at him but didn't shout. Growing up, I'd lived with my mostly deaf grandma. I knew the trick wasn't to yell, but instead to act like you were having every conversation onstage.

"Eh? Oh." He grunted and resumed his struggles to stand.

That was ridiculously easy, I thought to myself. I stayed where I was and watched the laborious process of getting Delbert off the couch.

"Well what are you doing still standing there, stupid? Wanna give me a fuckin' hand?" he shot toward me.

"Huh? Oh!" I rushed to the huddle and stood flustered, arms akimbo. Delbert grabbed me and spun me around. He planted a pasty hand on each of my shoulders and leaned on me like I was a walker. I could hear him raggedly suck in air and felt his warm swampy breath on the back of my neck.

"Well stupid, you gonna move or are we gonna stand here all day?" He jabbed a gnarled finger into my shoulder blade. I moved.

We took Aleksia's truck, and the evidence of her detective work was everywhere: empty bottles and wrappers on the floor, sticky-looking stains on the steering wheel, wigs and sunglasses in the back hatch. Delbert sat up front and Aleksia drove. Lynette and I sat in back and took turns fielding Delbert's questions.

"You like to suck cock?" Delbert threw over his shoulder at us.

"Delbert! None of your fuckin' business!" Lynette snapped, but she was smiling.

Delbert waited and I realized it was my turn.

"Well, if I like the guy," I ventured. It was true. "I don't usually do it if I don't like the guy. Then it's just work."

Delbert didn't say anything. I had no idea if he was satisfied with my answer or not.

Then he turned his head toward Aleksia in the driver's seat.

"Eh? Well stupid?" he asked.

"Well what?" she answered dreamily, eyes glued to the road. Imagining a surveillance chase with the car in front of her probably, I thought.

"Aren't you listening, stupid? I'm askin' questions and you're not even fuckin' listenin'. Stupid, stupid," Delbert clucked.

"Hmmm..." She murmured, never taking her eyes off the road.

"Do you like to suck cock, stupid?" Delbert cried.

"What?" Finally, she looked at him. "None of your fuckin' business, Delbert." She went back to staring at the road and hummed a little under her breath.

I stared out the window at the California hills rolling by. Once we'd escaped the City the fog had disappeared and now there was nothing but blazing blue sky above and green and brown fields gliding by next to us, like scorched patchwork on either side of the highway. I actually felt like I was in California, like I was seeing the real California that I'd pictured from the John Steinbeck novels I'd read when I was 12 years old and stuck on my porch during the long sweltering Michigan summers. This was the land by the edge of the sea I'd vowed to find.

"Yeah, it'll be soon now. Soon for me." Delbert stated suddenly. Picking up on the weight in his voice all of us kept quiet.

"Death is coming on. I can feel it. I feel it sitting on my chest. Do you know what it's like to not be able to breathe? Feels like you're being fuckin' strangled. Like God's choking you to death. Yeah, I feel it. You bet your ass I feel it. My own oncoming death. Feel it coming on like a fuckin' freight train." Delbert grunted a little after this speech, the creaking of a gate as he pushed it back into place. There was no feeling in that sound. Pissed off that he had to put up with God's hands around his throat, he was only as pissed as he'd

105

ever been at everything else in his life. I heard the echo of him talking to God in the middle of the night, sitting upright on his couch and cursing as he pumped the valves on his oxygen tank.

We didn't talk for the rest of the way.

When we pulled into Sacramento Aleksia drove through downtown and I glimpsed the Capitol Mall, anchored by the Governor's mansion and encircled with palm trees, like a green feathered headdress. I thought about how 30 years ago Charlie Manson's girl Squeaky had taken aim at Gerald Ford and tried to kill him. I wished we could get out and walk around.

Once we got to the fair sullen-looking guys holding signs and mopping their foreheads with their arms pointed us up and down aisle after aisle of cars until we found a parking space. We hadn't been outside the car since we'd taken off from San Francisco that morning. When we opened the doors, the heat hit us like we'd been clubbed over the head with a broiler. Aleksia and Lynette and I looked at each other and wilted back into our seats, defeated already. Delbert hadn't moved.

Suddenly he rolled his eyes wildly at the three of us. His face bucked and twisted like a spooked horse. Terror pulled at the loose skin of his cheeks, and that's when I saw what he'd been talking about—death really was coming for him.

"Can't...breathe..." he gasped. With one hand he clawed at his throat, the other squeezed desperately at the pump on the oxygen tank sitting mute and powerful between his legs.

"Shut...the...door...I can't—" He frantically tried to suck in oxygen and I heard a whistle start in his throat. It sounded like someone—someone who was very far away—was screaming.

Lynette and I hopped back in and slammed the doors shut and we sped out of the parking lot in a storm of dust, roaring past every guy we'd passed on the way in. I saw them in the rearview mirror. Coughing and choking, they bent over their limp signs. In that same reflection Aleksia and Lynette and I met each other's eyes.

We were idiots. Delbert would die in this heat. No way were we going to the fair.

"Plan B, Delbert." Aleksia said in a voice that couldn't be argued with. "We're going to a bar."

Delbert continued to hitch and gasp, but he nodded. The hand he'd been raking across his throat dropped to his side.

"Make it...a hofbrau," he wheezed.

"A what?" I couldn't help asking.

"A fuckin' hofbrau, stupid." he said, and took another gulp of oxygen.

I shut up. I guessed I'd find out what he meant whenever we got there.

●●●

A hofbrau was a German alehouse. Or a plastic-looking shell of a restaurant that was part all-you-can-eat buffet and part bar. Low and anonymous, it squatted hideously in a parking lot located on one of the major commercial strips feeding out of Sacramento.

Aleksia dropped the three of us off at the door while she parked the car. Lynette and I managed Delbert the same way we had when we left Rickenbacker's. She carried his oxygen tank and I functioned as a human walker. Stooped in front of him, he pushed me over even further as he leaned almost all his weight on me. His long, curled nails bit into my shoulders, his sour breath caressed the roots of my hair. My stomach clenched up and I gritted my teeth.

Inside the hofbrau, Aleksia, Lynette and I picked at colorless salads while Delbert dribbled gravy down his chin in between mouthfuls of oxygen and greasy stringy meat. When he finished eating he started in on the questions again.

"You got a steady trick?" Nasal and sharp, the question unexpectedly hooked me under the chin.

"Uh, yeah." I answered evasively. I didn't want to talk about James.

"Where's he work?" Delbert wasn't going to let it go.

"At a bar." I answered. I looked at the family sitting at the table next to us. Mom and Dad were almost as fat as Delbert. Their kid couldn't have been more than nine years old and he was a porker too.

"At a bar," Delbert mimicked me in a mean falsetto. "At a bar," he repeated in his regular picking-people-apart voice. "What's he, stupid? Yeah, probably." he said, answering his own question. "Probably a thief too." he added. I kept my face unreadable and went on staring at the family next to us. The dad was eating robotically, like a zombie. The little boy was picking his nose.

None of us said anything else. Aleksia started clearing the dishes.

"Two questions," Delbert fired off another round at me. "Have you ever been beaten up?"

"What's the other one?" I countered.

"Did it turn you on?" he smirked at me. Through the thick and cloudy windows of his glasses the glint of evil flashed at me like sun on a distant windshield.

Oncoming, indeed.

I took a deep breath.

"Well...yes. I have been beaten up. And it does turn me on...sometimes. But not when I got beat up around the head and face. When it happened like that—it didn't turn me on. I'm not stupid. When it happened like that it fucking sucked. But getting beat on the ass during sex is a different story. That turned me on..." Caught up in my explanation I stopped suddenly. Everyone at the table was staring at me. Delbert squinted at me like he was taking measurements.

"I don't know why," I finished in a small voice. Now I did feel stupid.

"Are you a homosexual?" Delbert changed the subject and relief swept over me as I realized we were back onto familiar topics.

"No, I don't think so," I said plainly. I faced Delbert without blinking and tried to stare past the filmy lenses.

"Well, how many women have you slept with?" he jeered.

"Zero." I waited for the next one. I got it now, got Delbert. He'd spelled it out for me already, after all. Oncoming. All of it was oncoming.

"How old were you when you started tricking?"

"Fifteen."

"Did he put it in your ass?"

"He tried to. It hurt. Then I didn't let him."

"Did you suck his cock?"

"Yes. I loved the guy."

"Anyone ever make you suck their cock?"

109

"No."

Delbert fell silent and seemed to ponder this. A grin crawled over the lower part of his face and he smacked his lips together. They looked like two strips of purple worm meat wriggling around.

"Somebody made me." he said. He looked around the table triumphantly.

"Oh yeah?" Aleksia spoke up. She cocked an eyebrow at him and leaned back in her chair.

"Yeah, stupid." Delbert snapped at her. "You betcha." He looked around at all of us again. "When I was a kid. In Singapore. It was this guy—this old fag—that used to drive me around. My parents sent me to live in Singapore, ya know." He kept his head turned toward Aleksia but glanced over at me, making sure I was up to speed on the Delbert legend.

"1943. I was ten. My parents sent me there and I use't make deliveries—food supplies—to the officers. Well this Jap guy was the one that drove us around to make the deliveries. He'd pull over and I'd run up and drop off the boxes. Guy was about 30. Boy was he a fuckin' fag. Used to make me blow him, used to blow me. Fucked me too. Liked my ten-year-old asshole 'cuz it was tighter—not only than a woman's pussy, though he didn't want none of that—but tighter than those blown out azzholes of the other fags he was fuckin'."

And again, Delbert made that almost inaudible grunting sound. A scraping in the back of his throat. And like before, no feeling in that sound. He was only as pissed off now as he had ever been. I cut my eyes toward Lynette. She looked bored. I pulled my eyes back to Aleksia and saw her watch Delbert, dead-eyed and lackadaisical. She pushed her tongue up under her upper lip. I heard her voice in my ear—*Delbert lies*—and knew she didn't believe a word of it.

Before we left the restaurant, Delbert had one last question for me.

"So what are you going to do with your life, stupid? You're not gonna fuck it up, are you?" He glared at me stony-faced and grim.

"I don't know," I said. "I might."

For a few minutes none of us said anything. Delbert looked off into space with the glare frozen on his face, and Aleksia, Lynette, and I took turns looking at each other and then staring at the table.

"Well Delbert, where are we going next?" Aleksia finally asked.

Without a moment's pause, Delbert answered her.

"To my sister's house," he said. "I haven't seen her in ten years."

12

Delbert's sister lived in the rich part of Sacramento, the really rich part. The neighborhood was what Delbert called "the forties" because all the streets were 40-something. More like Microwaved Mansion Drive, I thought to myself. The heat had climbed steadily since we'd been in Sacramento and I had no hope of it abating any time soon. I'd never experienced summer like this before. It wasn't swampy like the Midwest, and it was nowhere near the beautiful sun blanket that covered Seattle during warm weather. It was more like being trapped inside a car engine. The air above every football-field-sized lawn shimmered.

Delbert directed us up one street and down the next. Finally, he ordered us to park in front of one nondescript palace. The place didn't look exactly like the house next door, but it was pretty close. It wasn't that all the mansions looked alike, but more that they all looked like each other.

Since the house seemed to be set back roughly one mile from the road, it appeared impossible that Delbert had been able to read the address. I couldn't make out any numbers anywhere as we walked up to the gate.

All the houses were set back from the street. Like fortresses, they were fronted by hostile-looking gardens, studded with spiky-leaved plants and statues on guard.

Delbert's sister's house had all of that and a fountain. A naked little boy carved in stone flexed upwards on one foot. With his hands hidden behind him and his head thrown back, he showed pursed lips where presumably water was supposed to flow. But, spotted with searing patches of sunlight, the little boy and his lips were dry.

"Nice fountain," I muttered, nudging Aleksia. She glanced over.

"Water rationing." she said shortly.

This time out of the car I'd gotten lucky. Lynette had volunteered to be the human walker. I was assigned the relatively easy job of carrying Delbert's oxygen tank.

Somehow, the four of us made it through the gate and up the path. The plants bent toward us menacingly, like sentries blocking the way with spears. Aleksia hacked through them all with one hand, palm out, indifferent to cuts and welts. She cleared the way for Lynette and Delbert, who was huffing harder than ever. I stayed to the side with the tank, and with the length of tubing that snaked up into Delbert's nose looped around one wrist. When he gasped every minute or two and clutched desperately for oxygen my wrist was yanked forward like I was on a leash.

"Fuckin'...bitch...is worth...25 million," Delbert huffed. "But still no...fuckin'...door to...door...service."

"Hush Delbert," Aleksia tossed the words behind her. "She doesn't even know we're here."

Delbert opened his mouth to backhand Aleksia with something nasty, but nothing came out. Drowning without enough oxygen, he plipped and plopped his wet wormy lips together like a fish in the bottom of the boat. Sensing his distress with only a second's delay, like she really was a temporary extension of his huge crawling body, Lynette halted on the path.

"Aleksia!" she called. "Let's stop! Delbert's about to die."

Aleksia turned and looked at Delbert. Apparently deciding that Lynette was right and death was, in fact, whistling near, she stopped and backed up. She approached Delbert and circled him from all sides. He stared at her blankly, like he didn't know who she was, and continued working his mouth open and closed like a goldfish.

"Wanna sit down Delbert? Yeah? You wanna sit?" she asked. And then instantly her face was all military. "Find him a bench," she ordered Lynette. "There. No, over there. In the shade. Look."

She pointed to a bench that seemed to have sprouted up out of nowhere, growing like a concrete claw from the stone path. Lynette turned and then backed up slowly, getting Delbert into position. I followed with the oxygen.

"You," Aleksia pointed at me and motioned to the tank. "Give that to Lynette. Come with me." Obediently, I marched behind her as we went to scout the entrance. When we got there I lifted the brass knocker on the front door, but Aleksia's finger was already on the doorbell.

Soft footsteps came from far off, and then the door squeaked open. We stared into the dusky gloom of a house that looked like it had been shut up long ago like a mausoleum. A puff of cool air from inside wafted over us. It smelled like mummies.

"Hellooo..." A mild-faced old man with wispy sand-colored hair and square rimless spectacles answered the door. He smiled at us blandly.

"Uh, hi. We're um—well, I'm Aleksia, and this is Leah," Aleksia introduced us. "We're with Delbert."

The man maintained his expressionless smile. *Maybe he has Alzheimer's*, I thought. *Maybe we have the wrong house and this guy's some senile old man who's kept prisoner in the family mansion.*

"Hmm..." The man hummed lightly and kept staring at us. The smile never left his face. Was he on something?

"Uh, well see we brought him here and—" Aleksia started again.

"Whooo?" The man cocked his head, his eyes floating past Aleksia. He appeared to be concentrating on the hanging plant behind her.

"Delbert." Aleksia said. And then again, but louder. "*Delbert.*" The man's doped smile didn't shift a notch. And he kept looking over Aleksia's shoulder, at that damn plant. The guy was really starting to creep me out.

"You know, *Delbert.*" Aleksia seemed about ready to snap her fingers in his face. "He's—" And then she stopped. Instantly, I realized the mistake she'd almost made and wanted to laugh out loud. We had no idea what to call the sister. Here Delbert was, planted in her front garden, with three Manson Girl followers and an oxygen tank into the bargain, and we had no idea what her name was.

"Delbert's her brother," Aleksia said sweetly and smiled. She reached forward and clasped the man's hand. His eyes slowly wavered back to hers. "We've come for a visit," she said, and pulled the man out the door and down the steps. Once in the sunlight, he seemed to revive a little. He blinked at Aleksia like she was the first person he'd seen in years. I wondered if maybe she was. I still wasn't entirely convinced we had the right house.

However, a few seconds later I knew we did. The guy recognized Delbert.

"Why Delbert," he said, drawing near to him. "Heavens, how are you?"

"How the fuck do I look Bud? I'm fuckin' dyin' over here." Delbert sucked in a lungful of oxygen. His chest hitched under his greasy spotted overalls.

"Why, I'm fine Delbert. Thank you." Bud gave Delbert that same drugged, pleasant grin. He sounded like a tape recorder that only played one side of a conversation.

"Jesus," Delbert muttered under his breath. He shook his head like he was used to this. I inched back over to the oxygen tank. It was the most stable thing in this bizarre garden tableau.

"Lynette!" Delbert barked. "Go get me some beer."

"Right-o. I'm on it." She caught the car keys Aleksia threw to her.

After Lynette left to get the beer it was me and Aleksia, and Delbert and Bud. Even though Lynette hadn't been talking all that much it was like a huge hole of silence opened up anyway. Bud continued to smile hopelessly at all of us, Delbert licked his dry lips, which were beginning to resemble two snakes on a rock in the sun, and Aleksia and I stood awkwardly with the bristly garden plants and the dry fountain. Just for something to do, Aleksia fiddled with Delbert's oxygen. I shaded my eyes and checked the street. I didn't know for what.

"Well?" Delbert grunted after a few minutes. We all looked at him.

"Well what?" asked Aleksia.

"Where the fuck is she?"

Bud stared into the blinding sun, his grin frozen into place.

"Where's Norma?" Delbert demanded. He looked at Bud, waiting for him to answer.

"Hmmm..." Bud murmured and pivoted toward us. One foot caught in the shrubbery and he swayed, tottered, and then almost pitched forward.

"*Where* is Norma?" Delbert almost yelled.

Aleksia cupped her mouth around my ear. "Who's Norma?" she whispered to me.

"My Goddamn SISTER stupid! That's who!" Delbert snapped. "Now, where the fuck is she? I came to see Norma and I'm gonna see her."

"Hmmm..." Bud hummed again. His eyes wandered and then settled on us like drunk mosquitoes. "Oh yes...Norma. Why, right there. She's pulling up now."

Aleksia and I followed Bud's gaze to the driveway, where an overweight older woman with fried brown hair and gold-rimmed glasses was climbing her way out of a small bright sports car with some difficulty. She had the same deep lines of scorn cut into the bottom of her mouth and the same mean pig eyes as Delbert. Even from this far away I noticed they roved her immediate surrounding area in the same suspicious way.

Then, almost at the same moment, the front door of the house popped open. Aleksia and I turned to find a wiry guy who looked like a 45-year-old Boy Scout bounding down the palatial front steps. He had the short crisp-looking brown hair of the woman in the driveway and the defeated squint of Delbert. He must have been closer to 50 than 45, but the thin cotton t-shirt and baggy khaki shorts he wore really did make him seem like the world's oldest fifth-grade camper.

Aleksia and I turned back to each other. I raised an eyebrow and she made a face. What the hell was going on?

"Hi," the wiry guy bounced toward us and grabbed Aleksia's hand. "I'm Grayson. Nice to have you over ladies." Without letting go of Aleksia's hand, he grabbed mine and started shaking it too. "I see you've met Dad." I assumed he was talking about zombie Bud, still teetering right behind him and staring directly into the sun. "And oh, there's Mom." He smiled broadly at us, eyes flicking from Aleksia to me and back again, lightning-speed looks aimed down the fronts of our tank tops. He'd stopped shaking our arms up and down but still held hands with both of us.

"Uh, yeah, nice to meet you." I mumbled, extracting my hand and wiping it behind me on the back of my jeans. I backed up a foot and he turned full bore on Aleksia.

"Welcome, Grayson." Aleksia purred, switching on her spotlight smile. I knew what she was saying with that smile. *Welcome to the party. Welcome to the fun Grayson, and it's just the start of it all. Delbert planted like an evil toad in your garden is just the beginning...*

"Hello Grayson," Delbert growled behind us. Aleksia dropped his hand.

"Oh...hello Uncle Delbert. Didn't see you there." Grayson glanced warily at the bench but then went back to eating me and Aleksia up with his eyes.

"The fuck you didn't. Insipid piece of shit." Delbert threw the words on the concrete path in front of us and they made the shattering noise of icicles, falling miles to the pavement from a steep roof. Grayson went on smiling at us like he hadn't heard a thing. I peeked around him at Bud, who was still smiling at everything too, including his wife Norma. She was fully out of the car now and storming up the path like a raging bull, her face red as a river at sunset, running on fire. Unfazed, both men stared and grinned like idiots. I could definitely see the family resemblance.

"Delbert!" Norma had finally made it up the path. "What are you doing here?' The clumps of loose skin at her throat reddened and flapped like a rooster's. Her eyes bulged at Delbert, and then at me and Aleksia. She seemed not to see her husband, or Grayson, whose feverish looks were still crawling over us. I thought she might have a heart attack, or explode.

"Nice to see you too, Norma." Delbert stared past her, at the street out front. Then he looked at Aleksia.

"Where the hell's Lynette? Eh stupid? Where's my fuckin' beer?"

"Sshh...Delbert. It'll be here." She quieted him and then took a step toward Delbert's sister. She reached out a hand and gave Norma her most winning smile.

"Hi, I'm Aleksia. Delbert wanted to see you so, uh, we brought him."

Delbert's sister looked at the hand as if it were infected and stepped away from it. Picking her way around both of us carefully, like we'd rolled in something awful, she clamped down on Bud's arm. Her eyes said she wanted to draw blood. His smile didn't flicker. Whatever he was on, it had to be good.

"Why did you let him in?" she hissed under her breath, but loud enough for both me and Aleksia to hear.

"Fuck Norma, you already cut the sad sack's balls off, you gotta chomp on 'em in front of us too? Jesus.

Haven't changed a bit. He didn't do a fuckin' thing. We come on our own accord. *Our—own—damn—accord.*" Delbert said.

"Same as always," he added. "Insipid."

"And might I say you haven't changed much either, Delbert," she drawled bitterly, turning toward him and baring her teeth. "You're still the same. Disgusting. And lewd."

All of it was conducted as if the rest of us weren't there. Bud leaned floppily against his wife like a rag doll and Grayson continued to beam at me and Aleksia like we'd just jumped out of a cake.

"Well, hey, why don't we—" Aleksia began, and was mercifully interrupted. *Ooontz ooontz.* Lynette pulled up in front honking the horn. She cut out of the car in five seconds flat with a six-pack under each arm.

"'Bout fuckin' time," muttered Delbert.

"And who is that? Another one of your followers Delbert?" Norma demanded.

"Hello, hello," Grayson wiggled around all of us and raced down the path to Lynette. He scooped the beer out of her arms and escorted her back up to us. Ogling the back pockets of Lynette's shorts, he stooped and set the beer next to Delbert, who immediately cracked one open.

"It's fuckin' warm!" Delbert spluttered.

"No problem." Aleksia was at attention again. "We'll get ice. I'll go."

"Never mind that," Norma sighed deeply as she dug into the pocket of her polyester slacks. I could see she was beyond hating Delbert now. Maybe a third Delbert follower showing up had done it, maybe it was the way her son was dancing around all of us like he hadn't had any friends over in years, maybe it was the way her husband listed from side to side like a scarecrow in a coma. Whatever it was, I could see that she didn't care about any of it now. She just wanted all of us, Grayson and Bud included, to go away. She found what she'd been looking for—the key to the house—and handed it over to Aleksia.

"There's ice in the freezer. Kitchen's the first room on the left as you go in." She sighed again and now I felt sorry for her. It had to be hard enough being related to Delbert, I thought, without having him show up unannounced on your front lawn.

Aleksia walked up the path and climbed the steps to the front door. She bent to the lock and then straightened to turn the knob and then bent again. Then she straightened up again, and then bent over—*again*. Then she threw me a look and beckoned to me as casually as she could while everyone else was distracted. Norma and Delbert were still swearing at each other, while Bud sat mute in the middle and Grayson sniffed around Lynette like a Golden Retriever. I ran up the walk.

"What's going on?"

"I roke za ee." Aleksia said without moving her lips.

She'd broken the key. One sad jagged half stuck out of the jammed lock.

"Oh no," I looked back up at her. "Oh no...oh..." And suddenly I began to giggle and snort. I couldn't help it, it was just too funny. I laughed harder and then started hitching and gasping like Delbert. Aleksia screwed her eyes shut and her face turned as red as Norma's. Silent tears of laughter coursed down her cheeks. Her nose started to run and she snuffled and wheezed.

"Girls? Are you all right? What's going on up there?" It was Norma. Like a buffalo, she came huffing and grunting up the path.

"What are you girls doing?" she asked again, charging up the steps.

"Uh..." Aleksia began, but it was too late.

"Oh my God! What on earth did you do?" Norma stared at the half of the key that was left in the lock. Aleksia held her palm out to her, the other half sitting in the middle of it.

"Um...it broke." Aleksia said. She bit her lip, but a tiny giggle slipped out anyway. And then I broke, the giggles bubbling out of me in odd little choking noises. Aleksia struggled wildly to hold it in. Covering her mouth with one hand, she burped long and deep.

"We're...so sorry," I finally managed.

Norma glared at both of us.

"Well how in the devil am I supposed to get inside—" Then Delbert's voice cut her off.

"Stupid and stupid! Get down here!"

Aleksia and I grabbed onto Delbert's command like a swinging trapeze up on the high wire. We scurried down the steps and back into the garden before Norma could finish, leaving her stranded on the porch.

Delbert needed his oxygen adjusted. While we helped him, Grayson sidled closer to Lynette. He needled her with questions in spite of the evil eye she shot at him. Bud remained propped up against a stone pillar behind Delbert's bench. He smiled vacantly, waiting for whoever had propped him there to come back and move him around again.

A few minutes later Delbert finished his beer and then we left. We picked up our things and hoisted Delbert's oxygen tank out of a flowerbed as Grayson followed the four of us out to the car. He ignored Delbert's curses and asked for our phone numbers. Aleksia, Lynette and I ignored him like he ignored Delbert.

None of us said goodbye.

●●●

Delbert started talking again on the drive home.

"I met a guy in Europe, said he was a psychologist."

"Europe, huh?" said Aleksia. Strands of black hair blew up and stuck to the side of her face as she cocked one forearm over the steering wheel.

"Yeah, Europe. You know where that is, right stupid?" Delbert sneered. "It was during the war, when I met this psychologist guy."

But hadn't Delbert said he'd been in Singapore during the war? Hadn't he said he'd only been ten years old when he got molested by that other guy? Were we talking about the same war?

"He said some very wise things, that man. He wasn't no stupid. I been thinking on it for 50 years and still can't shake what he said."

50 years? If Delbert was ten during World War II that'd make him about 75 now, but if he was 75 now and met this guy 50 years ago that would be in the 1950s, not the '40s. Was he talking about the Korean War?

I glanced at Aleksia watching the road and remembered what she'd told me—*Delbert lies*. I stopped trying to figure everything out and went back to listening. I'd take what I could from him.

"This psychologist told me there's only three parts to love—bunch of dumb shits say there's all sorts of

123

angles to it but this guy saw stupid comin' from a long way off—same's me—and he said to me, he says, 'Stupid fuckers have no idea. There's only three parts.'"

"Well okay Delbert—" interrupted Aleksia. "What are they for God's sake?" Delbert fell silent and turned his head slowly toward Aleksia, like it was on a crank. He curled his upper lip at her.

"I'm getting to it. Boy...stupid, stupid. You need to learn some fuckin' patience."

Aleksia looked over at him, curling her own lip. "Oh yeah? Well sorry. I just want to know is all."

"No need to be like everyone else...no need to be insipid." he snarled.

I liked the way he used that word. *Insipid*. The way he called people out by it when they started acting like the worst thing they could be—just like everyone else. Delbert was the first person I'd ever met who said *insipid* out loud the way it sounded inside my own head.

"Well, what did he say?" Aleksia asked again.

"Jesus." Delbert paused and shook his head. But then he spoke.

"He said that there's only three parts to love. One, *longing*, and then two, *desire*. Now wait a second—" he broke in even though none of us had said a word. "Seems like longing—or *yearning* actually—is the same thing as desire. But it's not. The psychologist said the longing—the *yearning*—is the love of the idea of the thing in your head. The desire is the itch under the skin, that physical burn to get all over it. The desire's lust, like being fuckin' possessed. The craving the body gets to consume. That's true desire."

I nodded slowly to myself. Everything Delbert was saying jived perfectly with what I had experienced.

"So what's the third piece?" Aleksia broke in again.

"Suffering."

The car was silent, but Delbert said it again anyway.

"Suffering."

We drove into the setting sun, quiet the rest of the way home. The red light of the sunset washed over our faces, shadows bleeding from our eyes like ruby-red tears of blood.

13

As the foggy San Francisco summer ended and warm October days returned to the city, I started smoking cigarettes again, a habit I thought I'd quit for good over four years ago. My new favorite brand was the Djarum black variety. I convinced myself that because I was smoking clove cigarettes I wasn't really smoking. Currently, I was up to a pack a day and gurgled phlegm when I woke up every morning.

I mostly smoked when James wasn't home. At night when he went to work, I sat by the open window of our apartment, sniffing the salty air blown in from the Pacific Ocean just two blocks away. One night as I sat there, staring out into the dark, I kept one hand on my little black cigarette and the other folded in my lap. Then, a second set of hands—longer and thinner and more graceful—unfolded from the base of my wrists and reached behind me. Along the curve of the smoke they rounded down onto my back and felt for something I had already seen in my mind: two small bloody stumps, like tiny horns of bone breaking through.

I was growing wings.

I could already imagine them tearing their way completely out of my body. I could already see how they would appear fully outstretched, the limits of my vision outstripped by their unexpectedly majestic span.

And God, were they ugly.

A repulsive gray and mottled pink, covered in scales and feathers and shot through with veins of pure black, each wing was asymmetrical and off-kilter, clumsy and awkward. Embarrassing. They looked like tumors with a growth of radioactive peach fuzz.

I'd never seen wings like these before, anywhere. I sat and smoked and stared out at the night and I stroked my fingers over the bloody stumps breaking through the surface of my skin. I lit up another little black cigarette, and marveled at the feeling.

Ugly they were, and strange, maybe sinister, but goddamn strong.

Without even trying them, I knew they would hold me.

•••

The rest of that fall and all through the winter I did nothing else but eat, sleep, and work. Since Margaret had left, and Sal had decided to cut costs by not hiring a new secretary to take my place, the work at Pagliarani piled up more every day. And even though I drank a full pot of coffee every morning, it didn't seem to help. I was overworked and super stressed. By the time spring came around and the promise of my third foggy summer in the city loomed over me, just waiting to pounce, I knew it was time to find a new job.

When I started scrolling through the ads on Craigslist one afternoon in between editing reports, I didn't expect to find much. But then one ad caught my eye. It wasn't for a job but for something even better.

It was a writing group, and they were looking for someone to help with catering at their weekly meetings. The place was called Red City. I read the whole ad and then I read it again. Then I read it a third time. My heart thumped harder. Whatever this was, I knew I wanted it.

Are You a Writer? We Are Your Tribe.

San Francisco's most sought after writing group, Red City, is looking for a person to help us part-time at our weekly writing studios. We need someone who can assist with light cooking and setup of appetizers, as well as help with serving wine, tea, and other beverages.

Although we can pay very little, anyone who fills this position will have access to all of our writing studios every week at absolutely no cost. If you've never written before but have always wanted to, or stopped writing a long time ago because you got scared, this is the place for you.

In Red City you will find a safe, loving, and supportive space where you can get your writing done. Red City is filled with open, sensitive, interesting writers who would love for you to join us—whoever you are! No matter how long you've procrastinated on starting your book, or how many times you've told yourself you can't do it—that you shouldn't even try—we know that's not true. We know that your work is already there inside of you fully formed, just waiting for you to write it down.

Come join us and you'll see—you will start writing again. We believe in you.

At the bottom there was a number to call.

I wanted to read it again but I already had a good part of it memorized. I leaned forward with my chin in my hands and stared at the number at the bottom of the screen without blinking until my eyes started to water. Then I wrote it down. I shoved the scrap of paper scrawled with two huge inky words—RED CITY—into my pocket and closed the screen, turning to the stack of reports I still had to tackle on my desk.

Once, a long time ago, I had thought of myself as a writer. But then, after college, I stopped. Completely. And then Seattle happened and everything after and it seemed like I had shoved that writing dream so far down into a deep, hidden place inside of me that I had almost forgotten it altogether. But now here it was again. This weird ad that I had randomly found on Craigslist had dragged the dream back into the light, and seemed to be stirring up all sorts of other shit inside me too.

I thought about it all night and all the next morning. Finally, that next afternoon I took the plunge and called. A cool and elegant, gracefully polished voice answered. Not the author of the ad—I felt that much coming through the line—but someone close to the author. Ms. Cool Elegant Grace told me to come in for an interview and gave me a location and an appointment. Ms. Cool Elegant Grace let me know that it wouldn't be her I'd be meeting with, but she didn't say exactly whom I should expect. As nervous as I already was, it might as well have been Shakespeare himself.

That Saturday, I made my way to the Alamo Square address she'd given me. It was a sunny blue-skied afternoon in the middle of April and I inhaled the warm spring air as I walked past the famous row of Victorian houses known as the Painted Ladies and seen on all the San Francisco postcards. I found the number of the house on the next block down, only it wasn't a house. It was a mansion. An actual mansion, like something out of a fuzzy black-and-white noir film. I noticed it politely shadowed the street, sitting back on its haunches and breathing quietly so as not to terrify the ant-sized people passing on the street below.

Before I could even ring the bell a pretty, dark-haired girl answered the door, as if she had been watching and waiting right behind it. When she spoke, I recognized her as Ms. Cool Elegant Grace. She ushered me into a dim cavernous hallway that looked like a waiting room for knights and queens, and that was packed with people just like me—nicely dressed, fidgeting, and looking nervous. I wasn't the only one who'd gotten an interview. I groaned silently. Competition of any sort always made me feel like I wanted to crawl inside a hole.

Over the next half hour, I watched three different women disappear through an impenetrable dark mahogany door and then come back out again, looking happy and fresh-faced, like they were giving injections on the other side of that door and I didn't understand the look because I hadn't gotten mine yet. I chewed my lip and looked around. In spite of the gorgeous April afternoon outside, the moment I'd stepped into the mansion I felt myself slip into some sort of permanent twilight. The hallway was lit by chandeliers and the windows were narrow. Set deep into the stone walls of the building, it seemed they functioned more as decorative chinks in the masonry rather than a source of light. Rich heavy carpets covered all the floors, and colossal mirrors hung on the walls, nesting in frames made up of knotted clusters of gold.

I sighed and chewed my lip again. I checked my watch. The setting wasn't helping my nerves.

Finally, Ms. Cool Elegant Grace pushed open the mahogany door again and peeked her small sleek head around it. Like an elf, she twinklingly inspected everyone and gave a wicked half grin.

"Zacala?" she called. "Leah Zacala?" I jumped to attention, getting that uncomfortable feeling I always did when someone who didn't know me said my name out loud. It always made me feel—just for a second— like maybe my name wasn't mine anymore.

I followed her behind the door and found myself in a spacious room filled with sunlight. The walls were lined in pale green silk. The antique chairs arranged in the middle were done in silk too, but tinged a delicate apricot color. The windows were open and soft spring air wafted in from outside. The room was like a crystal globe where everything floated and sparkled on waves of invisible water, crashing against walls of glass curved to fit the world like the bowl of the sky.

In the center sat a woman, frozen in time. She stared at me.

"Leah Zacala." Ms. Cool Elegant Grace announced, and then she was gone. I could have sworn I heard her click her heels together and saw the faintest shadow of her parting salute on the sun-dappled wall to my left.

Only after my name was pronounced did the woman smile. Slowly, it spread across her mouth. Her red lips gleamed as they parted. A clear light diffused upward into her eyes, animating them and pushing her fine blonde eyebrows into a regal arch.

"Leah. How lovely to meet you." The woman rose and fanned out her hand at the chair in front of her, as if she were conferring a great favor upon it. "Please," she said through her smile. "Sit."

Mechanically, I moved forward and found the chair. I sat.

As the woman talked I found it was hard to look at anything else in the room. The spring sunshine, the warm air, even the green and apricot silks, all of it seemed to shrink and diminish the closer I got to her, like she was drinking them in just as I was drinking in her. Like every object in that room was magnetized to her, attracted to the small, separate universe she took from the space around her. Stuffed with furniture, paintings, and heavy velvet drapes, with that woman sitting in the center of it all, the room seemed completely empty.

"I'm Scarlet," she said. The smile never left her lips for a second. "Scarlet Monroe."

She was absolutely gorgeous. With her long blonde mane of hair, almost pure-white porcelain skin, those ruby red lips and the queenly arched eyebrows, it was impossible not to notice how beautiful she was. But her being beautiful didn't strike me right off the bat. It wasn't the first thing I noticed about her. What that first thing was, it's impossible for me to say. Any skull has a human face, but that's not the first thing anyone notices about a skeleton—that it was human once, and so still is.

"So, Leah." Scarlet looked at me and furrowed one eyebrow good-naturedly. "Tell me about yourself." I had a whole presentation prepared. But now that I was here I couldn't remember any of it. I opened my mouth. What could I tell her?

Why should she care?

But she was waiting, her smile stretched wide and her raised eyebrow held in place. Arched silently over me, it smirked.

"I...uh...well, I...I'm an alcoholic."

What the fuck? Why did I have to tell her *that* of all things? Alarm bells blazed inside me. Did I really just say that? But now it got worse. I could hear that I was still talking.

"See I came out here—to San Francisco—because I had to get out of Seattle. That's where I was before. In Seattle. For four years...and I, uh...I wrote a little but I...I drank a lot too." I stared down at my hands, unable to look at her.

"And uh, before that, I was in Michigan—in Ann Arbor. I didn't get into my college creative writing program...my writing professor hated me. And um...well, I don't even think she knew about the drinking part." I sighed and looked up again.

"So after Ann Arbor I went to Seattle. I didn't have anywhere else to go. And that's where I really started drinking—all the time I mean. And then I stopped writing, for good..."

Scarlet opened her mouth, exposing an upper row of perfect snow-white teeth. I rushed on before she could interrupt me. Everything was coming out now.

"And I'd always written before that. I mean—during college—I wasn't writing very much—but I was still writing. Something, at least. But then I met with my writing professor after the class ended, and she told me I should stop writing. She said I wasn't cut out to be a writer. So I did—I stopped. And I haven't written since. Even though before that—before college and—well, some things happened in high school, and uh, before, that sort of, uh, interrupted my writing then too, but what I mean is that I always wrote things. Always as a kid. I wrote my first poem when I was five years old, I wrote all the time growing up. You know, journals, diaries...I even wrote sex stories for the kids I went to

133

high school with. I charged five dollars a story!" I punched my hand into my fist and looked up, my eyes shining proudly.

The smile—and the eyebrow—hadn't moved.

"Well anyway," I hurried on. "The point is that I always wrote. All the time. I needed to write, had to write. It was my thing. It was what I did." I paused. "But then I stopped. Six years ago." I looked back up at Scarlet. "And I haven't written since."

I stared at her a moment longer and then threw my head into my hands. It was too late for appearances now. I might as well take the despair this experience had to offer, there was no way in hell I was getting this job. I'd somehow broken my old record of exposing myself as a lunatic in five minutes flat.

I cradled my head, listening to the rustle of spring air caressing expensive silk all around me. Somewhere outside, a bird called a lonely deep whistle, a strange warning cry woven into this beautiful warm afternoon.

"It doesn't sound like you need a job," Scarlet said. I looked up. Smile and eyebrow glued where they were still on her face, I knew she had to be laughing at me—or sneering in contempt—on the inside. I stayed quiet.

"But it does sound like you badly need to join our writing program." Before her words could even sink in, she leaned forward and clasped my hands around a folder full of materials that had been settled in her lap. Shocked, I bent my hands obediently around the folder and continued staring at her open-mouthed like an idiot.

"Look, why don't you take this packet home. Go over it when you have some time and then email me when you're ready and we'll get you set up to start coming to the writing studios. It's just one hour, once a week. Anyone can make time." Her words were polished and full, like ripe crystal apples. Succulent, reflecting a thousand small pinpoints of light from every facet, they were held out to me. And all of a sudden, everything seemed ridiculously easy. I only had to take what was being offered.

Scarlet leaned forward again and met my eyes. Her perfect teeth glittered.

"You will write again Leah Zacala. You are going to start—and finish—your book here, in Red City. I'll see to that."

And the smile broke across her face again.

14

Scarlet called them "studios" but we didn't meet at a studio, we met at the mansion. And all that happened was that we ate snacks and drank tea and then we wrote for one hour, silently and all by ourselves. That was it. We didn't show anyone what we were writing, and most of the time we didn't talk about what we were writing. It was a far cry from the noisy, smoky room I'd pictured, writers gritting their teeth and tearing out their hair, crumpled pages in their fists like sweaty dollar bills, red in the face and screaming at each other over the true meaning of art. I'd always envisioned this room full of writers somewhere, but without me in it. In my fantasy, they would never have let me in.

At Scarlet's real-life writing studios, I kept to myself. I didn't say much. But week after week, I showed up at Red City and wrote for one hour. I'd noticed nearly everyone had a laptop they brought with them, except for me. From the very beginning I brought a tablet of paper and handwrote everything. There was no question of doing it any differently. A few times my hand gave out before the hour was over. Red, cramped, and looking like a claw, it collapsed on me mid page and I had to hold it gingerly under the table until it stopped shaking and I could straighten my fingers again. I felt like an old woman with severe arthritis. But the page count kept mounting. Five pages, seven pages, finally ten a week, every week. If I lost my right hand but finished my book it would be worth it. I kept it under the table whenever it couldn't go on and told that hand the same thing.

I knew exactly what I was writing, and at the same time, I had no idea. I'd surprised myself by starting what looked like a ship's log, dating the head of the page with the precise day that I moved to Seattle and recording what had happened, piece by piece, from that day forward. My brain seemed to hold an infinite vault of records and files and information. The act of scratching my pen on a blank sheet of paper was the key.

Every Wednesday was like a magic day now. I looked forward to it all week. Walking into the mansion still felt like I was entering some dark ancient castle, but once inside everything glittered with light. Each mirror glowed with soft incandescence. Ms. Cool Elegant Grace was still answering the door, but now I'd come to know her as Katherine Ross—Kate for short. She showed each aspiring writer into the mansion and off with their coat, and then ushered us into a banquet-sized room, hidden behind another gargantuan mahogany door, identical to the one I'd passed through on the day of my interview.

This new room contained an enormous table, with the same antique chairs done in apricot silk dotting the perimeter. At the head of the table stood a chair larger than all the others, upholstered in deep red velvet, the color of drying blood. Bright but fading, it looked like a throne. It faced the room and the ebbing evening light glowed duskily behind it, silhouetting the figure that sat there. This was Scarlet's chair.

Every Wednesday I watched Scarlet mill around the room before we got started, flittering here and there like an opalescent butterfly. I saw her listen to an older lady who squeaked out short breathless sentences like a trembling little mouse. Smiling, Scarlet let the woman explain the difficulties she was having with her latest batch of poems. Arching one eyebrow, she ticked off advice on one, two, and then three long pale fingers. The woman's face brightened, and now she didn't look so much like a scared mouse as an eager mole ready to get to work. And then Scarlet moved on.

She was like that with everyone. Wherever she chose to linger around the table was a sacred place, if only for 30 seconds. The rest of us continued what we were doing—stowing purses, flipping open laptops, uncorking wine bottles—but all of us almost imperceptibly slowed our own movements. Our attention arrested here...and there...and here. Every place Scarlet stood for a moment became magic.

We all knew it. There was something in Scarlet that just wasn't in any of the rest of us.

At eight o'clock exactly, everyone was in their seats. Scarlet was always the last to sit down. Every session followed the same course: We all got to speak before we started writing, going around the table in order. It felt a little bit like an Alcoholics Anonymous meeting. Looking around the table at all those desperate faces staring at Scarlet—well, let's just say I understood. I didn't mind that Red City seemed to be a sort of recovery for artists. I knew we were suffering from chemical abuse too. Like a lot of other people on the planet, our drug of choice was fear.

But Scarlet wasn't afraid of anything.

She was sophisticated, independent, and intelligent, but there was something else too. Somewhere, inside, it seemed like she might be just like me. A girl who'd grown up in abnormal circumstances and so maybe grew up into something abnormal herself. The facts of my past were stirring and transforming themselves. My childhood years spent in a farmhouse with a broken family, the days and nights I'd given to roaming the fields that surrounded it, writing poems and making up stories in my head, talking to myself and pretending to be other people who didn't exist, or sometimes did—all of it had seemed strange before. Snapshots from my past that needed to be buried in a bottom drawer. But now, after Scarlet, things were different. I wasn't so hesitant to dig back into the past, and I wasn't so sure that my strangeness was something to be denied.

Now, after Scarlet, everything was changing.

At the beginning of each writing session, Scarlet called us to attention and then every pair of eyes at the table rested on her. We all got two minutes to talk, but Scarlet always talked way longer. Sometimes 15 or 20 minutes went by before she was finished. And Scarlet didn't talk like other people. You could tell she was proud of everything she'd ever done, whether it was a mistake or not. She talked about writing as if everyone knew it was a nearly impossible thing to do and the burden of it too much to carry. So heavy in fact, that only very special people were even allowed to try.

The more I heard her talk every week, the more I started talking myself. About everything. How hard it was for me to write, how I hadn't written anything in years before Red City, how I'd started drinking all the time. How there was something apparently wrong with me and how alcoholism was supposedly a disease. How it didn't feel like a disease but a real living, breathing parasite attached to my soul. How I just knew there was something, somewhere inside me, that didn't want me to make it.

No matter what I said at that table, they all listened. Scarlet listened. No matter what, they gave me my few minutes.

Then, when we were done speaking, we started writing.

For one silent hour I watched my hand rip across the page, defiling its pristine blank fields of possibility, soaking it in ink. Every session something else came out of me, and it felt simultaneously like vomiting and pushing a fetus out of my right hand. My fingers roared on, paragraph after paragraph, heedless of the cramps in my knuckles and wrist, contemptuous of the pain that ran all through my arm, shocking me into sitting up straight every few minutes, as if I were being struck by small bolts of lightning.

As the weeks went by, I learned a lot more about Red City. Scarlet included a little history at every session for all of us. I saw so many new faces come and go, in addition to the regulars I'd picked out, that I guessed everyone could use a little catchup.

"At first it was hard. It's always hard at first, of course," Scarlet began one evening. "I had to find a place—that was most important. And it wasn't easy. I talked to a lot of people and got nowhere. It took me a long time to find a location like this, fully furnished nonetheless, and convince the owners to let me rent it for just one night a week. Then three other people believed in me and started attending the studios, and my idea took off from there." Scarlet was silent a moment. She traced the screen of her laptop with two long elegant fingers. I saw the contour of her unpolished nails, curving delicately like a cat's claws.

"And now…" She turned halfway in her chair and made a sweeping gesture around the room with one arm. "Here we are. Red City brought me all of you." She looked triumphantly around the table and smiled, the rest of us nodding along with her. "Do any of you know why I started this program? Why I made Red City my life's work?"

The room was silent. Twelve pairs of eyes looked toward Scarlet.

"Well, it was out of purely selfish motivations, I can assure you," she went on. "I needed to write. And I couldn't. I tried everything—workshops, writing guides—" She sighed and traced the top of her laptop again. "Befriending famous writers in the hope that some of their magic would rub off on me…"

How did somebody do that? I'd always secretly wanted to be a writer, but I'd never had the idea to hunt down Stephen King and make him my friend. I marveled again at the perfectly groomed arches of Scarlet's eyebrows. I felt like she probably hung out with Queen Elizabeth on the weekends but was too polite to say anything about it. My heart racing, I waited for her to continue.

"Of course, none of it worked. And of course, deep down, I knew that none of it would. I knew what I needed, I just didn't know how to get it." She looked up again and flashed her eyes around the table. "Red City," she pronounced suddenly. "What I needed was Red City." The rest of us nodded with her, already on cue.

"What I needed was to sit down for one hour, at least once a week, and get my work done. What I needed was to stop the procrastination, the lies I was telling myself—that I couldn't do it. That I couldn't write a book and I never would." The two fingers she used to trace the top of her laptop trembled. She took a breath and continued slowly. "By creating Red City, I forced myself to sit down and write. I had to show up every week to *get* it going and then I had to show up every week to *keep* it going. And in doing that, I ended up showing up every week and writing for one hour."

She paused and looked around at the table again.

"And now I have all of you," she gave us her wide sparkling smile. "Now I show up every week to do this. I show up every week for all of you. Because it's only through you...that I can get my work done."

The setting sun threw its gold and pink striped cloak at her feet. I saw her white-blonde mane of hair lit from behind—*a shadow on a throne in a mansion*, my mind whispered. With an effort I pulled myself back to the real world. Back to Scarlet and what she was saying.

"Red City does work. That I can promise you," she said. As I'd been daydreaming, it appeared one of the regulars, an older man with a beard who I'd seen there every Wednesday, had asked Scarlet a question. All I really knew about him was that his name was Bernie and he hardly talked at all when it was his turn at the table. But what he did say was always simple and wise, and usually quite beautiful. I knew he was scared like me and he only made it here every Wednesday by getting through that first. The fear of showing up.

"Red City works not because of what it does, but because of what you do in it." Scarlet raised her voice as she looked away from Bernie and addressed the whole room. "If you show up here, once a week, every week, I promise you that within one year you will finish your book. I know what I'm saying is true because that's what happened for me. I was a blocked writer, just like all of you. A procrastinating artist. No matter what I did

I just could not do the one thing in the world that I wanted to do, get my work done. So, I created Red City, and I got my book done."

Dipping below the horizon, the last seashell-pale creamy glints of sun faded from the evening sky. The shadows in the room grew longer and colder. Suddenly they had more density. As if a tall man in a black cloak had just stepped invisibly into each one of them, they were somehow more real. I shivered and grabbed my sweater from the chair behind me.

"Finished a book? Really? But what—" Bernie's low voice ducked away shyly once it was out of his mouth, contenting itself with crawling across the polished table toward Scarlet. But before I could lean in closer to hear, Scarlet had picked up his voice and wrapped it inside her own.

"Oh Bernie! You would love my book!" she said. "It's all about San Francisco, it takes place in the heart of San Francisco. And the funniest thing is—" She stopped and looked around at all of us. "Every character I created in that story is me." Her red lips stretched over her porcelain teeth like a sunrise over the bleached dunes of a desert. "And I had no idea I was doing it at the time," she laughed. "But it will be like that for you too."

She looked over again at Bernie and clasped his hand. I saw him wince from the contact. He trusted Scarlet and he wanted to believe her, but yet...he couldn't be sure. Was he really a writer? When Scarlet let go of his hand he hid it under the table, concentrating on averting his eyes from the rest of us.

"No matter what you write about, no matter who you write about," Scarlet said. "It's always you in the end. It's always you. When everything is said and done, there's no getting away from it. There's no escape," she finished simply, and I saw an odd emotionless light emerge into her eyes.

"You will always come back to yourself."

Like Bernie, she looked down at the table and pursed her lips, as if that were the only thing she regretted.

Aleksia was head of surveillance now, which meant Sal gave her all the best cases. No one could keep up with her. In fact, it seemed we couldn't keep *any* new guy for more than two weeks before Sal erupted like a volcano on him, incinerating the unlucky rookie of the moment who had inevitably done the wrong thing in the worst situation. Two weeks was just enough time to learn how to aim the camera before Sal fired them.

Because Aleksia was so good at what she did, Sal was out of the office more. As the spring days got warmer he spent his afternoons down at the ballpark or out to lunch with business friends. I ran the office by myself while he stayed in touch with Aleksia and I kept contact with everyone else. And even though I was still halfheartedly looking around for a new job, for now, everything seemed to be working.

Until one day life snuck up on me, with events that started out innocently enough. Like everything does before it turns black and horrible. That morning, as Sal banged up the stairs into the office, I raised my voice over the sound of his feet.

"Hey Sal! Grove called! He's sick and had to bail on the Petrelli case!" There was no answer. "Sal?" I called again. "You hear me?"

The absence of noise was like someone had shut off a vacuum cleaner suddenly. The only thing I could hear was Sal's labored, stertorous breathing.

"Grove called in sick?" he finally asked. He stood frozen outside the door to my office and looked at me blankly. *Hmmm...preoccupied*, I thought. Must be new clients at today's lunch. Sal was in his good suit.

"Yeah," I said around a mouthful of coffee. "He said his stomach's bothering him." I swallowed and kept my eyes on Sal, still standing in the hall. I got the distinct feeling that he needed to be *dislodged*—like a nefarious chunk of food is *dislodged* from the windpipe of a person who's choking—before he could move from that spot.

"Hey Sal? You okay?" I asked, and then looked down. I wasn't in the habit of asking Sal questions, ever. Especially not personal ones.

"Huh? Oh yeah!" He sprang back to life like a movie reel starting up again. Snapping his fingers, he barreled into his office. I heard him digging frantically through his desk for the papers he needed, and then humming *Danke Schoen* by Wayne Newton off-key and out of breath.

Sighing, I went back to my coffee and stack of reports.

But it wasn't Sal's lunch with new clients that day that was making him act so funny. It was Grove. And it was me who had been preoccupied, not Sal. I was the one who missed what was really going on because I was too distracted by deadlines, the next report, the next client—all the smokescreens life throws up in front of us. At that time in my life I never saw the actual moment I was living in. In fact, when I stepped back and looked at the whole chain of moments strung together they didn't even seem to be something that belonged to me.

A few days later, Grove called again. This time Sal was in the office.

"Hey Grove," I said. "How's it going?"

"Is Sal there?" he cut me off without saying hello. "Can you put him on?"

Grove's voice rumbled into my ear like a small landslide. He coughed once, explosively, and all of a sudden, I knew. Something was off, something was happening. Imperceptibly, the last few moments had sped up and we'd crested some sort of hill. It was impossible to back up now, impossible to turn around and go back the way we'd come. The only thing left to do was to go down the other side.

I put Grove on hold and punched the button for transfer.

I heard Sal pick up, but I didn't hear anything after that. The pit in my stomach hardened, its circumference turned into a shell and the shell grew fine little hairs that morphed into teeth and began cutting into the lining of my insides. I cocked my ears toward Sal's office and strained for even a whisper.

I didn't hear a sound.

I looked down at the phone. The blinking red light was dark, the line dead. Sal had hung up without rushing into my office to grab the file for the case Grove was on. Something was up—way *way* up. Slowly, I rose from my chair and crossed the room. I paused for a moment at the doorway and then took the sharp left that took me to Sal's office and landed me in front of his desk.

"Sal—what's going on? Is everything okay?"

Sal sat rooted to his chair. Pale and bereft, his forehead had miraculously smoothed into the wide, accepting marble brow of a priest. The vein that ran down the middle of it, known for chugging maniacally along with Sal's red-hot fits of temper, had fallen back and gone limp. I saw only the faintest blue trace of it underneath this new skin that I'd never seen before. He seemed to be entirely emptied out, entirely out of hope. Sal looked as if the hand of God had smacked him down and he knew it would be futile to try to get back up again.

"Sal?" I repeated. "What is it? What's going on?"

"It's Grove," he said mechanically. "He's had some tests."

"Well, yeah? And?" I prompted.

Sal stared at me as if he were afraid of hurting me. He dropped his eyes lower, to my throat, with that same gentle fearful expression, like there was the black poison tip of an arrow lodged in me that only he could see. Then he winced, as if he was going to be the one to pull it out.

"It's bad, Leah. Real bad. It's cancer." Sal looked back up and then I knew, but it didn't matter because in the next second he said it anyway.

"Grove's dying."

He went back to staring at the wall again and I saw that delicate dawn-blue trace of the vein that ran down the middle of his forehead vanish completely.

I slowly backed out of his office and shut the door behind me.

●●●

Grove had three months to live.

It was pancreatic cancer, which was why his stomach had been giving him so much pain. His pancreas wasn't doing what it should be doing anymore, secreting enzymes into his digestive system to break down carbohydrates and protein, and so now bile from his liver was draining into his gut. Jaundice was one of the predominant symptoms he could expect and it would only get worse from there. He'd already dropped weight like an anorexic. Now that I seemed to be noticing everything that had been right under my nose for the past few months, when he stopped by the office I could see he looked like a tall guy who had suddenly put down the suitcases of pounds he'd been carrying all his life. Without all that baggage, Grove almost didn't look like Grove anymore.

The very next day Grove called Sal for advice. He had to start making decisions. Chemotherapy, or radiation, or both? Or none? If he was going to die anyway, why spend his last three months sick? Why waste precious minutes worrying about a few clumps of hair falling out? Why not go to Mexico and sit on the beach and drink tequila instead? I heard Sal's laughter thunder across from the next room as he joked with Grove about all of it that morning on the phone, but when he came over to my office later I could see fear haunting his face, his eyes glinting, wet and helpless. The corners of his mouth were dried out, crumbling into dust. They wouldn't stop twitching.

Grove had been his friend since they were 11 years old, did I know that? Sal asked. He looked right over me and kept talking to the air above my head. They'd seen Jefferson Airplane play in Golden Gate Park at the Human Be-In and called themselves "roadies" because the band let them haul some of their equipment. 1969, 1970...Grove's favorite neighborhood, Haight-Ashbury. They'd grown up together...Sal trailed off and I knew what he was thinking. Grove would be dead by August.

But the next day Sal seemed to be all right again. Grove sounded better too when he called.

"Hey Grove..." I said gently. "How are you feeling?"

"Me? I'm fit as a fiddle! Why do you ask?" Grove laughed and I forced a chuckle for him, silently thankful he couldn't see my face.

"Listen, Leah—" He was all business now. "I need your help, well Sal and I need your help, actually. We want to plan a party and it needs to happen in two weeks. Can you help us?"

"Sure," I said. "But what's the party for?"

"It's my birthday," he said. "I'll be 51. And it's also a goodbye for everyone—a going-away party of sorts, you see?"

My stomach dropped.

"Oooh-kay. We can do that." I let out a shaky breath and mustered myself. "We can definitely do that!" I said much more brightly.

"Good." Grove said. "I'm making up the invite list today, and all I need you to do is to write the invitation. It'll be two weeks from now, at a great little place outdoors that I know, down on the coast. We'll have beer, we'll have barbecue, we'll have good times and good friends. And..." Grove paused and cleared his throat solemnly. "We'll have some good ol' Mary Jane!" He roared with laughter again and I transferred him over to Sal. Then I sat with my head in my hands.

When I looked up again, Sal was standing in my doorway beaming.

"Doesn't Grove sound great?" he said. "He's doing great, just great—" he rushed on before I could answer. "I went and saw him last night, drove down on the motorcycle and picked up a couple of bottles of wine—a little red paint never hurt anyone! We popped those babies open and sat on Grove's roof and watched the sun set and just talked—about everything—about life—and dying—and how everything's going to be okay…" I winced at Sal's beatific smile. Was it really? Was Sal going to be okay?

"And look—" Sal strode toward me and held out his left wrist. "Grove made this for me. He's making them for the whole gang, me and the rest of the guys. Our buddies we grew up with, and the troopers who've joined us since."

I looked at Sal's meaty red hand and wrist and I almost laughed out loud. Peeking from beneath the sleeve of Sal's black casino-boss suit, scraping just past the 14k gold cufflink, was a simple bracelet made out of beads. Black, yellow, green and red, they clacked together softly as Sal shook his wrist and then withdrew it again. It looked like something a Rastafarian might wear—or a hippie—and in a million years I never thought I'd see something like that on Sal. He smiled and his eyes lit up as he glanced at the bracelet. Grove had made it and given it to him, his true-blue friend. I doubted now that he'd ever take it off again.

●●●

Everybody came to Grove's birthday party. Me and Sal and Gemma, and every single one of the detectives who'd worked for Sal and known Grove, past and present. Margaret and her husband and their toddler son even made it out. We all passed the kid around and congratulated Margaret on breaking out of the PI world and into motherhood. She burst out laughing as she readjusted her son on her hip, but I saw her face slacken, a phantom making its way across it, as Grove passed by the edge of the circle. We all felt it, and I shivered. Grove's death was here with us too.

Sal had ordered Grove a birthday cake in the shape of a giant marijuana leaf. In the center stood a tiny street intersection sign that read "Haight" on one side and "Ashbury" on the other. I wanted a picture of it. As I moved toward the table Aleksia stole up beside me.

"What do you think?" she asked bluntly.

"About what?" I replied.

She looked at me pointedly, lips pressed tightly together.

"All right, I'm a little freaked." I sighed. "It's weird."

"Yeah, I agree." Aleksia chewed on a piece of her hair and surveyed our group from the office. Then she leveled her gaze at the rest of the party, people straggling around here and there. Every few seconds sporadic laughter broke out across the lawn, like rumbles of distant thunder.

As usual, Sal was the one to interrupt us.

"All right ladies. Out of the way! Comin' through! Step aside!"

We turned to find four of Grove's friends carrying an enormous wooden chair with gilded arms and a purple velvet cushioned seat. Wobbling unsteadily to-and-fro, the chair bobbed and weaved through the crowd, swimming above everyone's head like a football player who'd just scored the winning touchdown and was being carried on his teammates' shoulders.

"Sal!" I shouted. "What is it?"

"It's a throne!" he called back. "A throne for Grove!"

Aleksia and I watched as the chair was finally planted at the edge of a shady copse of trees and Sal ran across the grass to fetch Grove. Within a few minutes, he'd settled into his throne and a line had formed in front of him. I snagged Gemma's sleeve as she passed by.

"Gemma—what's going on?" I gestured toward the line.

"It's for Grove," she said. "So he can tell each person goodbye face-to-face."

And then she was gone, hurrying to the end of the line to take her place in it.

I looked back at Aleksia, but her face remained unchanged. She squinted toward the throne, and the line, as if she were calculating the distance between two far-off boats out at sea. I backed up and walked around her, leaving her there to figure things out on her own.

A few minutes later I ran into another one of our detectives, Dwight Channing, who worked for us taking statements and investigating accident scenes. After making small talk we both looked at Grove and the long line that stretched away from him. I asked Dwight how he was doing.

"Oh, okay, okay. I mean, um, well...I just can't believe it, about Grove you know. I was shocked." Dwight's soft southern accent grew husky as he let his eyes linger on Grove, still cheerfully seated on his throne. Grove stood and clapped the newest visitor in front of him heartily on the back.

"I know," I said. "I couldn't believe it either. I don't know what to think. I don't know how to act, to tell you the truth. This is crazy."

Dwight nodded. "I don't know either." he said. "You know, I've never known anyone who's died before. Not one person."

"Really?" I asked, surprised. Dwight was at least 50 years old, just like Grove and Sal. And he'd never known anyone?

"Yeah, no one." he drawled. "All my family are still alive, all my friends. Grove's the first person I've ever known who—well, you know..."

"Wow..." I murmured. I thought back over my past.

"Have you?" Dwight brought me out of my reverie.

"Hmm...? Oh, yeah. Of course."

"If you don't mind my asking—who was it?" he blurted.

"Uh, it was my mother, when I was almost 12." I said, and then paused to get things straight. "Let's see...well, first really, there was my brother. He died when I was 8, almost 9, of leukemia. Then three years later my mom died of cancer, when I was almost 12— see, they both died in the fall right before my birthday. Um, then I lived with my grandma...but she died when I was 16, she had cancer too." Holding out one hand, I ticked each one off on my fingers, making a quick illustrated head count. Whenever I had this conversation, I heard myself from the outside of my body, like I was watching someone else explain it all. I ended up sounding like a robot, but how could I possibly sound human when every time I talked about my past I went into a state of deep freeze, where I couldn't feel a thing?

"So when my grandmother died," I went on. "Well, after that, I lived alone. Until I went away to college. Then I cleaned out the farmhouse—my mom's house—and moved to a different town where I went to school. Started a different life." I sipped my drink again and smiled encouragingly at Dwight, who was staring at me open-mouthed.

"Why Leah, that's terrible! I had no idea."

People always said that. They either said that, or something about what a strong person I must be. After so many years, it all sounded like the same thing.

"Yeah, well, it's okay. I'm okay." I smiled at Dwight again, this time a little more tightly. I was moving onto other topics. "Are you going to get in line?"

"I don't know," Dwight said. He looked over at Grove and I saw the same dark phantom flit across his face, the one I'd seen steal over Margaret earlier as she'd watched Grove when she thought no one else was looking. That phantom tore them from the present and hurled them forward, to a time when Grove was already in his coffin. Interesting, how death works. Always giving us reminders that time's almost up, but we ignore every sign. I looked at Grove and suddenly I saw it too, under the sunken skin on his face—the skull. And then I realized I wasn't seeing the future, but something that already was. Something that had been there all along, hidden under the façade of life. We all carried death, just under the surface, all the time. We all carried the future inside of us.

The line leading to Grove's throne diminished slowly throughout the afternoon and into the evening until there was only Grove left. When the last person stepped away a buzz rippled through the crowd as Grove raised himself majestically. The murmurs turned into whistles and finally all of us were yelling and clapping, some of us crying. Grove shakily got to his feet and lunged upward, the fingers of one hand stretched into a peace sign pointed at the sky. A second later he sank down again, exhausted, and the crowd grew quiet. Everyone looked down at their paper plate of abandoned picnic food, sad and limp, and there was a rush at the trash cans as everyone migrated in that direction. Sunken and silent, Grove slumped back down into his throne.

Darkness crawled across the violet twilight sky as we made our way to the parking lot. Aleksia and I talked with Margaret as she went about strapping her son into the car—a million little buttons and snaps until the kid was officially safe—and watched Sal at the other end of the lot surrounded by his and Grove's old gang of friends. Sal splashed into the gravel on his knees and started crooning old 1950s love songs, cracking a smile at Aleksia. She looked over and laughed and Sal jumped to his feet and sang louder, wiggling back and forth under the edge of the moonlight like a lounge singer. We walked over to him still laughing.

"Hey Sal—has Grove seen your performance?" Aleksia asked sarcastically. But suddenly it was the wrong thing to say. The phantom that had been with us all day filled the air. An invisible fog with an evil mind and damp, caressing fingers. I crossed my arms and shivered.

"Grove went to bed," Sal said quietly, and grimaced. "He's not feeling too well."

The rest of us fell silent and then dispersed back to our separate cars, the stoic crunch of the gravel under our feet. The lonely song of a night bird called out somewhere nearby. Like Sal, he was performing a one-man show under the moon. I felt like we were all thinking the same thing.

Grove's party had come and gone, and now we could only wait.

●●●

A few days later Grove sent Gemma a thank-you note in the mail. As she walked through my office that morning she was striped with wide swaths of late spring sunlight, flooding through the windows and over the floor like shimmering waves of water. Wrapped in shadows and liquid gold, she walked toward me, handing me the small card.

"It's from Grove. Read it." she said. She stood resolutely in front of me, smiling and waiting.

Dear Salvatore and Gemma,

I'm writing this letter to say thank you for the party, and all that you've done for me during this time, but also to say thank you for being the best friends a guy could ever have.

As I write this, I'm watching a bumble bee fidget and buzz around, working his way into a newly opened flower in the spring sunshine. It's June and I'm happy. I'm grateful to be alive.

I looked up and saw Gemma holding something out to me. It was the violet-colored flower that Grove had pressed into the envelope with the card, as delicate as an old silk dress unearthed from an attic trunk. She held it up to my nose.

"Smell it," she said, and smiled again. "It still smells pretty."

I sniffed. Mechanically, I smiled back. I didn't feel a thing.

But later at home, I locked myself in the bathroom and cried. Leaning against the door to brace it—just like I always did, just in case—I sobbed so hard I shook and the wood shook with me. So I guess I did feel something, then.

16

Whenever anyone asked me about my childhood, I told them I grew up in farmhouse. Those words were old now though, decaying. Rotting boards holding together a disintegrating bridge. The bridge stretched across the deep and violent waters of a dark river churning on a raw February day. I had always kept both feet firmly where they needed to be, negotiating my way across to the other side, never looking at what roiled beneath. *I grew up in a farmhouse...* is what I always told other people. *And during that time, it seemed like everyone in the whole world died...* is what I always told myself.

My brother died when I was almost 9 years old, my mom when I was almost 12. After my parents had divorced and shortly before my mother died, my dad had gone off and started a new family. He stopped in to see me still, but he never stayed for long. I lived with my grandma in the farmhouse after my mom was gone, and she took care of me. She died when I was 16.

Now, all these years later, I was going to Red City every week, and every week it seemed like I tripped over another box of memories that I thought had been buried long ago. The boxes popped out of nowhere and sprang wide open without warning. They looked like they were decomposing just as badly as the old wooden bridge in my mind. They smelled rotten.

I found filing cabinets too. The files were organized by date, and some dates had more information than others. Certain files contained very specific information, like pictures of who was wearing what that day, or tapes that played recorded bits of conversation. Some files contained nothing. It appeared that I had tucked a lot of files away and then never looked at them again. Others—I was now realizing—I took out and examined all the time.

As I dug further, I discovered that the boxes were full of dates that had *never* been filed. Information that had apparently never been processed. As I began to comb through them I found one box labeled with the name of my brother that read: *Charles: Dying.* I sat down to get comfortable, pulled the box into my lap, and started pulling out what I found.

I tugged out the first piece of a memory— something long and sharp that looked like it could be deadly, if wielded in the right way. Along with it came tiny loose fragments of time, as if some part of the original memory had broken off in storage and been pounded into dust by the stacks of other boxes sitting on top of it over the years. The long sharp piece now glinted at me, the bright white light of morning twinkling on one side, and the glare of a red evening sun setting fire to the other.

I didn't know what to do with this thing. Finally, I turned it in my hands. Then I turned it again, and again, until I was turning it so fast that it became a blur of spinning red and white light, a shower of sparks, and then, I felt what I realized I had been waiting for, the memory had cut me with its gleaming blade. Slowly, it worked its way across my skin, forcing an entrance, forging a new bridge.

The day my brother died I got out of school early. It was one of the first days of fall and the leaves were already turning. My grandma had come to pick me up from school and that was odd, but I didn't much think about it. I was lost in the leaves and the change in the air, the slant of the sun that was so different from yesterday, when it had still been summer.

When we arrived home to the farmhouse, my mom was waiting for me on the porch, and here I paused and held the memory up to the light. I considered how fragile it felt, how much like a very delicate, antique glass, and how it seemed to have its own inner illumination, although I couldn't discern the source. My mom had something to tell me, she said, and she pulled me over to a chair, not letting me go inside. *Charles is going to die. By this time tomorrow he will be gone.* She held my hands as she said the words and the memory blinded me with its brilliance for a moment, as if a flashbulb had gone off.

I lowered the memory back down to my lap and it began to crumble, dissolving into shadows that ran through my fingers like grains of glistening black sand. I heard myself screaming at my mother. I heard myself call her a liar, even while I knew what she said was true.

Then the memory gelled back into shape, into a particular form that I could hold and examine again. My dad came out of the house. He walked over to me, and he was crying. And now I knew that something was so completely crazy wrong because my father was *crying*. I saw his cheeks slick and cloudy with tears. I'd never seen him cry before. *He's gone. Charles is gone,* he said. When he squeezed his eyes shut even more tears spilled down his face.

A lasso made out of light reached out of the memory and encircled my neck. Tight and sticky, it choked me until I felt like I was being strangled by flypaper. I turned violently, away from my mom and dad, away from the memory, and a vicious warm red light flooded my vision. I was blinded, my eyes filled with blood.

When I blinked I was back, sitting on the floor of my mind with the box in my lap. The memory in my hand glowed fiercely for a second and then winked at me like a dying coal and went dark. I dived back into the box and pulled out handful after handful of flat and glossy black squares that looked like defective Polaroid pictures that hadn't come out right. Images that had never been recorded. I knew that meant there was no more memory after that.

Not for a long time.

●●●

Every time I finished another session at Red City, I ripped all the pages I had written off the legal pad I brought with me every week and shoved them to the bottom of my backpack, burying them underneath all the other junk accumulated down there. The next morning, at the Pagliarani office, I yanked the pages out of the backpack and hid them in the bottom drawer of my desk. I slammed the drawer shut and locked it. Then I forgot about it. I forgot that I was writing anything, for the rest of the week.

But on the weekends, instead of spending my time walking around the city now, I snuck into the office and sat at my desk, with all the shades drawn, and typed it up.

Scarlet had started her own company a few months before, some sort of online media service for published authors. Her time was stretched so thin these days that she didn't even talk for her usual half hour at the table before we got started writing. As warm spring turned into chilly, foggy San Francisco summer, Scarlet became more distracted every week, until finally, she showed up one night with someone new. A woman named Una, who she said would be leading the writing program in her absence. And from the moment she was introduced, none of us were happy about it.

What would I do if I lost Scarlet? How would I ever finish my book? I already knew the answer. I wouldn't, not without Scarlet. I needed her. She made me feel like maybe all the bad things I'd thought about myself for years and years was just a silly mistake, like when you have the map turned the wrong way and go down the wrong road. The way Scarlet explained it, anyone could back up and turn themselves around again. She saw something in me that I couldn't see, but that I'd hoped had been there all along. Scarlet was the first person, ever, to make me see that maybe, just maybe, I was born to be a writer.

Even Scarlet's name sounded like something out of a story. It was something I'd name one of my characters, if I could ever write something good. And sometimes I did doubt that she was real. Her huge eyes and sculpted cheekbones gave her the look of a 1930s movie star—Katharine Hepburn carved out of ice and infused with fire. Scarlet strode into a room like a lioness, her hair floating around her china-white face like a mane. Everyone at Red City chewed their fingernails and sat on their hands waiting to talk to her. We could never get enough. She was the only one who saw the writers we could be. She'd delivered every one of us from an unremarkable life, and there wasn't a person in Red City who didn't know it.

Determined not to let my feelings show, I remained stonily cheerful as I watched Scarlet at the head of the table with the new woman, Una, sitting right next to her.

Tall and dark-eyed, Una reminded me of a Native American medicine woman. She wore her long black hair loose, and among the few strands of iron gray peeking through like stars on a stormy night, I imagined feathers and combs carved from wood. Una's face looked like it was carved out of wood too, serious and somehow sad, almost immoveable, fixed like a marionette's whenever she glanced over at Scarlet. Seeing them side by side, I couldn't help but notice that as pale as Scarlet was, Una was brown as the sunbaked earth. Scarlet's white-blonde hair caught the light on every strand, reflecting hues of snowy gold, while Una's hair was a nest of ravens at midnight, stealing sharp silvery glints from the moon.

Scarlet's voice boomed around the table as she introduced Una, loud in just the right way, like when an actor performs his soliloquy in a packed theater. Una mumbled hello and then darted a few nervous glances at us before staring down at the table again. Scarlet swiveled her eyes around the room, big as dinner plates. I looked up and down the table at the other members. Everyone looked as stoically resigned as I felt.

"All of you are going to love Una," Scarlet said. She straightened her back, pushing her shoulder blades together, and looked at Una, who then straightened up too. "And I hope that you do," Scarlet went on. "Because she's going to be my permanent replacement."

The room had been quiet before, but now it went dead silent. Like one of us had accused another of doing something horrible.

"I know all of you were counting on me to be there with you until the end of your finished sloppy first draft." She licked her lips and popped her laptop open. Compulsively, she began tracing its contour with the tips of her long milky fingers. "But now it will be Una," she said. "She is highly competent and—" she turned to Una, focusing the two huge lamps of her eyes on her. "There's no one I trust more." Scarlet fixed her beautiful smile on her. A hesitant grin flickered weakly at the corners of Una's mouth.

"And of course—" Scarlet slammed her laptop shut. I was sure I saw Una jump, just the tiniest bit. "I will still be delighted to be a first reader for any of you. I just won't have the time to give feedback. But that's why Una is here, to fill my shoes." She opened her laptop back up. "Una is now my right hand. I trust her completely." She smiled winningly at all of us again.

I needed additional information. Somehow, I had to get closer to Scarlet. There was a secret there somewhere, I was absolutely sure, and that secret was the key. It was the thing that had called me to San Francisco, I just knew it. It was the thing I'd been searching for the entire time.

●●●

Over the next few weeks I got to Red City early, stayed late, got to know Una, and dropped countless hints. Finally, at the end of July, I got the email I had been waiting for. Una said Red City's resident volunteer had quit, and she was wondering if I was interested in the position. They needed me for both nights of the week,

Tuesdays and Wednesdays. *More writing for me*, I thought to myself and smiled, and wrote back that I'd start the very next day.

Now, from the moment I arrived at the Mansion on both evenings, Una put me to work.

First, there was the food. The fruit had to be washed and cut and then put out, along with the crackers, cheese, nuts, and candy. The hot appetizers had to go in the oven and the tea had to be brewed. Then we uncorked the wine, set up the candles, and ran all the extension cords we needed under the banquet table. 30 minutes later I was in front of the door, ready to answer it before the bell could even ring. Scarlet hated the sound of doorbells, Una said. Since Scarlet wasn't even there most weeks, and neither were the actual owners of the Mansion, I was puzzled why it mattered, but obeyed Una's orders nonetheless. I made sure the doorbell never rang.

So far, I liked Una a lot. She had a quiet, capable air about her that said she could do anything. I pictured her in mechanics' overalls covered with grease under her car on Saturday mornings and then writing her theories on the history of magic late into the night. No matter how tortured the new Red City writers were, she shared their pain. No matter how scared any of us got along the way, she held our hand. In another life, I was sure Una had been a nurse during the black plague. She seemed unafraid of any form of contamination.

About two weeks after I had started as the resident volunteer, Una gave me a ride home one night.

"So how do you know Scarlet?" I asked. My voice came out sounding relaxed, but I kept my eyes nervously on the road. For as unobtrusive as Una seemed to be in person, she made up for it in aggressiveness when driving. The speed limit was 35mph but it felt like we were going about 80.

"Through Makiah," she said. "You know Makiah, yes?" I'd heard this Makiah person's name before, but I couldn't remember her exact link to Scarlet.

"Yeah...I think I've heard you and Scarlet mention her name, but I've never actually met her."

"Oh. Well, she's amazing." said Una. "I met her when I was working for the DA's office downtown. She's a lawyer and..." Una glanced casually to her left as she floated over to the other lane and blew through a stop sign. "She's just—well, she's amazing. She's hard to explain...and she's Scarlet's new business partner." she added.

"Oh." I didn't know what else to say. How did anyone get to be Scarlet's business partner? Makiah *must* be magic, I decided promptly. As if she'd heard my thoughts, Una sighed.

"Makiah *is* magic." she said.

Then she punched the gas pedal.

17

When Sal got into it over the phone one afternoon with one of our rookies, his yelling escalated until it was broken by the sound of splintering blows that always let me know another one had bitten the dust. I tiptoed in to see the latest casualty, the demolished hulk of plastic that used to be a phone, trickling to the floor in shattered pieces. Not for the first time, I wondered what supernatural material Sal's desk could possibly be made of in order to withstand so many constant and unrelenting attacks.

"Rookies, huh?" I said.

Sal looked up sheepishly.

"Ah—yeah. Fuckin' A—" He shot a glance at me. "Pardon my French, sorry. It's just..." Clenching his forehead with both hands, he stared down at his desk. "The client's gonna have my ass for this one. Fuckin' rookie screwed up big time. Burned the guy so bad *nobody'll* be able to work him for the next ten years. The client's gonna freak when she hears about this. And she's no box of chocolates on a good day, know what I mean?"

Sal looked up and smoothed one hand over his hair. He fisted the other and slowly brought it down on the impenetrable desk. For a moment I saw what Sal would look like when he was dead. The same face, but without all the fire; without the tornado energy, the zest for life that moved at 150 miles-per-hour. I could see he was tired now, but when I looked forward in time I saw him age, slump, and grow pale. I saw him as time moved through him, killing him slowly.

"Fuck," he whispered. His eyes went somewhere else. And suddenly I knew we were both thinking about Grove.

I backed out of the room like a ghost. Back at my desk, I closed my eyes. I was tired too.

●●●

Grove died at the end of August.

Aleksia texted me the news on a Saturday morning and I called Sal first thing. No answer. I left a message but didn't expect a call back.

When I got into the office that Monday it was business as usual. Sal stomped up the stairs and into his office. He gave me a short wave, but didn't say hello. I understood. Part of him wasn't here right now, it was with Grove. And all of Grove wasn't here anymore. He was somewhere else. I didn't know where. And in spite of being a die-hard Catholic who attended church every Sunday, I was pretty sure Sal didn't know either.

He was on the phone the whole morning. From my office I heard him make calls to every single one of their friends from the old gang and ask about the funeral. No one knew anything. Then he called Grove's ex-wife, and then his kids. Grove had a son and daughter who were grown now and lived up north in Humboldt County, which I pictured as a jungle full of friendly yet monstrous marijuana plants, bobbing playfully in the breeze and sucking people in like Venus flytraps. I wondered if Grove's kids knew that he'd died before Sal tracked them down. I thought about the Humboldt jungle again and had my doubts.

Nobody knew anything about any funeral.

"GOD FUCKING DAMMIT!!!" Sal screamed as he slammed the receiver down for the last time. The floor shifted and creaked with his outraged weight. I kept my eyes down at the keyboard, but it wasn't more than a second or two before Sal burst into my office and I had to look up anyway.

"Can you fucking believe it? What the fucking FUCK?" Sal shouted at me, and then backed up and grabbed the doorframe as if we were experiencing an earthquake. "A man's gotta have a funeral! I mean, what the *fuck*? Gemma! Get in here! It's not right—THIS is NOT right."

Gemma scurried out of her office and stood hesitantly beside him.

"Sal? What's going on?" Compared to Sal's bellowing, Gemma's voice was like a flute being played by someone having an asthma attack.

"No one's planning a funeral!" Sal shouted. "That's what's wrong! Not anybody! How could this happen? It's not right!" He let go of the doorframe and swayed. But then he clutched the sides of his head and steadied again. "Well, I won't have it." Sal dropped his hands and looked at me like I'd just challenged him to a duel. "I won't have it," he repeated. "In fact, I won't stand for it. We're giving Grove a funeral. We are burying that man properly if it's the last thing I do. If no one else will do it, by God, Grove can count on us!" he yelled, pounding his chest with one fist. Gemma nodded with the slight quivering of a mouse twitching its whiskers.

I went back to typing.

●●●

The morning of Grove's funeral opened onto a beautiful sunny California day. It was a day like in the travel guidebooks, where the sky is so blue it looks solid and like it's made out of ceramic. Funerals in movies always happen on rainy days. The rain comes down so hard that it just spills over people's faces, so that they practically have to mop it out of their eyes as they're talking to the villain they're supposed to have their standoff with, the one who comes to the funeral just to mock their loss, or to try to heal old wounds that are predestined to stay open, festering for eternity.

There's too much water in the rain in movie funerals. That's how you feel the fakeness underneath it. When the actor breaks his concentration and you can see irritation cross his face. That's how you remember it's only a movie, that it's not real. All that water dumping from above reminds you that it's not like that in real life, nothing ever comes all at once. Destiny is insidious and slow. Movie-funeral rain puts you back into the safety of your chair. Because you know it's just some guy poised above an actor on the movie set, dumping a bucket of water over his head.

I walked up the church steps, a little unsure where to go. Aleksia came running to meet me and then we made our way into the church and to a secluded pew in the back, away from the family and close friends. I saw a lot of the same faces I'd been introduced to at Grove's birthday party, just a few months before.

Grove's cousin delivered a eulogy, and then his ex-wife. Grove's son was third in line and when he got up and spoke I felt the tremble move through the crowd, the pews squeaked and sniffled. Then, Sal got up to speak.

I felt Aleksia stiffen beside me. I looked up toward the front of the church and saw Gemma's back, as straight as a poker. All of us were holding it in, Sal just barely. He told all the stories I already knew, but hearing them wrapped up in a funeral eulogy they were all new again. Seeing Sal up there, in his good black suit, red in the face and trying not to cry, it was like hearing an entirely different person tell the tale. Through the tears, I couldn't help but be happy. I loved stories more than anything.

Two weeks after Grove's funeral Sal still wasn't right with the world. I could tell his game was off. In those two weeks, he'd only yelled once, and that was when he dropped the typewriter on his foot. When I questioned him on cases he was distracted, his usually pink and shiny face drained of color.

"You think he can hear us?" he asked me one afternoon. I'd stopped by his office to let him know I was heading out for the night. Without warning, he'd looked up and fired the question at me, like it was a conflict of probability that he'd been grappling with for the past two hours. Rolling the dice over and over.

I knew how it went. I loved to roll some dice myself.

"I don't know," I said truthfully, buttoning my coat. "I think so. Don't you feel him sometimes?"

Sal didn't answer. I heard a soft plastic clicking and looked over to where he sat at his desk. It was the bracelet Grove had made for him. Feverishly, he jostled the beads together, as if he needed to count them unconsciously over and over again. "I wonder..." he muttered, but then he didn't say anything else. I shrugged inside my coat and left him there, running his fingers over the beads Grove had given him.

Sal wasn't on the phone half as much now. Instead, he spent most of his time contemplatively staring out his office window. He didn't even slam the phone down with as much ruthless vigor as before. He still assaulted it, yeah, but now his attacks seemed to come from a guy who actually cared whether he had to buy a new phone or not. It was totally out of character.

And then, Sal got a sign.

"Leah!" He blasted through my office door one morning, nearly ripping the doorknob off with his entrance. Distracted by the latest shitty rookie surveillance report, I took more than half a second to respond. Sal pounded the wall with one fist and amped up the volume a couple of notches like he always did when I didn't pay instant attention to him. At times like these I wondered if Sal thought I was actually partially deaf. He always used the same method to "get through to me," as he said. First, he'd hit the nearest wall as hard as he could so that I'd feel the vibration—like I was an old deaf dog under the family's dining room table—and then he'd widen his eyes and project his already booming voice while making slow exaggerated lip movements—like he thought my hearing aid had conked out and I'd resorted to reading lips.

"LEE-AAH...YOU...WILL...NE-VER...BEE-LEVE...THIS..." He mouthed to me, his giant pink hands fluttering and framing the words in the air. I sighed and stared at him. Sometimes I was convinced that if I could only choke the shit out of Sal once in this life I'd die happy.

"Sal. I can hear you. What is it? What happened?"

"It's Grove!" Sal didn't so much as run from the doorway to my desk as take an actual flying leap. In a twinkling, he was right in front of me.

"What about Grove?" I asked. The way Sal was acting, I thought there was possibly a small chance he'd come back from the dead.

"He gave me a sign! I knew it! I knew ol' Grove would come through!"

"Sal," I started again. "What in the world are you talking about?"

"It's the Zodiac. It all comes back to the Zodiac Killer. I told you about that, didn't I?"

He had told me about that. At least a thousand times it felt like. About how him and Grove had just been kids that year—the same year he'd claimed the two of them had also been roadies for Jefferson Airplane. But Grove and Sal had been into more than psychedelic rock bands that summer, they'd also been obsessed with the Zodiac Killer. No one could find the gunman that terrorized San Francisco, shooting lovers dead on the spot and in cold blood as they parked or picnicked. No one could find him and no one could stop him. The Zodiac Killer was never caught.

And Grove and Sal never forgot it.

"Yes, Sal." I said. "I remember. That was your thing, your thing with Grove. The Zodiac Killer." Sal nodded frantically. Practically choking on the words, he forced them out of his purple straining throat.

"Well, last night, last night after I went to bed," he spluttered. "I was lying there thinking—about Grove of course! And I sez, I sez to myself, but really to Grove too, well, really just to Grove—I sez, 'Grove give me a sign. Just so I know you're all right. Just so I know you're somewhere. Just so I know.' Ya know what I mean?" He paused and looked at me, his throat still working. I nodded.

"Well, so I said, 'Grove—give me a sign—and it can be *anything*. Just so long as I know, just so that I know when it happens—I know that it's from you, just so I know it was meant for me.'"

"Yeah?" I prompted.

"And then today—just right now, it happened. Leah, I swear to God, it happened." I raised an eyebrow. Sal may have had a sailor's mouth, but he didn't swear to God lightly. The little muscles in his neck pumped up and down. His eyes goggled out like a flounder's.

"Well what? What Sal?" Exasperated, I stood up all at once from my desk. "What happened?"

"So I went into this shop, see, right down from my house on the corner, see, and I'm talking to the salesgirl, you know, when I got up to the counter, so we're talking—" Sal paused to get his breath. I looked at the vein beating time in his forehead and the way his wrists bulged out of his suit cuffs. I was having serious doubts that Sal would make it through this story.

"So she sees my bracelet, see—" Sal shook his wrist free from the suit, and shook the bracelet in my face. It was the one Grove had made him, the one he'd been compulsively fondling since the funeral. I'd grown well-accustomed to hearing the *click-click-click* of the beads every time I passed his office.

"Yes, Sal. I see." He dropped his hand and continued.

"So she sees the bracelet and she's like, 'I love that bracelet. Who made it for you? It must have been a good friend.'"

Something went cold inside of me. Sal saw the look on my face and slowed down. "I know, creepy right? But that's not all of it..." He sped up again, spittle and words flying everywhere. "Then she says, 'Good friends are hard to find. And when you lose one they can never be replaced.' But that's not all either—" Sal rushed on before I could interrupt. "She goes to hand me the change and she turns her hand like this, see..." Sal made a fist and swiveled the thumb side toward me, as if a face was painted on his hand and he was going to make it talk like a puppet.

"And right here—" He drew an imaginary circle with his other index finger right below the joint of the thumb, where the lips would have ended on that painted-on face. "She's got a tattoo...and I see that tattoo and Leah—I tell you, I almost fell over right there. You'll never guess what it was."

I was sucked into his story now. Sal stared at me hard and dropped his hand. The face that had never been painted there fell away.

"It was a sign, from Grove." he said. "It was the sign of the Zodiac."

I sank back down into my chair as Sal made another leap off the ground.

"Grove made it!" he yelled, and ran out of my office.

I let out a shaky breath. Silently, I thanked Grove for sending Sal his last goodbye. And then I did what Grove would've wanted. I dived into making a shitty surveillance report better.

18

In my old life back in Seattle, when I was drinking and when Lo came out to play, I attracted a certain type of person, usually male. Someone who wanted me to hurt them. Whenever they showed up, Lo drew them in further. Then she started cutting them, just a little at a time, and pinching them, just hard enough to bruise, and then kept upping the ante whenever she got bored. These masochistic strangers who had somehow found me, who wanted pain and saw it in Lo's chameleon face, could never resist her siren song.

But with every new day that passed in San Francisco, with every day that I was sober and away from Lo's influence, I was more certain that I had it in me to be a better person. I was determined to at least give it a try. However, every so often a masochist still showed up on my doorstep.

There was a guy at Red City, a handsome guy with gray hair and wire-rimmed glasses. We talked one night before the writing started about the art of cartoon illustration, but under the surface he handed me something else, a warm, dark, pulsing egg, ready to be broken open. The image of a brutal black boot flashed into my mind and I saw that the boot bristled with dangerous silver, as if it had been mated with a Swiss army knife and produced some new instrument of torture.

Boot in the face, I thought. And I knew…it wasn't my thought. It shot into my brain like a satellite signal, clear as a bell. I blinked hard and looked at the guy.

I want a boot in the face. I locked eyes with him. It was real. And it was coming from him. Then it faded out. We were back again in the conversation about illustration.

The guy gave a final opinion and then sniffed and smiled weakly. I remembered that look from my days with Lo. They always smiled like that when it was over, or looked around nervous-like and then bolted, like they couldn't get away from me fast enough. Like I'd stolen their private information on purpose. Like they hadn't had any hand in delivering it to me, and like they didn't expect me to carry it for them now, at least for a little while.

How weird, I thought. I knew this guy was a good friend of Scarlet's. Masochists were usually attracted to sadists, like Lo, so I didn't get the Scarlet connection at all. But what I did get was that people were still coming to me with their pain, looking for someone like Lo to cut and pinch and up the ante, just like they had when I lived in Seattle.

Only now, I didn't want to do it anymore.

●●●

I had to get out of Pagliarani. No one person could do all the stuff I was doing on less than three pots of coffee a day. I handled all the cases, edited all the reports, and did all the background checks, locates, phone and plate traces, burned all the video for clients, and kept on top of every investigator's deadline, too. I woke up every morning in a state of panic, three hours before I had to be at work. But that was probably from all the coffee. I drank it nonstop, from the time I opened the office until I walked through the doors of the mansion into Red City that evening. I was so wired I fairly hummed while I was writing.

Una didn't seem to notice. If possible, she seemed to be even busier than me. She wasn't only working as the head of the writing program, Scarlet had also hired her as her personal assistant. All she talked about was Scarlet, and every night it seemed like she had a different checklist to run down. One evening, as we cleaned up in the kitchen of the mansion after a writing session, I asked her about it. She picked up a plate, started wiping it, and smiled grimly.

"Scarlet's building a company from the ground up," she said. "There's so much to do it's unbelievable. And we barely even have five people on staff yet, so I have to do a lot of it." She smiled again. "Or it won't get done."

For months now, I'd been waiting for my chance. I'd been listening, considering, and calculating. An opportunity would open up for me, I was sure, and when it did, I had to be ready. Some people are given a thousand chances and never take any of them, but all I needed was one. Now, here it was.

"Una, I'd love to work for Scarlet." I met her eyes and refused to look away. "What do you think? Would she go for it?"

Una drew back and stared at me. *Fuck*, I swore to myself. Now she was really offended. And honestly, I couldn't believe the nerve I had either. A worm like me working for a goddess like Scarlet Monroe? Yeah, right.

"Leah, yes..." Una hissed at me, quick and intense. "Why didn't I think of that? Yes, of course. You'd be perfect!"

"Really?" I ventured. "You think so?"

"Oh Leah! Yes—of course! Why didn't you ask me before? You'll do perfectly!"

She set the plate she'd been wiping down on the stainless-steel countertop, almost dropping it. It clanged on the surface, the sound echoing down the huge dark kitchen of the mansion. I winced. Una, however, appeared to hear nothing. Something in her face tensed and set like clean cement, nothing could walk through it now.

"I'll talk to Scarlet tomorrow," she said.

●●●

When I got to Red City the next week Scarlet was there, and I had the feeling she'd been waiting for me. As soon as I sat down she went into motion, stalking around me like a lean white panther. I could feel her presence crackling with electricity.

"Where are you working now, Leah?" she asked, making half a circle around me.

"Uh, at the private detective place," I stuttered.

"Oh yes. Yes, yes. I know that." She smiled, and I noticed for the first time how her red lips pooched out just a bit when she did. Anxious and half out of my wits, I thought absurdly how it made her look just a touch predatory.

"How do you like it?" she asked, completing the circle. Now she was on the other side of me. I had to turn almost all the way around to face her. "How do you like it?" she repeated, as if maybe I hadn't heard her. "Are you happy there? Are you happy working for them? Are you happy with your life?"

It sounded like a lot of questions but all of them meant the same thing. *Are you happy Leah? Are you really?*

"No," I confessed. "No, Scarlet, I'm not happy at all."

"What do you want to do?" she asked and abruptly stopped in the middle of one of her circles. I held my breath. She was making me dizzy.

"Well, I want to write," I said truthfully. "I don't know what or how, but that's what I want to do. I want to write." God, I sounded pathetic. *I want to write.* Well didn't everyone? But not just anyone could be a writer. You had to be special. You had to be someone like Scarlet Monroe.

"Come work for me." she said.

"Wha-what?"

"Come work for me." Scarlet stood still for a second and then resumed pacing her endless circle around me. My mouth hung open stupidly.

"Come work for me and help me save the world," Scarlet said. "This company I'm building is going to be like no other company anyone has ever seen before. We're bringing writers together and we're bringing their work to every dark corner of this country, and then beyond—to the entire world. Somewhere out there, there's a little girl—maybe in Kansas, maybe in Michigan—maybe in the desert of New Mexico—but wherever she is, she's waiting for us. She's a little girl who's got no one but the stories she reads and lives in—and she needs us. She needs us to show her that she can get out, she can escape her little dark corner of the country, she can make it to somewhere like San Francisco, this place that's made for people like us. But she needs us to light up the darkness first. So she can see where she's going. Do you see Leah? Do you see why we need a company like mine?"

I'd never seen anything so clearly in my life. That little girl was me. Back in my past, and also right here and now, sitting in the magical land of San Francisco but still stuck in a dark corner of my own mind.

It suddenly dawned on me that I had no idea what Scarlet's company did. All I knew was that it was a start-up, and somehow based around a website for writers. As if she'd read my mind, Scarlet started answering all my unspoken questions.

"What we're going to do is build a network of famous writers." She stopped circling and stood directly opposite me. She raised her arms and I had that feeling again of being presided over by a queen. "We're modeling our website—RedCity.com—on social networking sites like MySpace and Facebook. The set-up will be similar. With one crucial difference, it's by invite only. It's only the famous writers, the really famous ones, that are allowed...at first. Of course, only at first. The really famous ones will draw the others in."

She closed her lips over her teeth and I saw her go inside of herself, away where I couldn't see. She was thinking something over that was just between her and...well, I didn't know who else. Not Una, I suspected. Definitely not me. And then she was back. Like she'd never been gone.

"It's going to be huge—it's going to turn into a worldwide phenomenon, that's what I'm counting on." She started pacing again as she talked. "And then everyone's going to be into it, all the writers, everywhere. It'll expand until it becomes the place where writers get famous. And that's where that little girl comes in."

Scarlet plunked down into the chair next to me and turned my way.

"Come work for me, Leah. Quit your job tomorrow. Climb aboard RedCity.com and let's save the world together. What do you say?" she asked, giving me that glittering smile again.

"Yes...oh Scarlet, yes. Yes!" I managed, and then my throat closed up altogether and I choked on my own hidden tears.

●●●

That night, I waited up until James got home and then told him all about my job offer from Scarlet. Although it felt like maybe we were more distant than ever these days, I knew he was happy for me. We still sometimes smoked a joint together in the middle of the night and during those accidental nocturnal meetings the connection we had flared to life again. During those 3:00am hours we shared what was most important with each other, the book I was writing and the music he created. To other people it might seem odd that we devoted hours and hours to scribbling words on a page or picking out notes on a guitar, but to us, there was no higher purpose in life. So, even though a rift had grown up between us that was getting wider every day, it was possible to bridge that rift all in one leap. At the deepest level, at our most secret hidden core, we were the same as each other, and different from almost everyone else. This was the glue that held us together, and somehow, I knew that it would take more than any amount of time or distance to pull us apart.

After I went to bed, I thought about how tomorrow I had to go into Pagliarani and give Sal my notice. He'd probably go ballistic. He'd definitely scream at me and he might throw something at my head. But I didn't care. It was beyond crazy, but it was true. I just didn't care.

I imagined myself working for Scarlet in a glorious office with gleaming gold walls like a big open castle. I saw Scarlet sitting at a red desk, patting my hand and telling me that we'd made the dream come true. We'd united all the writers in the world. The little girl had been freed from her dark corner and she was writing her own book now. I saw famous writers walking through that magic office door. I saw what I wanted to be one day, a real writer myself.

I fell asleep, still dreaming of Red City. Sal and Pagliarani, all the work and stress of the past couple of years, had ceased to exist. It had fallen away.

Tomorrow was another life.

19

When I told Sal I was quitting he shocked the hell out of me for the last time. He didn't freak at all. In fact, he was as calm as I usually was in the face of his tornado tirades.

Quietly, he asked me if I was following my dream. When I said yes, he nodded gently. He said "ok," and that was all. Over the next few days I helped him hand my job over to Aleksia, who'd decided to quit surveillance and work in the office instead. She'd had enough of chasing people, she said. A week later I was free of Pagliarani.

My first day working for Scarlet I took the same train I usually took to work, but instead of walking down to the Castro, to the Pagliarani office, I walked up into the Fillmore District, where Scarlet lived. I'd felt exhilarated stepping off the train, but that had evaporated by the time I got to her door. I could smell the anxiety coming off me, like my armpits and the special little glands in between my toes were already working overtime. I raised one trembling hand to ring the doorbell and shifted from one foot to the other, the insides of my shoes already beginning to squelch.

Someone buzzed me in from above. It was like being let into a prisoner's visiting room, I thought, and suddenly noticed that iron bars covered every door and window of Scarlet's beautiful Victorian home.

Maximum security. I wasn't surprised. It wasn't so different from a lot of other houses in the City. San Francisco could be a dangerous place.

As soon as I pushed open the door, I saw Una running down the long staircase. "Leah!" She clapped her hands softly and smiled like a happy little girl. "I'm so glad you're here."

I managed to grin through my nervousness. "Yeah, me too," I answered. I couldn't believe I was standing in Scarlet's house. I sort of felt like I might throw up.

"Come, come, come—" Una grabbed my hand and pulled me upstairs. Before we reached the top step, Scarlet's voice wafted down to us.

"Una? Who is it?"

For a second, I thought I picked up on an odd touch of helplessness in Scarlet's voice, high, with an edge of desperate. But that was me. I was the one knocked off-kilter by the fact that I was actually standing in the middle of Scarlet Monroe's house. It was almost too much to believe. I looked around, trying to take it all in and prove to myself it was true.

Her home consisted of the entire top floor of a sprawling Victorian. The wood floors shone luxuriously, the walls were a thick milky cream color. Antiques furnished all the rooms, and artistic masterpieces— some expressly dedicated to Scarlet—decked the walls. Floor-to-ceiling bookshelves lined the front parlor, jam-packed with everything from paperbacks to leather bound volumes. Probably all signed to Scarlet too, I thought, from writers she'd helped on their way.

It was like a smaller, more intimate, version of the mansion.

But I didn't have time to gawk much longer. Una still had my hand, and she'd dragged me clear across the hall into Scarlet's office.

"She's here, Scarlet. It's Leah. Leah's here." Una said rapidly.

"Well, she'll need a workstation Una. That's first thing. You can put her next to me for now. That should work best, as I want to make sure to set her up for success on her very first day." As Scarlet waved a hand to her left I suddenly realized the room was stuffed with furniture. Five desks and two filing cabinets. Not an inch to spare, literally. The desks were all smashed right up against each other.

Una led me to the desk next to Scarlet and gestured for me to sit down.

"You'll sit here—for now—just as Scarlet says. I sit over there—" She pointed to the desk right across from Scarlet's. "Makiah sits here, and this last desk is empty for now." I shot a glance at that one, tucked into the corner opposite me.

"Don't worry—" Una rushed on. "It won't be empty for long. We have new people starting every day...in fact, I think there's another one coming in...today?" she faltered and looked toward Scarlet.

"No, no one else today." Scarlet answered without ceasing to type or take her eyes off her computer screen. "Just Leah."

Una bent down quickly and began rummaging through the drawers in my new desk.

"Let me just clear this out, and this...oh—and these things...we had someone in here up until a couple of days ago...a designer...she didn't work out though...just want to make sure all her stuff is out of here..." Una murmured apologetically, almost half to herself, as if she were moving distractedly down some internal to-do list.

"No, she certainly didn't work out," put in Scarlet from where she sat, still typing. She threw her smile toward me again and then went back to the screen. "A lovely woman. But completely incompetent."

"Oh, I'm so sorry," I said. "That must have been awful to have to fire someone right away like that."

I watched the top of Una's head as I waited for her to clear out the desk. It bobbed unsteadily as she continued to whisper to herself, too low for me to hear. Scarlet appeared to be thoroughly engrossed in whatever was on the screen in front of her. Probably super important business CEO stuff, I thought. I didn't want to start talking too much and make it plain I was a nuisance on my very first day.

When the door buzzed I practically jumped out of my chair. Since I'd gotten inside, for some reason, my anxiety had only increased. "Una?" Scarlet wailed softly, even though Una was right there. Her eyes stayed on the screen. I figured she assumed Una must have walked out of the room.

"Got it, Scarlet," Una answered, still rustling through drawers. She looked up at me. "That's Makiah." she said, and jumped up to let her in.

A moment later the small quiet room turned into a big boisterous party.

"You're Leah!" Makiah pointed at me and giggled. "Welcome to Red City!" She ran at my desk and clobbered me, hugging me so hard the seat I was in bent backwards. I heard a small sharp crack from the chair's spine.

"Uh, hi Makiah," I managed, muffled by her coat and her long bronzey-brown hair spilling over me. Even though we'd never met before I could already tell she was like the popular kid in class, cracking jokes everyone loved and giggling in a way that made everyone else happy. When Makiah laughed it did more than warm up a room, it made you feel for just a few seconds like it was the first day of summer and school was out. She laughed again now, and all of a sudden I felt better about everything. I'd get over being nervous. It would all work out.

"Makiah, you'll never guess who signed a check yesterday." Scarlet said, her voice a cool jetty of rock jutting into a warm frothy ocean.

"No!" Makiah froze in mid-giggle, her eyes wide behind her square black glasses. She looked exactly like a teenager, hearing about how *you-know-who* had been caught doing *you-know-what* behind the school parking lot.

"Oh yes. Definitely yes." Scarlet cut her eyes away from the screen and snapped her keyboard tray under her desk with a final flat-handed push. She rolled her chair around in one fluid movement to face us.

"He did." she said. "In fact, I have it right here." She patted her breast pocket and smiled, moving her eyes from me to Makiah and then finally to Una. "And it's everything he promised. We can finally start expanding with this. We can launch the site with this."

Makiah jumped straight up and billy-goated onto her chair. Then, before I could blink, she was standing on top of her desk.

"Eeeeee!" she squealed and did a little jig. "Eeee! Eeee! Eeee!" Heels clicking and hair flying, she bleated and sang, and knocked over a cup full of pens. Una crossed the room and began picking them up. As she bent down, she whispered to me.

"It's an investor. Scarlet and Makiah have been working on this guy for months. It looked like he wasn't going to come through. But I guess he did..." She shot a glance at Makiah, still hoofing a square dance on her desk. "Now the company's not only guaranteed to stay afloat, but we can finally get the website off the ground too." Una said. She moved away again, stooping to pick up pens as she went.

"Eeee!" cried Makiah. "Hallelujah!" A lone stapler kept time with the rhythm of her heels.

"Makiah," Scarlet said sharply. "Get down." She turned back around to her computer screen. "You're making a spectacle of yourself."

"Eeee!" Makiah shouted, and kept right on dancing.

I could barely make sense of anything that morning. It wasn't the same kind of chaos as Pagliarani—no phone ringing, no reports to write, nobody to chase down and nail with a particular piece of damning video—but it was chaos all the same. The front door buzzed constantly. There were deliveries, messengers, carpenters coming by to work on the house, and consultants coming to work on the website. Plus, Scarlet told just as many stories when she was working as she did before we got started writing at a session of Red City. I wasn't sure exactly what she was doing on her computer, but whatever it was didn't appear to take great levels of concentration because she was able to type a little, talk a little, type a little and then talk a lot, all morning long.

And Makiah never stopped dancing. She didn't repeat the number she'd done on top of her desk earlier, but she danced to any tune that happened to be playing at the moment. She popped CDs into a stereo crushed under a stack of binders, wedged into a corner of her desk, and cranked it all the way up. She sang along to every song at the top of her lungs.

Una didn't tell stories and she didn't sing or dance, but it seemed like she had a thousand questions for Scarlet and every question she asked seemed to open up ten more. Already I shuddered at the thought that I had ever been jealous of Una for being Scarlet's assistant. It made me dizzy just to listen to her.

But I still had my work cut out for me. It was my job to manage the office, and even though right now that only consisted of this one room and a few stacks of files, I already knew everything was about to explode like dandelions in May. At the beginning of April you see a couple yellow specks on your lawn and then three weeks later it's like someone's splattered 3,000 egg yolks all over the grass. I had a nose for things like that. I'd been the victim of change too often not to recognize its long black shadow on the horizon. If I didn't get this one little room under control now, I'd never get my footing on the ship back. I'd be seasick for the entire journey.

Early that afternoon the front door buzzed again—for maybe the 86th time since I'd gotten there that morning—and I happened to be out in the hall. "Leah, can you get that?" Una called. I checked the small screen that showed video from the surveillance cameras outside and saw an Asian guy with short, spiked black hair and an impassive face. He was also wearing a full three-piece suit. Something about him struck me as outrageously calm. He reminded me of the jagged rocks usually planted at the foot of oceanside cliffs—the ones that the most thunderous waves can't budge an inch.

"Who is it?" I piped into the intercom box.

"Benjie," the guy answered. "Benjie Hong...I am here for an interview." I was positive Scarlet had said just a couple of hours ago that no one was scheduled to come in for an interview today. But, shrugging my shoulders, I let him in anyway. I couldn't very well leave him out on the stoop dressed in a suit like that. Scarlet's house may have been a gorgeous Victorian, but as often occurred in San Francisco, it happened to be not in the best neighborhood.

The guy clomped up the stairs and when he got to the second floor I checked out his shoes. They were big, and shiny black like his hair, polished to a glossy sheen, and just as solid as the rest of him.

"Scarlet?" I poked my head into the room that served as the office and raised my voice. Makiah was rocking maniacally back and forth in her chair to the newest album from the Killers, the volume thrown to full blast. "Scarlet? There's someone here to see you. An interview? He says his name is Benjie Hong."

"Makiah, the music." Scarlet said over her shoulder. She kept on typing. I looked helplessly at Una.

"Scarlet, I think there's someone here to see you..." Una started.

"Makiah, turn down the music—Makiah?" Scarlet kept talking over her shoulder.

"Scarlet, there's someone out in the hall...are you sure you weren't supposed to interview anyone today?" Una swiveled her chair closer to the doorframe and peeped around the corner at Benjie Hong and his suit. "There's someone here—and he definitely looks like an interview..."

"Makiah? Makiah!" Scarlet raised her voice but it didn't seem to make a bit of difference. Makiah shook from side to side frantically. I wondered briefly if she was secretly epileptic.

"MAKIAH!!!"

"What? Oh, sorry Scarlet." Makiah shut the CD player off. "Did you say something?" She shook her damp hair off her forehead and beamed. Scarlet scowled at her for a moment and then put on a pouty face.

"I am trying to hear myself think Makiah and with the music like that, at that volume—"

"Scarlet, there's someone here to see you—" Una started again.

"Yes, I KNOW UNA!" she snapped. Suddenly her eyes were blazing. "Would you just stop *yammering* at me like a whining dog!"

Una shrunk into herself like a penis dunked into a bucket of ice water.

"Oh God, my head..." Scarlet closed her eyes and massaged her temples. "Una, you know you're the best assistant anyone has ever had...there's just so much going on, I'm so swamped," she moaned. She pinched the bridge of her nose and then her eyes snapped wide open again, like a jack-in-the-box springing to spooky life.

"Well now, where is this person?" she demanded brightly. "Who are they exactly?" And the smile was back on—the ruby-red glistening smile I knew so well. Suddenly I felt cold all over.

"Benjie." I fairly whispered. "Benjie Hong."

She strode past me to the hall, delivering that same smile up to Benjie himself, standing still as a stone in his stiff black suit.

"Benjie," she said warmly, and her voice was all honey now. Scarlet clasped his hand like they were long lost friends. "So good to meet you," she purred.

With only the barest flicker of hesitation rippling under his imperturbable mask, Benjie smiled right back.

●●●

Scarlet took Benjie and Makiah into the office with her and booted Una out into the hallway with me. I glanced at her but she looked away fast, before I could read anything on her face.

"Well, into the dining room we go!" she said cheerfully. I followed her over to the dining room table. As chipper as she sounded I felt the crack running along the length of her voice.

"This is our temporary workstation," Una explained. "Scarlet and Makiah have a lot of meetings, you have to understand, and some of what they talk about is confidential...sooo..." She waved a hand over the table. "Here we are."

Two laptops, a pile of folders, and an overflowing in-basket clustered for space on the small mahogany surface. With all the papers scattered over it and the mishmash of other random crap, I didn't see how it could possibly function as a temporary desk for anyone.

"Here," said Una as she handed me a folder. "Take this—and this—oh, and this one—" Folders and binders and stacks of scrawled notes came at me until my arms were full. "As long as we're out here we should start on this pile," Una said. "Scarlet won't like it if we're wasting time. She's very conscious of productivity. We have to make the most of every minute."

My arms sagged with the weight of all Una had given me. I saw quickly that she was right. Everything had to get done, and fast. Shit, some of this stuff was supposed to already have been done. We had no time to lose, seconds were slipping by. My mind whirled with the gravity of the situation. Sobered, I opened the first folder and plunged in. Una was already way ahead of me. Out of the corner of my eye I saw her head pecking ferociously at the air as she scanned the contents of a binder.

A few minutes later—or maybe an hour, I had no idea how much time had passed—our concentration was broken.

"Una? Hey Una?"

"Yes Danica? You need something?" Una asked as she kept working.

I turned and met with the owner of the voice. It was a girl who looked no older than me, somewhere in her late 20s or early 30s, with long black hair streaked through with electric blue, pulled into low pigtails that rippled over both shoulders. Her eyes were big and innocent-looking, and just as blue as the streaks in her hair. In fact, I'd never seen such blue eyes on anyone, anywhere. Not even on Paul Newman in the movies.

"I just need you to look over this form, Scarlet signed it but she didn't date it. Could you get her to fill it out when she has a chance?" The girl—who was named Danica apparently—said as she handed Una a sheet of paper. I noticed she had the same kind of energy that Benjie Hong had—a quiet imperturbability. Just the thing I'd always wanted to have, but never did. In my daydreams, I pictured strangers meeting me and then saying afterward to one another: *That woman is unflappable.* Unfortunately, the truth was I flapped like a sheet on a clothesline in a wind storm. I'd never have anything like a quiet imperturbability in my nature, ever. But that only made me so much more curious about those who did.

As Danica stepped closer to me, I saw her walk was just as confident as her voice.

"Hi, I'm Danica," she said simply, extending one hand.

"I'm Leah," I smiled at her. "Where did you come from?"

"Where did I come from?" Danica repeated with a sardonic grin. "Well that depends on if you're talking biological or geographical. Or, if you mean in the last few minutes. In that case I came from back there—" She cocked a thumb over her shoulder. "From the back room."

"There's a back room?" Scarlet's place was full of surprises.

"Oh yes," Danica smirked and winked at me. "And there's a trapdoor and a dungeon, too."

I liked Danica.

I looked over at Una. Her eyes swung back and forth over the page she held in front of her like an amped-up pendulum. When I looked back at Danica I saw her looking at Una too. Somehow, I had the feeling they already knew each other very well. As if she'd heard my thoughts, Danica answered my unspoken question.

"Me and Una went to college together, down in SoCal." she said. "Isn't that right, Una?" Danica spoke a little louder and tapped Una on the hand. Una gave no sign she'd heard. As if in a trance, her eyes swirled over the contents of the list in front of her.

Danica chuckled and shrugged, like she experienced this with Una all the time. *How weird that they're friends*, I thought. I was starting to see how high-strung Una was, while Danica was the epitome of cool, calm, and utterly collected. As if to prove this point, she sat down and kicked one converse sneaker up on the chair beside me.

"So how do you know Una?" Danica asked. But before I could answer we were interrupted by Scarlet, Benjie, and Makiah, who poured out of the office in a froth of noise and exclamations. I saw Scarlet pumping Benjie's hand furiously.

"Excellent. Then it's settled. You're hired and you'll start immediately," she said. Una and I jumped up at the same time and rushed to Scarlet's side.

"He's starting with us? He's on board?" Una asked, breathless.

"Should I start an employee file for him?" I asked at the same time.

Scarlet gave a sophisticated tinkling laugh, like she might melt into velvety-soft cinematic shadows at any moment. "Ladies, please. Give Benjie some room. And yes, he's on board with us and RedCity.com, and yes Leah," she glanced my way. "You'll definitely need to start a file."

"When does he start?" Una gasped and smiled at the same time, if that was even physically possible.

"Why, today. Right now, in fact," said Scarlet, looking around at all of us seriously. "That is okay, isn't it Benjie?" she asked, a worried crease working its way between her two perfectly arched eyebrows. Not for the first time, I was reminded of how those eyebrows sometimes made her look like an evil queen out of a Disney movie.

"It has to be today, Benjie. I mean it," said Scarlet. "There's work on the computers that absolutely must be done right now, without a moment to lose."

"That should not be a problem," Benjie said in his soft formal English, tinged at the edges with his beautiful accent. "Not a problem at all. I will begin at this very moment." He began unbuttoning his suit cuffs and rolled up his shirtsleeves, smiling for the first time at all of us now, everyone but Scarlet unable to look anything but astonished.

●●●

Benjie wasn't joking when he agreed to start working right away. He got down underneath Scarlet's desk just like he was in sweatpants instead of a suit and immediately began fiddling and fussing with every little wire she pointed out to him. Scarlet kept both eyes glued to the back of Benjie's head and told him exactly what to do, every step of the way. After watching the convoluted process, I was surprised she had hired Benjie to do the job. She had such specific instructions for him it seemed she could just as very well have done it herself.

Between Makiah's radio, Scarlet trumpeting commands to Benjie like a histrionic war general, and Benjie's blocky maneuverings under Scarlet's desk, his suit getting dustier and dustier every time he came up for air, I figured the safest bet was to stay out in the dining room. Una was still poring over list after list like a zombie worker bee, but Danica, who'd settled herself into the chair across from both of us, cracked jokes and told me the story of the first time she and Una had met each other in college and how they had hated each other's guts. Danica didn't seem in any hurry to return to the mysterious back room she'd mentioned, which was just as well, because even with Una sitting right beside me I suddenly felt all alone.

When I looked back at the clock on my laptop I was surprised to see it was already 7:00pm. I'd been at

Scarlet's for a solid 12 hours. Wearily, I started packing up my stuff to go. Scarlet had told me earlier to start working on the employee handbook tonight. *Not a minute to waste*, she'd said. Yawning already, I wondered where I'd get the energy to even begin. I was exhausted.

I tapped Una on the shoulder.

"Hey, are you staying? Una? Are you staying? It's seven o'clock," I said. But she barely nodded to me.

"Have to," she said tersely. "Have to get things done," she mumbled, and went back to counting whatever it was she was counting.

"I'm with you! Hold on! One sec—don't leave! I'm coming!" Danica rapidly gathered up her things from where she'd set up camp next to me. On our way out, we stopped by Scarlet's office door.

"We're going Scarlet. Have a good night," said Danica.

Scarlet glanced at her watch. "Already?" she asked, her eyebrows dipping down in disappointment. Before I could make an excuse Danica jumped in smoothly.

"We want to get good and settled in at home, start all those projects you gave us on the list and get as far as we can tonight. No use starting them here and then having to deal with the distraction of driving home." I threw Danica a look when Scarlet turned back toward her computer screen. The look Danica gave me back was a kick under the table. I felt it and kept my mouth shut.

"Well, don't forget about tomorrow night." Scarlet said.

"Why? What's happening tomorrow?" I asked.

"Litquake." Scarlet pronounced it coldly, as if it were Christmas Day and I'd been too bone-headed to notice. "Kick-off is at the Make Out Room. I expect you and Una to be there."

"After all," she gave me her shark smile again. "You are my team."

20

The very next night I took the train to the Make Out Room in the Mission, the bar that was hosting the Litquake kick-off event that Scarlet had required me and Una to attend. Litquake was a weeklong literary festival founded by June Sorehl, a woman who was a friend of Scarlet's (because Scarlet knew everyone) and who now also worked with us at Red City occasionally. Litquake happened every year in the middle of October and during that time the streets of San Francisco rang with poetry and rocked with prose. Lightning bolts of spoken word zigzagged between Victorians, in through windows and out through skylights. I was sure there had probably been more than a few sightings of Allen Ginsberg's naked ghost dancing down the sidewalks.

Tonight's show was a reading from San Francisco's hottest new emerging authors and I didn't know what to expect. As I walked into the Make Out Room I found the inside dark as a cave, or some cool-kid teenager's basement. Revolving round discs of red light swirled along every wall and silver disco balls spun from the ceiling. A few basic black tables and chairs were scattered about, but the décor was mostly made up of plush aquamarine couches and bright pink, fur-covered stools. I was beginning to get the name.

I sort of felt like I was trapped in an '80s movie, or my own life four or five years ago, when I would have loved this place and flounced straight up to the bar to order a martini, wiggling my ass and throwing a wink to the bartender all in one blow. But that wasn't me now. I didn't know where to look or what to do. Uneasy, I shuffled back and forth near the entrance, dodging the people who did know where they were going and wanted me out of their way, while my eyes adjusted to the darkness.

Then I saw someone waving to me. It was Makiah, sitting by herself at one of the small black tables right by the stage. I shouldered my way over through the thickening crowd.

"Leah!" Makiah squealed as I approached. "Sit sit sit!" She patted the chair next to her as if she were putting out a fire with the palm of her hand and giggled with delight. Relieved to see her, I sat down.

"Hey Makiah." I said. "Where is everyone?"

"Scarlet and Una are on their way. Scarlet's late as always," she explained. "And the Red City readers are backstage—getting ready for the big performance!" She giggled again and waved to someone walking behind me.

I'd nearly forgotten the very reason we were there. Every year Scarlet got to pick two people to read from her flock of writers at Red City. This year she'd managed to get in three by selling two of them as a mother-daughter team. Marla, the daughter, was an alternative girl with a serious prairie-flower face and golden hair that had one violet streak worn in a tiny braid running through it, and her mother, Rose, was a Czech immigrant who'd left Marla's father after 40 years of marriage and moved from their drab little Pennsylvania town out to magic San Francisco—and into Marla's cramped apartment with her. A situation that caused no end of laughs—and story ideas—in the weekly Red City writing sessions.

The third reader was a long-time friend of Scarlet's, the handsome guy with the gray hair who had so unwittingly handed me one of his dark secrets months ago.

"Oh! Here they are!" Makiah said. I turned and saw Una clearing a path to our table for Scarlet, who was following behind her. The way all eyes landed on Scarlet and floated along with her, as if some part of everyone's gaze had snagged on a fold of her clothing and was being dragged out of their heads against their will, well, I could tell everyone knew who she was. I'd seen those same looks a million times in my old life, in dark rainy-night bars in Seattle.

They got to the table and Una aggressively brushed the top of it clean, as if she'd seen crumbs littering its surface, when there hadn't been anything there at all. Scarlet descended regally into her chair as if she hadn't noticed.

"Scarlet, what can I get you? Sparkling water with lemon?" Una asked intently, like she was afraid of already fucking up the order.

"Thank you, Una. Yes, that would be lovely." Scarlet smiled demurely. I marveled at how all traces of the petulant rage I'd seen the day before seemed like something unimaginable now. She was once again Scarlet as I knew her, as I'd always known her. Perfect as a dream.

Una bounded away to fetch Scarlet's water just as the performance began. Everything went dark and the room fell silent. When the lights went up a few seconds later I saw Una slip like a shadow between tables, delivering Scarlet's drink to her and then squeezing covertly into her chair.

The first writer up apparently knew most of the members of the audience because he kept cracking inside jokes and dropping names while winking at a couple of people in the front row. I could tell the guy was kind of drunk by the way he was so red in the face and sweating under the lights, pulling and groping at his limp expensive tie. When he read his stuff I found it just as obnoxious. Pompous, overblown, and as carefully analytical as a math problem.

I felt a tug at my elbow. It was Scarlet. I leaned forward apprehensively, tilting my ear toward her. "He's pretty good but your writing's better than that," she said.

Really? Did that really just happen? I shook my head, my eyes watering. The stage suddenly grew so bright it fuzzed out at the edges. Everything became muffled, distant and unreal, everything except the compliment Scarlet had just dropped in my ear.

Your writing is better than that.

She'd said it so casually, like it wasn't even a question. Like I should have known it all along. Not only was my writing good, but it was *better than that.*

Better than someone who'd made it to the Litquake stage.

I sat and shivered with exhilaration, hoping it was too dark for Scarlet, or anyone else, to notice. But at the same time, something else tickled the back of my brain, something on the tip of my tongue, a piece that didn't quite fit. Something that didn't belong.

Then another reader took the stage and I forgot all about it.

The girl was young, in her very early 20s probably, and wore plain jeans matched with a white t-shirt. Her chestnut brown hair was pulled low and she wore no makeup. I could tell she was nervous by the way she kept wiping her hands down the front of her pants and when she spoke her voice shook. But when she started telling her story I was immediately sucked into it. I was with her, in her body, and looking out through her eyes. I grew up in the Mission and went off to the championship volleyball tournament in LA when I was a freshman in high school. I was sitting with the wealthy sponsor family at their gigantic dining room table in their Bel Air mansion. I was making a fool of myself by commenting on how amazing I thought their lawn was, it was just so big.

"Why?" asked the rich, droll father. "Don't they have grass where you come from?"

Everyone at the table laughed, including the other girl my age, the girl from the sister LA team who'd volunteered to let me stay at her house so I could play in the championship game. Everyone laughed except me. I was humiliated.

Then I was back at the Make Out Room, pushed out of the experience and back into my own body. I was standing, clapping my hands so hard I was sure welts were probably popping up all over them and the tears in my eyes were serious crying tears now, because that girl had been so good. That girl could *write*. Her story hit me so hard it was like a nail had gone through my heart.

Next, it was Rose's turn. She got up on the stage and began telling us in her sad, beautiful, broken English about how she had left Marla's father to find herself in San Francisco, and when she got to the City she started picking up pennies wherever she found them

205

because pennies were good luck, and after a while it was like there were pennies under each one of her footsteps, in the corners of stairwells, rolling down the steep hills of the streets, everywhere flashes of copper light glimmering in the California sun, until she didn't even have to look anymore because now the pennies found her and her life was filled with luck.

After Rose, Marla was on, and everyone laughed uproariously all through her reading. She called herself Alien Girl and used big pieces of black poster-board illustrated with neon glitter drawings of her and her cat, her drunk at a party, her and her mom drinking together and Rose putting on a wig and getting silly. I laughed so hard my eyes started to tear up again.

The last writer was Scarlet's long-time friend and the piece he read was about lost love. Him walking on the beach by the Bay with the woman who was his soulmate, kisses at twilight, promises exchanged at dawn, and then her leaving and him left all alone. Heartbroken and empty. Trampled. I felt the audience sigh behind me. I didn't sigh with them. I looked at his eyes as he looked out at all of us and remembered what I'd seen inside him. I suspected the girl in the story didn't exist. Somewhere I knew, there was a shoebox— or maybe a hidden folder on his laptop—with the real story. Him in a basement, tied to a bed, and a woman in leather with a whip standing over him with one black stiletto boot planted squarely on his throat, giving him exactly what he wanted.

Trampled, indeed.

●●●

Sunday morning, I dragged myself back to Scarlet's to tackle another grueling day. I'd stayed at the Make Out

Room late the night before with Scarlet, Makiah and Una, and the local San Francisco writers we hoped to snag for RedCity.com. This morning we had a new girl starting—our editor—and Scarlet said she needed me there to put the girl's file in order, make sure her desk was ready, and "set her up for success." It was a phrase I was fast learning was one of Scarlet's favorites.

I thought it was kind of weird that our new editor was starting on a Sunday, but like Scarlet said, not a moment to lose and all that, so bright and early that morning, still digging the mascara out of the creases under my eyes, I showed up at Scarlet's place and plunked down next to her ready to start another day of work. When the door buzzed just a few minutes later I got up again. I was exhausted but I didn't have to be told now who needed to answer it. As the newest arrival made her way up the stairs and I got a good look at her I was even too tired to evince the slightest surprise that she appeared to be doing her best impression of Jackie Onassis.

"Hi. I'm Stephanie. Here to see Scarlet?" The words came out clipped and brisk, and the voice came from behind a pair of giant black sunglasses that covered half her face. Her olive complexion was set off by a sensual pink-lipped mouth that was perfectly glossed, but somewhat sharp too. A broken seashell. I glanced down at her faux-casual, obviously expensive, green silk smock and black tights. A simple silver band circled her upper arm. She looked like she'd just stepped off the runway for Seventeen magazine, beautiful but something too-young about her. Like a little girl in a beauty pageant.

"Uh yeah," I croaked, covering a sneak-attack yawn. "Scarlet, Stephanie is here," I called as I brought her into the office. I was looking forward to depositing the new girl at a desk so I could concentrate on more pressing matters—like the employee handbook. Since I'd started Friday, worked Litquake Saturday, and today was just Sunday, it was technically only my third day. But Scarlet had already sent me 12 emails about the deadline for getting the handbook done. She'd sent two on my first day, four yesterday, and then six already this morning. According to the unpromising pattern in front of me, the frequency and length of the emails were only going to increase.

What was worse was that every email said the same thing, that the deadline for having the whole thing finished was tomorrow.

I hadn't even had time to start it.

But today, with nobody else at the office except for Scarlet and Stephanie, there would be no distractions. I'd banged out 30-page reports for Sal in less time and with the phone ringing off the hook. No problem, whatsoever. Piece of fuckin' cake.

However, about five minutes after Stephanie got there, Scarlet decided that she needed to introduce Stephanie to her favorite singer of all time, Frank Sinatra, and his greatest hits. So, instead of having Stephanie fill out employment paperwork or briefing her on her job duties, Scarlet popped a CD into the stereo crushed under the stacks of files on Makiah's desk and turned up the music.

Stephanie took off her huge sunglasses and I caught sight of her eyes, wide and innocent and brown. She nodded eagerly, wagging her tail at Scarlet and begging to be scratched behind the ears. Inside, some tiny part of me crawled off and died. That was exactly how I'd looked on Friday morning, just two days ago.

Scarlet turned the volume even higher, and then higher still. The walls vibrated, the tops of the desks shook. Scarlet started talking but I couldn't hear her, and I doubted Stephanie could either. Helplessly, I smiled and shrugged my shoulders. I looked at Stephanie. She had the same expectant look on her face that I did. What did Scarlet want next?

Scarlet seemed to be announcing something. She raised her arms to the ceiling, as if commanding rain to fall, and both Stephanie and I reacted at the same moment, facing each other like a mirror image. Our mouths opened, our upper lips curled away from our top teeth. We weren't just surprised—*this was lovely!* Not just pleased—but *utterly delighted!* By a series of unscripted, unconscious signals we aped each other like two fawning women at a Victorian tea party put on by the Mayor's wife.

Even though I'd only just met Stephanie, and even though it was hard to think about anything with my eardrums being blasted by music that was so loud it sounded more like a jack hammer, still I knew. Stephanie, in some way that I couldn't discern yet, was just like me. No normal person would agree to start a new job on Sunday. No normal person would show up to that new job and not think it was weird that instead of filling out tax forms, like everyone else did at every other job, they were expected to sit and listen to Frank Sinatra at 300 decibels. No normal person would sign up to work at a company run by someone like Scarlet Monroe.

When Stephanie and I left that evening we walked down the stairs together, but we didn't say goodbye when we parted ways at the street. I think we both knew we wouldn't have been able to hear each other anyway.

That night I fell into bed half dead, my mind swirling with the events of the past few days. Starting at Red City, the show at the Make Out Room, the deafening sounds of Frank Sinatra's greatest hits in my ear all day long today, my brain spun faster and faster with it all until it finally sputtered out in exhaustion and I started to drop off to sleep. But right as I teetered at the edge, something came to me. The thing that had tickled my brain at the Make Out Room when Scarlet had said my writing was *better than that*. Right before sleep took me fully it leapt into my mind, all blazing lights and alarm bells, shoving me totally awake again, mind on overdrive.

Scarlet had never read my writing. I had never shown anything I had written to *anyone*, ever. So how could she possibly have known it was "better than that"?

Worse, what did she have to gain by saying that she did?

21

The next day, Monday, I showed up at the office at my now customary time of 7:00am. We had another new person starting, but Scarlet wouldn't be in the office that morning. Although I was sure I'd see her that evening when I was still there toiling away at the employee handbook. I'd only had the energy and focus to piece together 20 pages so far. From Scarlet's numerous emails, and all the information she'd included in them—entire cut-and-pasted sections from books on self-help and organization and lists that went on for dozens of pages—I knew that handbook was going to turn out to be longer than the longest report I'd ever written for Sal.

When the new guy got there, I gave him his paperwork, showed him around, and then moved him to the tiny desk Una and I had wedged into the storage room, behind piles of boxes and other assorted junk. He looked it over with a rueful grin and settled into the pint-sized chair.

"This is my third start-up," he said. "I'm just so thankful you guys even *have* a desk to put me at."

"Sure, no problem." I said, examining him more closely. His name was William and he had deep brown skin the color of a Hershey bar. His black hair was short and curly and he had two sparkling intelligent eyes that looked at me curiously from behind small rimless glasses. Although he seemed gentle, there was something like grit in him too. Something way down deep that was stronger than all I was seeing now. William would do well with us. Whatever "well" meant in this kind of place, this Red City world.

The next few weeks flew by.

That October, Indian summer came to the City again. It was hot enough that it felt like July in the Midwest. Bright sun and blue skies banished the fog. Girls wore sundresses and straw hats, the beaches were packed, the smell of barbecues floated over the City late into the night.

Inside Scarlet's Victorian, hot October sun fell through the tall windows and their rainbow-colored panes of stained glass like a shower of gold. The warm breeze playfully lifted the gauzy curtains in the dining room, where Danica and I sat typing away at the table that had become our permanent desk. Makiah turned up the stereo in the office, rocking back and forth in her chair and singing at the top of her lungs. Una dug around William in the storage room trying to clear space in another corner for another desk for another new hire, and Benjie crawled around underneath us all, trying to disentangle a wire or connect just the right one.

Even with all the work we had to do, the eight of us swam together in a golden bubble. We all knew it: Red City was going to go big. We were in the process of creating something no one had ever seen before. We were standing at the beginning of a dream unfolding. These warm October days were just the start of it all.

And even though the cold voice of doubt nagged at the back of my mind, I knew most of us still believed that with someone like Scarlet at the helm, we couldn't possibly be steered wrong.

●●●

In addition to working every day in Scarlet's house for RedCity.com, I also still worked at the mansion every Tuesday and Wednesday night, as a volunteer for the writing sessions. And still, every time I sat down and wrote, the words poured out of me, pooling like oil all over the pages. What I had so far looked like a book, or at least, it seemed long enough to be one. The stack of paper I'd hauled out of my bottom desk drawer when I'd quit Pagliarani had been heavy enough that it took two hands to hoist it up.

I wasn't sure if it was a novel or a memoir or something else. The story was a long rainy night, cut through and scarred with silver streets that bled thin ribbons of streetlight orange. Deformed and screaming, the book had staggered up on two misshapen hind legs and clawed open a hole from the inside of my head as I wrote it, extricating its slimy girth inch by inch in soft wet pieces that hit the paper with obscene *plap-plap-plap* sounds. My pen had left glistening trails behind it, like a dying slug twitching its way to the end.

I'd never written a book before. I didn't know if this was how it usually happened, coming out all fucked up and ugly. Hurting so much I wanted to scream along with the deformed creature still halfway inside my head, but at the same time, feeling better than anything I'd ever experienced as it pushed its way out of me. When I finished a writing session and felt I'd squeezed out as much as I could for the night, then I felt empty. And happy. Really happy, without drinking or even thinking about drinking.

But it wasn't easy. Even though the words flooded out of me during every writing session, I still had work to do outside of the mansion. The boxes of old memories in my mind still needed to be excavated, pried open, and confronted. If I left them to rot where they had lain neglected for so long, then all the writing I was doing was for nothing. Because I knew, sooner or later, I would just end up back in that old life, trapped in the long rainy night of Seattle.

●●●

The day my mother died, my dad told me that she probably wouldn't make it through the night. She had been in the hospital for the past few days and just had her last surgery. I found out later, as an adult, that the doctors had opened her up and knew instantly there was no hope. She was filled with tumors, they told my dad. There was nothing anyone could have done.

My mom had been battling ovarian cancer for the past two years. After my brother died, it came on her aggressively, determined to have its way. She'd gone through breast cancer years before, and gone into remission, but now it was back. The doctors said that it might be linked to the original cancer, or it might not. No one knew for sure. But I knew. After losing my brother to leukemia, my mom was at her weakest, in her most vulnerable, defenseless state. It wasn't surprising that the cancer she thought she'd beaten took the opportunity to strike her again.

My mother died in the early afternoon and that evening my dad held a summit with me and my grandma at the farmhouse. The three of us posted ourselves on different sides of the big wooden kitchen table as my dad asked me what I wanted to do. He said I could stay in the farmhouse with my grandma—it was mine now, he added, my mother had made that clear in her will—or I could go and live with him and my stepmother. I already knew my answer without thinking about it. I said I wanted to stay where I was and my grandma reached over to clasp my hand.

Since my mom had been sick for the last couple of years, my grandma had pretty much come to live with us full time anyway. I couldn't have asked for a better guardian. Now, as I looked at her across the table I already knew she wanted me to stay with her. I knew that without even having to study her soft and wrinkled, tear-creased cheeks. She loved me more than anything, and even if she had lost her daughter on this day, I knew she was grateful to still have me. And I was lucky to have her, because my father was a busy man and I didn't see him much. He had four other children, my stepmother, and a career as a surgeon that demanded 90-hour workweeks. No one ever saw him for long.

I assumed that my father's workaholism was a result of the pressure placed on him by his own mother. Everyone who knew my father's mother knew that she had to have things done a certain way. She was particular and her standards were high. A grade point average of 3.8 wasn't enough, it had to be 4.0. Good manners weren't satisfactory if the candidate was caught chewing gum, even once, because well-bred people kept their mouths clear of debris at all times. She was never *grandma*, always *grandmother*. No one was allowed to answer her with a sloppy *yeah*, even if they were only three years old. In her house everyone said *yes* and *yes* only, even if they had just learned to speak. With my grandmother, there was no compromise. It was all or nothing.

In my grandmother's house it was important to know the difference between similar-sounding words like *etymology* and *entomology*. It was essential to remain at your ideal weight, whatever figure had been decided upon for you, and not go even two pounds over. It was vital to go to college, to conduct yourself accordingly, to fit into the lines drawn out for you.

Whenever I was in her house it seemed like there were a thousand rules, and the only way to discover them all was to keep fucking up. Luckily, in my grandmother's presence it was possible to fuck up at least once per minute, so I was able to constantly update the nebulous lists of rules that floated over my head like acid rain clouds. The poisonous storms that resulted from these clouds soaked her children their entire lives—my father, his twin brother, and their older brother. They all had daughters. We girls shivered and huddled under cold dripping trees for most of our childhoods.

Something lived in my grandmother's eyes, something that could smack us across the room with just one look. It couldn't be named or grasped. It was as invisible as the virulent lists of rules. Whenever I was around my grandmother I had visions of gloppy severed heads kept in some back room, clumps of skin and strings of glubby black blood flapping off the ends of the necks, like the frayed tassels that hung off the lamps in her living room.

The owners of those heads had trespassed in places they didn't belong. They had observed, examined, and questioned. And then they had dared speak against her. I figured that was why I never saw my dad or his brothers contradict any of her rules. The fear of decapitation was too great.

I felt, too, that those heads very possibly kept her awake at night because she hadn't been able to make a perfectly clean cut on every single one. Maybe that was one of the reasons she was so happy that my father had turned out to be a surgeon. He had grown into someone who was specifically trained to saw through human flesh in an unassailably perfect straight line.

I wasn't sure if I loved my grandmother, but I knew there was something about her that thrilled me way down deep. It was like she was protected by that magic circle of heads kept in her secret back room. My grandfather and her three sons all steadfastly ignored me. Or, they smiled politely when I talked but never really looked at me, except to judge whether or not I had, in fact, gained two pounds. But their eyes went alive and searching when she entered the room. As sick as it made me feel, I loved seeing it happen too. The way their eyes danced with fear in her presence, that was power. And with some of her blood in my veins, I dared to wonder if someday I might be able to do that too.

22

At the beginning of November Una and I got sick. It started out as a harmless cold and then bloomed into a possessive, festering flu. Feverish and freezing at the same time, our foreheads were burning to the touch and our hands ice cold. We shivered and we sweated and oh god did we cough, until our lungs clacked together like two dry boards, tears streamed down our cheeks, and our ribs ached constantly, as if we were being beaten by a jealous lover every night in our sleep.

Needless to say, taking a sick day at Red City wasn't an option.

In the mornings we drank a special concoction of tea that Scarlet's personal chef made for us: lemon, honey, ginger, and loads of cayenne pepper. The ingredients floated to the top like chunks of pollen. We resolutely stirred the mixture before bolting the whole thing down. We kept pills on us at all times and popped some every few hours, swapping them between each other's pockets like kids exchanging Pez candy on the playground. Scarlet abhorred the smell of menthol so we sucked the organic grainy pellets of an herbal brand she had pre-approved for our sore throat relief.

Oddly, Scarlet didn't get sick. She didn't flag for a second, and the machine that Red City had become rolled on without pause.

At the end of that month we moved into a real office. Scarlet had driven by an old restored Victorian in Hayes Valley, painted a stately deep pink—or a distinguished pale red, as she liked to say—and recognized the place. She said that she'd suddenly remembered she had told herself when she was young that one day she would have her office there. With five rooms and an entryway that looked out directly onto the busy street below, it was perfect for our burgeoning Red City staff. We were slated to move in that Saturday, the day after tomorrow.

"I have to meet with an investor in New York this weekend, unfortunately," said Scarlet. She smiled at me and Una and Makiah. Danica and Benjie edged into the doorway just behind us. William and Stephanie were stuck out in the hallway, trying to squeeze in closer to hear.

"It has to happen this weekend, of course. There's no time." Scarlet flashed her snow-white teeth at us again as she pinched her black patent leather purse shut with a cruel snapping sound. "Everything must be moved," she finished. "Absolutely everything."

I caught Benjie's eye and pursed my lips. I saw the crease in his brow deepen into a worried furrow. There was a shitload of stuff in this office—and all the files, all the computers, all the frigging wires—how would we ever make it happen in just under 48 hours?

"All right troops!" Makiah cried, up on her feet in a flash. "Let's rally! Heave ho! Left right left! We'll get 'er done!" She sounded like a cross between a trucker with war on his mind and a Girl Scout leader on methamphetamines.

The rest of us looked around doubtfully at each other and stayed silent. Scarlet had already turned away and was now looking at her laptop screen, lost in new email messages, oblivious to the fact that any of us were even still standing there.

Under Makiah's military-style command mixed with her dance party music, we managed to move everything into the new office by Monday morning. Scarlet strolled in just before 11:00am that day. She paused in the entryway to look around and stretched luxuriously. She'd been forced to spend all her time in New York getting massages and facials, she said. The investor she had gone to meet had canceled at the last minute, but by then she'd already checked in at her hotel and was belly up with cucumbers on her eyes and an exfoliating skin peel slathered all over her face. She'd really had no choice but to stay. I glanced over and caught a look from Danica, then from Stephanie, the same thing on all of our minds. Had there even been an investor in New York to begin with?

●●●

A week later Scarlet gave me a new project. She wanted everyone on staff to turn in an official to-do list every Monday morning.

"You do know what I mean?" she asked. I sat across from her in her new office, the wide, smooth expanse of her new black desk between us. The room glinted with flashes of what she called *Red City Red*. The curtains, her folders, the stacks of business plans, even her paperclips were a deep red. Not brick, not magenta, and never, *never* anything with the slightest hint of pink. Scarlet was obsessively particular about the exact shade of red in Red City. It was always, and nothing less, than the color of spilled blood.

"Sure, I know what you mean." I said. "Like a list of things you need to get done, right?" I smiled and instantly a wave of nerves hit my stomach. With Scarlet, I couldn't be sure of even the simplest things.

"No. That's *not* it." she snapped, crossing her arms in irritation. "It *is* a list, and it *does* include all your work, but it's much more complicated than that." Her eyes narrowed and flickered toward the open office door. "Close the door," she said quietly.

When we were alone she started smiling again.

"The problem is, frankly, that the employees are not performing up to their potential. I really don't know *what* is going on. I do realize a certain amount of time will be frittered away on useless tasks such as eating, pouring coffee, and visiting the restroom. But the amount of time I currently gauge our employees are throwing away is absolutely unacceptable." She leaned back in her chair and brought her hands together in front of her, making a tent with her fingers. Sometimes, without trying, she reminded me of an even scarier Christopher Walken.

"The to-do list nips procrastination in the bud, Leah. In—the—bud!" She leaned forward and snapped her fingers at me with every word. "The to-do list contains a reference of all tasks, finite and ongoing, and all projects, finite and ongoing. A project is a larger model of work consisting of a series of tasks, the smaller steps to take in order to complete the project. The to-do list also holds all responsibilities, which are different from tasks, sometimes part of a project, but also able to be divided either into finite or ongoing. All projects, tasks, and responsibilities are to be listed in one column, directly related to three other columns listing—respectively—total estimated time of completion, actual time spent thus far, and estimated time remaining until completion of the task, project, or responsibility. All to-do lists will be done in Excel spreadsheet form. All columns will be totaled automatically by formula. All cells will be right justified."

I wrote furiously, recording every word she said. I already knew how Scarlet felt about mistakes. As she continued, she ticked off points on her five outstretched fingers.

"Every project will have a heading, every group of tasks a sub-heading. Responsibilities will be grouped separately, with their own headings and sub-headings as apply to each sub-group. To-do lists will be in Times New Roman font, 12 pt. They will be due no later than 8:00am every Monday morning. Not 8:01, not ten minutes after. *Not* 8:30. 8:00am and not a second later. You will collect them and I will rate them. To-do lists will be graded on a scale of one to three, with three being a cause for immediate termination. I will rate them according to employee initiative and the employee's ability to be proactive in regards to projects and responsibilities, neatness, and strict adherence to all to-do list formatting rules and content regulations, and of course—" she smirked malevolently, ticking the last point off on a single upraised index finger. "Time well spent."

Seconds after she finished speaking my hand fluttered to broken rest.

"Very good." I said. "Shall I tell the staff?"

"I want instructions from you, first. Written, detailed instructions. No mistakes. The staff will receive both the instructions you write, and a detailed memo explaining the purpose of the to-do list and how they can *all* be more productive, manage their time more effectively, and in general and overall be better Red City employees by using the to-do list religiously, which memo and instructions you will email out, once approved by me of course—" She smiled and dropped both hands into the contemplative finger tent again.

"But it will all come from you. The to-do list is your project Leah, and I expect you to own it. We will grade them *together*," she said. She practically purred the words as if she was considering something deliciously sinful. Her eyes flicked behind me again to the latched entrance to her office.

"Behind closed doors, of course."

Every Monday after that Scarlet asked for a full report on to-do lists, making sure everyone had turned one in to me. Without exception, I doctored them all. Because no matter how many times I went over all of Scarlet's crazy technical rules with everyone, no one could ever get it. Some came really close, but no one ever got every rule down perfect. No one except me. Apparently, I was able to memorize roughly 95 different and contradictory rules of format, guidelines for guaranteed insanity, and carry them out without a single error. What did that say about me? What did it say really? I didn't want to think about it.

So instead of thinking, I collected to-do lists. My own and everyone else's. And I made sure every one of them was perfect.

●●●

Both Benjie and I got to the office every morning before 7:00am. While the place was still quiet, we sat in the deserted conference room and talked, ducking our heads out into the hall every minute or two to make sure no one was coming. Strangely enough, the person we were most worried about catching us was the one person who most probably wouldn't. Scarlet didn't ever get into the office until close to noon, even though she lived only a few blocks away. But sometimes Scarlet knew things that no one had any way of knowing. And sometimes she popped up in the most unpredictable of places, sneaking up on you when you least expected her.

To play it safe, we kept a constant watch.

In between checking the hallway and munching on whatever junk food either of us had brought to share—sometimes I brought donuts and sometimes Benjie brought instant noodles—I found that I liked Benjie. He told me how both his grandfather and grandmother were doctors, how much he respected his parents and wanted to make them proud, and how none of his friends back in China had any brothers or sisters. Like him, they had all been born after 1978 and into China's one-child policy. He told me what it had been like to live in China until he was 16 years old and then come to California—and then crazy San Francisco—and grow up the rest of the way here. Benjie's eyes stayed flat throughout his stories, showing no emotion, and his lips hardly moved when he talked. But behind the calm plane of Benjie's face I saw a tumultuous dark ocean, the flashes of lightning that gutted it the only illumination between sea and thundering sky.

Shortly after we moved into the new office Scarlet hired two more people, a product manager and an assistant editor to Stephanie and William. The assistant editor was in his mid-40s, quiet and likable, with a dragging weight to his steps. He laughed at all of Scarlet's jokes and his name was Worthington Pike. I built him a mail-order desk from Office Depot and squished him in with William and Stephanie in the front room.

The new product manager was Jess, a girl who smiled easily and had a voice that was melodious and earthy, with a face that was wide and fleshy and pleasant. She had the air of someone who moves through each new thing completely unruffled, satisfied that it too would pass. Just by looking at her I could tell Jess never laid awake at night worrying about anything.

I couldn't imagine how that was going to work out with Scarlet. Scarlet's whole racket was spun entirely out of the stuff people lie awake at night worrying about.

I gave them both the memo and the instructions on how to create their to-do list, waiting it out as Jess scanned the small stack of papers and then looked at me with one raised eyebrow. Her stare made me uncomfortable, but I would wait that out too. I was picking up Scarlet's lessons fast now. Everyone had to drop their eyes sometime. I'd rather have a few long seconds of being uncomfortable rather than lose my head to Scarlet's wrath, one severed tendon at a time.

And, as I expected, even Jess got tired after only a minute. Because normal people didn't get into stare-downs with people they hardly knew. But from Scarlet, I was also learning now that the parts of me that were the most abnormal were actually my strongest gifts.

●●●

After Worthington was hired was when I really started catching Scarlet in lies. I'd caught her fudging on details before, in Red City writing sessions and in front of the staff. Small things like the number of years she'd lived in New York, the time it took to write her first book, how

225

close of friends she was with so-and-so. She'd tell it one way the first time and then slightly alter it the next. Or someone would question her on a certain point and she'd have to backpedal. She'd give her smile and an excuse and change the subject fast.

I recognized it because I used to do it. I'd picked up lying when I was young. I'd learned long ago how important it was to memorize the telling of a story completely—the structure, the order of events, especially the numbers. It was best to tell the story a couple of times, see what emerged, and then stick with it. It was a bad idea to re-tell too many stories to the same people, or repeat a story to a group in which some had heard it and for others it was totally new. Big mixed groups and tall tales were a bad combination. The absolute best recipe was never-been-heard-before paired with one-on-one.

But the rules didn't apply to Scarlet. She broke them every time. So, when I first started catching her in lies, I knew they were lies and I didn't hold them against her. Being someone who'd been a liar myself, in greater and lesser degrees, for my entire life up until the last few very recent years, lying was not something that conflicted with any deep sense of morality I held, or even offended me very much. Lots of people had lied to me before, and I didn't hold it against any of them either. But now that I was trying to be a better person, I did notice it a lot more.

In fact, when I saw Scarlet put on her fake voice and the smile and saw how perfectly it worked, and also thought about how it had worked so well for me all those times in the past, well, now I felt kind of sick. Something deep in my gut pinched at me and I never wanted to do it again.

Working for Scarlet, I was constantly pulled between wanting to run, and wanting to stay. When the front room was full and I heard the editors arguing over books and authors, I smiled to myself, glad to be where I was. Red City's popularity had exploded and the writers poured in so thick and fast now it was all our little team could do to keep the site updated. I laughed when I heard Stephanie yelling at Worthington and Worthington grumbling to William and William trying to make peace with everyone.

"Stephanie, we cannot let her on the site—she writes porn for God's sake," Worthington complained.

"Porn? You're *not* serious. Worthington, she ties men up and gets on top of them—obviously she's a feminist." Stephanie shot right back.

"A feminist? Are you joking? Stephanie, are you *high*? All her stories are about shaved balls in a sling and a fist up the ass. It's really too much!" Worthington yelled. "Are we seriously defining the limits of porn as to which of the genders climbs on top?"

Out of the corner of my eye I saw him collapse back into his chair, running both hands through his graying hair.

"Now, now children," William sweetly intervened. "Let's talk about some real sex. I've got a 91-year-old woman who's just published her first memoir. It's her list of lovers and she's had just as many men as she's had years on this earth." He giggled naughtily and swiveled his laptop toward them both. A kindly old grandmother flashed a toothy grin from his screen.

"William! Gross!" Stephanie shouted, reverting from Jackie O to peeved Valley Girl in an instant.

"Really, William. Your taste is alarming to say the least," said Worthington in a haughty tone. But I saw the beginnings of a grin at the corners of his mouth.

Every day was like that. Danica cracked her sarcastic jokes, Makiah shook and rolled, gyrating in a nonstop dance party frenzy, Una counted and stacked and whispered things endlessly, as if she had an eternal number of rosaries to say, and Benjie ran around in the middle of it all, ducking and dodging under everyone's desk trying to connect every wire in his labyrinthine network of cords that had become somewhat of an electrical tape city, all leading back to a behemoth monster of a server, chugging and gasping and dumping hot air out of the back room, where we kept the window open all the time to prevent the entire office from turning into a sauna.

It was chaos, every single minute. And I loved it.

But I didn't love Scarlet, not anymore.

23

Before I met Scarlet I had already had a vision of what my kind of superhero would look like. She wasn't young and she wasn't shapely. She didn't wear tight black vinyl clothes and have a mane of flowing red hair that cascaded around her face in thick cartoon waves when she took off her mask. She was no Playboy centerfold dressed up in fetish gear.

My woman was plain, with a face like Jane Eyre. Small, slitted eyes, skin that was rough, a little weather-beaten. Sometimes looking middle-aged, and sometimes like a flat-faced, cruel-mouthed teenage boy. Her hair was short, clipped into little more than brush. Her trade was violence; she didn't have the luxury to mess around with long hair.

My woman played by no rules, she knifed you where she could. She waited for hours in closets. She went straight for the throat, the balls, the eyes. She ripped into any exposed soft tissue. Her face never changed while she was doing it. She was exquisitely skillful at what she did. She waited and she killed. She hacked into the guts. She plunged both hands into dying bodies like a child into a mess of wet pumpkin seeds, carving a jack-o-lantern. She felt no remorse.

My woman was also a woman without a past. Or rather, her past was buried deep and never allowed to surface. She was someone who lived her life in segments; someone who compartmentalized people and put any emotion on deep freeze at will. She was a woman who had been hunted once, in some other time, and knew how to run; a woman who knew how to hide and rest, and then emerge fully transformed, so radically altered that her hunters never knew as she passed them by, on her way to somewhere else.

And now, I had Scarlet, and she was a different sort of superhero: a Red Avenger. Clad entirely in that blood-cut shade of red she insisted was just hers, with bedraggled red wings trailing behind her, her white-blonde hair swirling around her wide cold eyes, she strutted onstage inside my mind. She delivered monologue after monologue, sometimes forgetting the lines completely, and at other times reciting the words perfectly, like a wind-up doll. The performance was definitely weird, but the monologues were interesting.

"The deeper the wound, the more concentrated the gift," she always started. She used the same opening line every time. "It is no coincidence that anyone chosen to be a superhero is cut down by tragedy before they receive their superpowers."

Case history was then presented in a list, Batman first. He witnessed his parents' murder when he was just a little boy. Second came Spiderman, bitten by a radioactive spider, pain spreading into every cell of his body as he resisted the change rippling over him. Then the Hulk, a victim of the blast of his own homemade bomb. On and on went the list. Each hero went through hell to become more than other human beings. To get to where they were now, they had to be ripped to shreds first.

Onstage, Scarlet the Red Avenger said that was the source of all superpower.

"The deeper the wound, the more concentrated the gift," she repeated.

But the Red Avenger's knowledge came at a price. For all the high moments I had—listening to the editors argue, dancing along with Makiah, seeing the numbers go up on the site every day, going to the literary events I had to attend every night, my life a blur of work and words and Red City—despite all of it I couldn't ignore the fact that I wasn't so much falling downhill as I was flying.

Both Una and I were still coughing. When I talked I sounded like a 60-year-old woman who'd smoked for 50 of those years. I was getting so thin that my tits had collapsed into sad little bags of skin that hung off my ribs. My face was greasy and pale in the mirror, accented sharply by the charcoal rings under my eyes. I kind of looked like I was seriously ill. I was always tired but never sleepy, I was always too wired to get the sleep I needed.

I was always too worried.

●●●

At the end of December, Red City put on a Christmas party at the mansion that was like no other office party I'd ever attended. Scarlet had invited all the employees, all the writers from the program, and all her friends too. The night of the gala, I met Benjie and Danica at the door. Benjie had agreed to act as the party photographer and a boxy black camera now hung from his neck, crumpling the lapels of his suit. Danica's blue-streaked black hair was in an upswept do, bringing out her azure eyes even more under the soft twinkling lights. As we walked in, we ran into Una, who was taking coats and simultaneously balancing a tray of hors d'oeuvres on one hand.

"Hey Una—I thought Scarlet hired a catering crew to work the door and serve food?" Danica asked with a frown. She moved behind Una and the precariously balanced tray of pâté, hanging up her own coat.

"Of course, of course she did. But they need all the help they can get, and it's never a bad idea to be too helpful." Una tried to smile but over the past couple of months she'd lost weight and gotten dark circles under her eyes too. When she smiled now it looked like she was trying to swallow a hard ball of food with spikes in it.

"Oh, okay." Danica shrugged and let it go. Benjie dutifully snapped a picture of the three of us together and we moved on.

I'd never seen the mansion look so beautiful. Green garland stretched from all corners and over all the doorways. Red and gold glass ornaments spun from the boughs, softly emanating a lazy golden shimmer as they moved above us. Wreaths hung on every door. The whole place smelled like a crystal clean snow-bright forest in winter. Huge Christmas trees stood in every room, decorated exactly as if they had been stolen right out of Macy's in the middle of the night.

It was as if we'd been transported to a sumptuous Christmas ball back in the 1920s. Cultured voices tinkled through the rooms, playing elegantly alongside the gentle clinking of ice in crystal goblets. Some of the women wore shining gowns and their cheeks and lips glowed like rubies in the dim light, their eyes flourishing like coals turned over in a fire. Hors d'oeuvres circulated among the guests on shining silver platters, and as

Scarlet had instructed, every hors d'oeuvre had been colored red.

I had to admit, Scarlet had really outdone herself.

Glancing around I saw June Sorehl dressed in a stylish black suit and huddled in a corner talking with Makiah, as well as a number of writers from the Red City writing sessions milling about. Even if I hadn't known all of them personally I thought it probably would have been hard not to spot them. Strangely, even though they were the guests who had to be the most familiar with the mansion, they were also the ones who appeared the most out of place. All of them stuck to the edges and wilted on the sides of the room, talking to almost no one.

My first stop was Makiah and June. As I approached, I caught the end of their conversation.

"She's gotten worse," said June.

"Gotten worse? She's a black hole!" Makiah slapped her forehead with the palm of her hand. It would have been comical if I hadn't noticed how even she was a bit paler than usual, her cheeks slacker than they had been a few months before.

"Hi ladies." I smiled and moved in. They froze. Slowly, a small pressed grin stamped itself on June's mouth while Makiah gave me her classic reassuring smile. After mumbling how great the party was, both of them bolted within seconds. *Odd*, I thought. But then again, not so odd. The longer I worked for Scarlet, it seemed the less people wanted to talk about it.

I moved onto a woman I recognized from the writing sessions and the man she was clinging to, who appeared to be her husband.

"Hi Cheryl," I said warmly. "Happy holidays."

"Oh hello!" The petite lady squeaked. She smiled politely and shrank further behind her husband. I tried asking some questions to open her up, but her husband either answered for her or she looked to him before answering. At the end it felt more like de-programming a cult victim than casual conversation.

This Christmas party was the strangest I'd ever seen. In fact, the only people who were acting anything like normal were Danica, sarcastic as usual, and Benjie, zipping around like a hummingbird, snapping pictures every two seconds.

"Nice party," Danica joked to me a few minutes later. "Everyone here's like a robot or a scared kid. Look. It's weird."

I nodded as we looked around the room. There was something I couldn't quite place. I felt a pattern in front of me, so close I couldn't see it. But frankly, right now I was too tired to figure anything out. I'd been up late at the office the past two nights finalizing the details for this party. I could barely keep from swaying on my feet, much less analyze one-of-these-things-just-doesn't-belong-here in the room at large. I stifled a giant yawn and shrugged at Danica.

"I don't know. Isn't there always a certain element of fucked up at Red City?" I replied. But then our conversation was interrupted by an announcement coming from the other room. We heard the whine of a microphone and Una's voice breaking in over the static.

"Please everyone, I'd like your attention."

Danica and I shuffled over with the rest of the crowd. Una stood at the bottom of the immense winding staircase. A red velvet piece of curtain had been pinned to the bottom steps, fashioning it into an impromptu stage.

"Uh-oh," whispered Danica. "I think Vampira is going to sing."

Scarlet mounted the steps, smiling and effortlessly pulling the microphone away from Una. Unsure of the timing, Una wobbled slightly and then started down the steps, almost missing the one at the end but then catching herself on autopilot. I noted how blank and glazed her eyes were. I knew Una was tired too. She did double the amount of work I did for Scarlet, and I felt like I was going to fall over.

When Scarlet started singing, I really almost did. She was awful. And the song she was singing was weird, even for Scarlet. Even for me. She sang most of it in a falsetto little girl's voice while fluttering her huge eyes at the audience like JonBenet Ramsey. The song was about how she'd do anything for her daddy, and she repeated that line over and over on a loop. I glanced over at Danica, whose face had gone pale, her eyes big and frozen. I looked back at Scarlet warbling out the incestuous lyrics on her red velvet stage. This was a nightmare.

But to my astonishment, when I turned around everyone in the audience was smiling, some even nodding their heads enthusiastically. They were loving it. They grinned like happy children let out into the yard for their noon recess hour. Everyone except for me and Danica, rooted in horror to where we stood.

But not everyone was smiling. Stephanie stood in the corner, her eyes dark, and hectic pink patches staining her cheeks. I saw Benjie almost hidden behind the crowd with his camera. His face stayed flat and emotionless as usual, but I knew Benjie now and I could read his indecipherable eyes. As I searched the crowd, I realized Makiah was gone. June Sorehl stood next to me and now she smiled politely up at Scarlet, rocking slightly to the beat of the music. Worthington and William clustered close by too and when Scarlet glanced down at them they clapped their hands silently with delight. She winked and swung into another round, stronger than before.

Later that night, after everyone including Scarlet had left, I stayed to help Una clean up. We found the 300 gift bags that Scarlet had instructed us to put together as party favors for the guests stashed away in the back of the coat closet. Without saying a word, we packed them up, knowing already it was Scarlet who'd hidden them. At the last second her fear of any possible flaws had been too much. She'd decided to have nothing rather than hand out something that might be imperfect. I transferred handful after handful of the elegant gold foil pouches to Una and watched her dump them into a big garbage bag.

All that energy, straight into a black hole.

24

In the first week of January Scarlet ordered me to purchase seven different framed portraits of the Eiffel Tower. She wanted the staff to see the magnitude of what we were building with Red City, she said. The bill had come to just about $2,500. I could see the symbolism plain as day, but what I didn't see was how a startup company fast running out of funds, with not one new angel investor in sight, could afford to blow over two grand on what amounted to cheap posters of some overdone icon in France.

If there was a ridiculous thing to spend money on, Scarlet found it. $300 dinners, at the fanciest places in town, Egyptian cotton sheets, a cartoon artist who drew adventures based on his clients' real lives (Scarlet had herself and the founding of Red City immortalized, of course, and then framed under glass and hung in her office), massages, spa visits, hair treatments, exfoliation rubs, enemas.

Outside of me, Danica, Una, and Benjie, I wasn't sure how much anyone else knew. Makiah had to have a pretty good idea, I supposed. And the way Stephanie's face was looking nowadays I guessed she definitely had her suspicions. After all, it wasn't like Scarlet tried to cover her tracks. One day suddenly seven huge framed pictures of the Eiffel Tower appeared on our walls. (I'd hammered them in place at 6:00am when no one was even stirring in the streets yet, much less in the office, no one except for me and Benjie.) Once they were up, Scarlet never mentioned them again, but everyone knew they had to have come from somewhere.

When a story on Red City made the front page of the San Francisco Chronicle, Scarlet sent me and Una to patrol the whole city for leftover newspapers. She told us to wait until the evening hours, after the vast majority of San Franciscans had bought their paper for the day. We were instructed to find every newspaper receptacle, every newsstand, and every little corner store that sold newspapers, and buy all the copies they had left. The next day she had me call the Chronicle's distribution center and buy all the copies they hadn't sold too. That night Una and I carted in the stacks and stowed them in a back closet.

"What's she want with them, Una?" I asked, staring helplessly as the shelves groaned with the weight of all that newsprint. My fingertips were inky black and left smudgy prints on the doorframe.

"Well, it's great PR." Una chirped. "We have to think about the investors."

I raised a disbelieving eyebrow. "What investors? We haven't had a bite in months."

"Well, Scarlet's going to turn all that around. With this story. She'll send it out and people will get interested. You know Scarlet, Leah. She's got a plan."

For a moment I was reminded again of how much Una had changed. These days she functioned in eternal robot mode. I was beginning to feel like I could say, "Hey Una, I think Scarlet eats the hearts of newborn babies to keep her strength, she's found their clean blood really gives an energy boost," and Una would only blink rapidly at me, like she did now, like a mouse caught by a flashlight in a corner, and answer: "Well, it's all about organic health, right?"

A day after the story ran it was published online and all of us read it again. Since eavesdropping had become instinct in me now, I absorbed Worthington and William whispering in the next room without even trying.

"Look at all the comments—" William said breathlessly.

"God, I know. Over three hundred. But have you read through them all?" Worthington asked gloomily. "Not all of them are good."

Instantly I swiveled my screen toward me and clicked downward rapidly, scanning each comment, filtering through the words like I was panning for gold. Did anyone—anyone at all—see what I saw? Anyone else besides Benjie and Danica? Or was I really crazy? Were the three of us truly suffering from some sort of shared paranoid insanity?

Good comment, another good one, crap comment, something obscene, something just bad...good, good, bad...good. Crap, crap...crap.

And then there it was, almost at the end. Made just two hours ago by an anonymous user. It was someone else. Someone who maybe saw her for what she was, or maybe someone who already knew her. I didn't have to search, it jumped right out at me. One of the shortest comments in the whole list, it said more than all of them put together.

"Scarlet Monroe—" it taunted.

"—is that even your real name?"

•••

One week later, Una came through the front door of the office huffing and red in the face, carrying a trophy almost as big as she was. It got stuck halfway in the door and as she grunted and pulled at it, I rushed to help her. But I was too late, she and the trophy popped through all at once and, clattering across the entryway floor, she landed with the thing on top of her.

I pulled it off, flakes of metallic gold paint sticking to my hands.

"Una, what is this?"

"For Scarlet—" she puffed, still gasping for air as she picked herself up from the floor.

"Well, I know that." I rolled my eyes. Who else would have told Una to bring a six-foot-tall trophy into the office? "But why?" I asked.

"I don't know. Didn't ask. Tell her it's here, would you? I have to go." Then Una was back out the door again, checking off something else on her endless list. Sometimes I had dreams about her with that list, and in my dreams it spooled around her legs in piles of looping, narrow white paper, trying to drown her. Like unused cash register tape, it was blank, Una the only one who could see anything on it.

A day or so later Una dashed in again, her car idling out at the curb. She dropped a men's white vest, a white skirt, and a white pair of high heels onto my desk before running back out. An hour later she did the same thing, only this time with a white blouse, a pair of men's white slacks and—of all absurd things—a white top hat.

"Una—*stop*." I commanded. "What is going on?" I held up the white hat in front of her. "What is this?"

"It's for—" she started.

"Scarlet. I know." I finished. She nodded and blinked.

"I mean why, Una. *Why* does she want these things?"

"Uh, I don't know…" she mumbled.

I took a deep breath and came at her from another angle.

"Una, what exactly did she tell you this morning? What were her exact instructions?"

Una's face relaxed. We were getting somewhere. By now, she was an expert in exact instructions.

"She said, uh, that she needs white clothes. She's going to play croquet."

"So, she needs these clothes to play croquet?" I asked.

"Yes!" Una almost shouted, triumphant at finding the thread holding up the end of her list for today's work. Una was kept so busy moving a pile of sand between one place and another that she'd lost all ability to see the big picture. And sometimes, especially after I had that dream about her and the cash register tape list, I wondered if she'd ever be able to see it again.

"Ok," I set the hat back down. Una looked at me and I could see her vibrating, coiled like a spring. With a sigh, I released her.

"Go get the rest of the stuff."

She bounded back out the door, like a rubber band soaked in rocket fuel.

Meanwhile, things with Makiah were getting weirder too. She didn't dance anymore and she wasn't nearly so cheerful. Now she came into the office late, really late. Sometimes she started the day at five in the afternoon and sometimes we didn't see her at all. In the mornings I'd find a half-eaten sandwich on her desk, folders belonging to a project I knew she was working on moved around, and the smell of cigarette smoke lingering in the air. I cleaned all of it up before Scarlet got in.

Back in October, Makiah ducked out two or three times a day to have a cigarette on the rickety fire escape attached to Scarlet's Victorian. It was her second office, she joked, where only smokers were allowed. Back in October, Makiah came to work with her long chestnut brown hair carefully curled and put on mascara in Scarlet's bathroom. Back in October, she'd been as clear and playful as the San Francisco Indian summer skies.

Now, it was January, and she was as bleak as the cold rain.

Makiah ducked outside to smoke every ten minutes now, when she came into the office during daylight hours at all. And I knew she was smoking nonstop at night too, the smell of it in the office betrayed her as loudly as greasy pink lipstick on a collar. When she showed up during the day her hair hung limp and draggled, and without makeup the crow's feet at her eyes stood out in sharp relief. Her lips were dry and chapped like weathered rocks on the beach, small crusts at the corners like salt left behind by the tide.

Her usual outfit now was a beanie hat pulled low over her eyes and baggy clothes. One afternoon when she forgot her key and tapped on the glass for me to let her in, I mistook her for a homeless woman.

Every time me or Benjie or Danica tried to ask Makiah about Scarlet she evaded the subject. She had to know all that we knew, and more. She was Scarlet's partner, and they still worked in the same office even if they were there at opposite hours. But no matter what we asked, no matter how we phrased it, she remained as tight-lipped as a member of the Mafia.

"Stick with me kids," was all she'd say, sucking long and hard on a cigarette. "Stick with me. I'll find a way out of this. The dream isn't dead, not yet."

I wanted to believe. I really did. I wanted to so badly.

But Scarlet was the one I never doubted anymore.

●●●

In February, Scarlet hired Kristy, who she said was an old friend, in a careful sort of tone. But I knew that in Scarlet's world there were no friends. There were only people who could be used. So, when she started gushing about how rich Kristy's fiancé was, I wasn't surprised. Scarlet needed more money, badly, and that was the way Kristy would be used.

Along with Worthington and William, who were still Scarlet's two biggest admirers, Kristy helped make a cluster of three in the fan club. "A coterie of sycophants," Stephanie called them as we walked to the train together one night after work. We'd been leaving the office at the same time lately, giving each other secret glances and then cutting out the door when it would be least noticeable. Lately, it seemed like Scarlet especially had it in for Stephanie. They were in Scarlet's office together a lot now, with the door closed, and I knew what that meant.

"And then she started comparing me to my mother," Stephanie went on, and I pulled myself back to the conversation with no small effort. It was hard to stay focused when people talked to me these days. "Her exact words were, 'Now Stephanie, you don't want to be like your mom, do you?' And that's when I knew—what an evil bitch she is—and how stupid I've been. How stupid to tell her all that stuff about my childhood, my stepfathers and how...how..." Stephanie sniffed, the dark circles underneath her eyes tinged with a deep despairing red, tears wobbling dangerously on her lower lashes. "Well, I just *crumbled*. I just couldn't handle it. It's like she *knew*, she knew right where to go. Right where to stick the knife and how to twist it. I should have known better, than to *ever* let her in."

I nodded but stayed silent. We all should have known better. But now every one of us was at the mercy of the hook, the lustrous blade that Scarlet held and turned within us, making slow revolutions without end, cutting away a little more of us each day. The most fantastic perpetual motion machine ever made.

25

By spring our staff had swollen to almost 20 people. One day when Una was out running errands, and Makiah's desk lay abandoned in silent piles of crumbs and ash, Scarlet called me into her office and had me shut the door.

"That Valerie is rough," she said, talking about the chic and sophisticated designer we'd hired just two weeks ago. At the time we'd hired her Scarlet had said the woman's style was the "epitome of exemplary taste."

"Rough?" My pen paused mid-air over the checklist I was holding.

"You know," said Scarlet. "Sloppy. Unkempt."

"Oh?" I recited my reliable responses with perfect execution. Noncommittal and short, their brevity was an agreement in itself.

"Yes. She sounds like a man when she speaks. And she's hairy. Her arms are horrid." Scarlet shuddered as she turned back to her computer screen. I flicked my eyes down at her smooth forearms, as white as unblemished porcelain. I scratched one ankle with the heel of my other foot through my sock and tried to calculate the last time I'd shaved my legs. Three weeks ago? A month? Every time I tried think about the past all I saw were dancing to-do lists swimming in front of my tired eyes.

"And Janine...That one is awful. Where did we find her?"

"Hm..." I murmured, pretending to be engrossed in one particularly urgent item on the list on my clipboard. Scarlet had found her—and hired her—just two days ago.

"She's beastly." Scarlet pronounced the word as if she were spitting something out of her throat. Beastly? Who even used a word like *beastly* outside of Victorian novels?

I cleared my throat at just the right pitch, distracting her without annoying her.

"Oh yes, the list. I know. It's just—" She slammed her palms down on the desk, her keyboard clattering between them like a pile of plastic bones. "I have to do something about this staff!" she shouted. "They're lazy! Rude! Insolent!" She paused and fixed me with glittering eyes.

"Disgusting," she breathed. I swore I saw flames—tiny and blue, but flames nonetheless—shoot faintly out of each of her nostrils.

I gauged my position. Assent was required.

"Yes," I whispered.

"It's time to clean house." Scarlet said.

●●●

Scarlet fired five people, and then she fired five more. Then she hired another ten. I couldn't keep track of the employee files anymore. My desk looked like a dumpster fire. Then, a few days later, Makiah vanished. That morning we got an email from Scarlet that she was gone, for good.

Good Morning Red City Team:

I'm pleased to announce that Makiah has been handed the opportunity of a lifetime. Her novel, which she's been working on diligently for over a year in the Red City writing sessions, has been picked up for a movie deal.

Working on diligently for over a year? Was she kidding? I still worked the sessions every week with Una and I hadn't seen Makiah there once.

Makiah will be dearly missed, of course, but how can we hold her back when she's following her dream? That's what Red City is all about after all, making dreams come true.

That's what Red City was all about? Making dreams come true? I looked over the avalanche of my desk, clipboards and lists scattered everywhere, ruby paperclips glinting at me here and there, like cruel red eyes.

Gag me Scarlet, I thought. That email was really too much.

That morning, I watched everyone arrive and saw clearly from the expressions on their faces how they felt about Scarlet's bullshit story. Jess, Una, Danica, Benjie, Stephanie—they all stared with disbelieving eyes, their lips sewn together like stitched-up wounds. Worthington, William, and Kristy—and all of the new staff—were buoyant and bright-eyed, smiling with an altogether different form of disbelief.

When Scarlet got to the office shortly before noon she ordered Una to vacuum up all the leftover crumbs and ash that decorated Makiah's desk. "We need the desk as soon as possible," she said, as Una boxed up the last of Makiah's belongings. "I've already filled the position."

I knew she hadn't found another partner. That wasn't what she was looking for. Like everything else that Scarlet created, the job was a sham. The position she wanted to fill was a cover for something else that she needed. And now, I knew, what Scarlet always wanted was just another *someone*. It could be anyone as long as they sat in that room with her and agreed with everything she said, something Makiah had never been able to do, and as long as they had a warm body from which she could siphon her energy.

Of course, I wasn't surprised Makiah had left the company. She had been a thorn in Scarlet's side for a while now, just like everyone was, sooner or later. But I was surprised that all emails to her went unanswered. Phone calls went to an automated answering service. Una said she'd driven by her house a couple of times and her car was gone from the driveway, her windows shuttered. Later that week, when it had become obvious that Makiah had vanished entirely and we wouldn't be hearing from her anytime soon, Una threw the box of her things into the trash.

●●●

Every year Danica had a huge birthday party up at Stinson Beach. She said that she and a bunch of her friends rented a cabin right on the ocean, everyone hung out for a whole weekend and did nothing but eat, lie around, and color.

"Color?" I asked. "Like with crayons?"

"No, not crayons," Danica rolled her eyes. "With markers."

I looked at her and raised my eyebrows.

"You should come...you need it," she said, giving me a wicked little grin.

"Oh yeah?" I joked back. "Do I look that bad?"

"Yeah." And suddenly Danica wasn't joking anymore.

"I don't even know where Stinson Beach is," I mumbled, unable to look her in the eye.

"That's ok. I'll write you directions. Stephanie's coming too. You can catch a ride with her."

That's how I ended up speeding erratically around curve after curve of the beautiful Northern Coast of California that weekend with Stephanie Ciccone, a pair of giant black sunglasses poised just under the bridge of her nose, and a fat green bottle of champagne sitting between her legs, a ribbon the color of a lime curling around its neck, a birthday gift for Danica.

On the way to the cabin, Stephanie filled me in on her past, a catalogue of already-finished trauma. Much like my own, I mused, marking the similarities on an inward checklist. Everything was a checklist now. No more simple lists. Now I saw, it was important to check things off. Scarlet was right. It helped you figure things out a lot faster.

"And then there was stepfather number two..." Stephanie drawled, slamming around another curve and knocking me into the passenger side door.

It was the same story I'd told a thousand times heard from someone else's lips: A broken home, early sensitivity leading to adolescent low self-esteem leading to a series of toxic relationships and then...but that was where my story went dark. On the other side of the tunnel lay Scarlet. It appeared Stephanie did not have that same tunnel. Instead of the period of blackness I'd experienced during my Seattle years she'd found a job and managed to keep it to two glasses of wine a night.

But it was all the same in the end. We were both here now in Red City.

We slung around another curve and I slammed back into the door.

When we arrived, Stephanie swung the car into a patch of gravel like it was a skateboard and was almost halfway to the entrance of the cabin before I caught my breath and shakily pulled myself out of the vehicle. I followed her inside, hanging back a bit and looking for Danica.

It wasn't long before we found her. She sat with a few others, all gathered around a black and white poster that stretched across a long wooden table, each of them coloring in parts of it. Lost in their own little worlds, they squinted and sighed happily, picking out different-colored markers to shade in tiny sections. A tall honey-blonde girl in a thin black dress slouched from the table into the kitchen, picking a handful of blueberries out of a creamy white bowl as she passed, a dreamy look in her eyes. Two guys sat in wicker armchairs in the living room, chatting about not much at all.

Leaving Stephanie to find room in the packed fridge for the bottle of champagne, I pulled Danica aside. "What's going on?" I whispered. "Why is everybody so…so…"

"Relaxed?" Danica filled in for me. She smiled and shook her head as if I were an adorably stupid child. "I told you. It's Stinson. Things are different here." She winked at me. "You can get off the hamster wheel."

I looked over her shoulder to the coloring table. Soft light the color of lamb's wool fell gently through the big round window facing the table, sort of like a giant porthole that swept the ocean and the beach into the room without disturbing any of the cabin's inner

250

tranquility. Outside that window, I watched tall pale-green beach grass tap playfully against the glass, blown in waves by the wind. Beyond was sand, and then sea, stretching on without end, living as it did through waves of its own.

Later that afternoon Stephanie and I went for a walk on the beach. Stinson had a strange effect on Stephanie, she didn't quite know what to do with herself. There was no work to be done and in a place like this her designer clothes meant nothing.

"I hate her," she breathed vehemently as we made our way along the edge of the water, leaving dark heel prints in the wet sand behind us.

I didn't have to ask who.

"I know," I agreed.

"She's all lies, and it never stops. The whole thing is lies—" She gritted her teeth in fury. "All of it."

"I know," I said again.

"But why?" Stephanie wheeled to face me.

"I don't know. I…" I tried to explain what I felt and then faltered. I could still see only the barest shadow of the pattern, the truth of why Stephanie and I had ended up with Scarlet. We shared something in common, something more than our similar pasts, something that Scarlet wanted above all other things, but what that was, I couldn't put into words.

"I really don't know, Stephanie. I'm sorry." She deflated like a flat tire.

"Oh, I know you don't. Who does? It's just that it makes me so mad I could rip my own eyes out. I get that she's greedy. I get that she wants to hook all these writers in—convince them it's their art that matters when really it's just their famous name she's after—and then when we have them all, or at least enough, she

251

wants to capitalize on all those names, and sell the site for millions of dollars. Just old-fashioned greed."

As she finished her little speech her entire upper body shook. None of us had laid it all out like that before, so bald and plain, but it was true, every word. Scarlet had tricked us all, including the famous writers, into thinking we were going to change the course of the world, that we were going to help people. All she'd ever wanted was the money, and now she'd mow down anyone who got in her way.

But there was something else to it. Something beyond the money, and that something was the reason that Scarlet kept me around, and Stephanie. And Danica and Una and Benjie. There was something about us *specifically* that was different from other people, and Scarlet wanted that thing.

I shivered in the warm sunlight falling across the beach.

Scarlet Monroe, was that even your real name?

26

A few days later, during the usual Wednesday night session of Red City, Una looked preoccupied. She looked a lot older than she ever had before.

"What's wrong, Una? You look down," said quiet, thoughtful Bernie. He never said much but when he did it was full of insight. Every time he said anything at all I prayed he'd finish his book someday and share his beautiful thoughts with the world. But as far as I knew he'd been working on that book for 25 years. I wasn't sure if I should hold out hope.

"Hm...? Oh—nothing. Nothing." Una answered resolutely. She shook her head and gave him a wan smile. But then unexpectedly she blurted, "It's Makiah. Makiah's gone. A couple weeks ago was—well—it was her last day."

For a moment I thought Una was going to break. Never, not once, had we broken character. We played our parts flawlessly. We were happy. Scarlet was amazing. Red City was going to save the world. We fielded questions like expert witnesses, used to a thousand courtroom trials. We deflected any probing about Scarlet like mirrored glass, it was impossible for anyone to see what was on the other side. We grinned until the corners of our mouths shoved themselves up automatically, lips on Viagra. And always, always our eyes remained shut, guarding what was within.

And so, for a moment, I almost panicked. I thought Una was going to break character and I didn't know what to do. Yeah, I was miserable and in pain, but Scarlet still held every writing dream I'd ever had. I'd put everything into her and Red City. If she went down, the deepest part of me died with her.

But Una didn't break. There was that one moment, that one second of losing her balance on the high wire, and then she caught herself. She launched into the spiel about Makiah's book getting a movie deal and I listened to her story of the bullshit dream coming true and followed the familiar cues as prompted and relaxed. I was back to the pain I knew, familiar ground once again.

As I answered the door that night, I thought about how everything was so different from last spring, only a year ago. Back then I'd waited to show up at Red City all week, it was the high point of my life. It was the hardest thing I'd ever done, even harder than quitting drinking, showing up week after week, pushing so much out of my core, onto the pages in front of me. But it was the best thing I'd ever done, too. I wrote things down that I'd never told another living soul, and when I'd written enough I didn't want to drink so much anymore. The book I was writing was one of the ugliest I'd ever seen, but also the most beautiful, because it was the only good thing I'd ever done in my life. It was the only proof I had that I could stand and fight.

And…there it was.

That was it.

The last piece of the pattern, the clue that knit everything else together. It was a bolt of lightning that electrocuted me, and almost split me in two. Suddenly, I saw it.

I saw it all.

Scarlet fed off creative people, specifically writers. And writers who had already been broken in some way opened their veins without a fight. Me, Una, Stephanie, and all the other writers in the program, we all had different pasts but somewhere along the way, something had broken us, and we'd never been able to heal ourselves.

Then Scarlet came along and collected what she needed.

It made a weird sort of sense, because after all, we weren't using the maximum of our life force anyway. None of us were going anywhere. Deep down, we all knew that. That's why we let her take our energy without a fight, without the sort of resistance a whole human being unleashes when someone tries to steal his personal will, his freedom and his light.

None of us believed in ourselves. And believing we were broken, believing we would never go anywhere ever again, we willingly gave up our essence to the one we believed *was* going somewhere. Scarlet Monroe.

●●●

Scarlet worked for the dark side, but she was also my greatest teacher. She taught me how to practice magic— and I say this literally—when she taught me the power of writing.

Writing is magic. That's something most writers don't talk about, but it's true. Writing is a kind of holy practice, and there's both white and black mixed up in it. You're never really sure what you're going to get. It's my belief that if a writer is able to exorcise most of what's inside and needs to come out, down onto the page, then he's been successful in turning the trick. He's taken the black that lives within him, practiced the magic, and turned it white, where it harmlessly settles, captured and tamed, down onto the page in black on white again.

I took a couple of creative writing classes in college even though I had stopped writing altogether when I was 16. I had this feeling that *not writing* was doing something to me, something that made me want to cry like an injured animal whenever I thought about it. I had to start writing again. But I didn't know how—how to begin, or how to write. So, I made my first mistake and approached it logically. I signed up for two creative writing classes my junior year.

In the first one, we learned all about writing down the details. The professor said the most important thing was to be realistic. He was a small, neat man with black hair and long beautiful fingers that tapered into clean oval fingernails. I looked down at my own hands that first day of class, cut up, as usual, from being drunk so much. I tended to hurt myself accidentally when I was drunk. My nails were dirty, cuticles torn.

I sighed and looked up again at the professor. Details, right. Details were the most important thing.

Over the next few months we wrote short stories and passed them around the room to everyone else. Then we all got a day where everyone else critiqued our stuff. We got very good at picking out the unrealistic details. If a can of soda entered the story, it had better be 12 ounces. Because that's what cans of soda weighed in real life. Not 7 ounces, not 5 ounces, not 16. It had to be 12. The class was very precise about stuff like that—catching obstreperous cans of soda trying to be maverick beverages, wanting to be any weight, any number of fluid ounces imaginable. Before the can of soda—or the writer who'd written the can of soda into being—knew it, our class had nailed that detail to the wall. Another one bit the dust.

I tried to keep all weights, numbers, and brand names out of my stories. It seemed safest. Before this class I'd never even noticed the weight of a can of soda. All my life I'd had a lot of trouble picking up on that sort of thing.

But even when I'd combed through all my details, making sure everything was square, I hated the critiques like nothing else. The whole time I squirmed on the outside and spasmed violently on the inside, wishing I'd just let this not-writing problem kill me at the start.

My stuff was horrible, and that was no surprise. I knew it was horrible. It wasn't at all what I wanted to say. But that was why I'd taken the class in the first place. Because I couldn't write. Once, a long time ago, I had written. And I'd loved it and some of it had been good. But now what came out of me sounded wooden and stilted, like a painfully-recited book report. So now, I sat in that circle of 30 people like I was sitting through torture. Every one of them had a copy of my horrible writing, and went combing through it for details, like they were looking for a body in a field, in complete orderly lines with sniffing dogs, and then afterward the same look flashed over everyone's face—*this is bad, really, really bad. I feel sorry for you. What are you doing here? How did you get into this class?*

By the time my hour was over I had been reduced to a quivering red-faced pile of meat jelly. Sweating and shaking and feeling like I was going to vomit out all my insides. Dirty fingernails the only thing intact.

The entire four months I sat in that torture ring of 30 desks I lived in constant fear that I might lose control of myself, stand up and scream at the circle, waving my cut-up hands. But I didn't have the words to say what it was I wanted to scream. And that was why I was in the fucking class in the first place—because I didn't have the ability to express what I needed to express. *I couldn't write.*

Second semester was worse. This time 30 of us were settled around a super-sized conference table instead of the ring of chairs. My hands with their dirty fingernails left foggy smears of sweat on the laminated wood, even when it wasn't my work being critiqued. I wasn't ever comfortable with that many people facing me at one time.

The professor was a middle-aged woman with close-cropped, beauty-shop gray hair. She wrote stories about horses and ranchers in Wyoming. She never stopped talking about how she was published.

She hated everything I wrote.

Not that I could disagree, I hated it too. It sucked. I knew that. That's why I was there. To learn how to write. But so far—not in this class and not in the first one—had I gotten one word of instruction on how to write. Other than pointers on realistic details and the oft-repeated phrase *write what you know*, I didn't get anything at all but criticism. 30 people telling me my shit sucked. 30 people telling me something I already knew.

Then at the end of the semester, the problem was solved for me. I met with my professor and she told me I should never write again.

"Really?" I asked, numb but still somehow alarmed that I might give the appearance of blinking back tears. My professor sighed and tapped my papers together as if she'd already been tired of the idea of me before I'd even walked through the door.

"It's just not for you. You're just—well, it doesn't appear that you have any...talent...in that area. It would probably be a much more productive use of your time if you went after something you might be really good at." She pursed her lips and blinked rapidly at me.

"But—I mean—couldn't I get any better?" My words ended in a dry squeak. I knew that would be the last sentence out of my mouth in that office. I was incapable of saying anymore.

"No." She pressed her lips together even more tightly and tapped the sheaf of papers on the desk again. "I'm afraid not."

Slowly, I nodded. Slowly, I collected the papers she held out to me. I took them and she rubbed the tips of her thumb and index finger on her smooth pressed jeans, as if she'd smudged them on something greasy. Her silver and turquoise necklace glinted contemptuously at me in the cool spring sunlight.

I slunk out of her office, already crumpling the corner of those ugly pages.

That night I got drunk. Wasted. Through the booze it all seemed like something that had happened to someone else, or to a younger me, a long time ago. Now I could laugh at it.

"Like a fish—she slit me like a fish," I announced to my friends and roommates on the porch of our rundown off-campus house.

"Wow," said one of them. "You okay?"

"Doesn't matter," I smiled and winked. I lifted the bottle in a toast.

"Guts all over the floor," I said.

●●●

I didn't write all senior year. I didn't even try.

After graduation I moved to Seattle. Mostly because a guy I'd met was moving there and I was in love with him, but also because I had nowhere else to go.

The only times I ever tried to write in Seattle, the whole four years I was there, was when I was drunk. I'd look over what I'd written the next morning, sober and in pain, everything too cold and too bright, and I'd crumple it up cringing, just like I had when I walked out of that professor's office.

I never, ever talked about it.

I read everything I could get my hands on, always talking some stranger's ear off about my latest favorite writer at whatever bar I happened to be at, but I never talked about my writing. If someone brought it up I changed the subject. If they kept talking about it I left the table, jumped off the bar stool, walked away. Refused to come back.

When I got to San Francisco I quit drinking, and then I couldn't ignore the pain anymore.

That was the state I was in when I reached Scarlet Monroe.

27

A little over a month after Makiah disappeared, the Red City office was as beat to hell as our staff. Piles of crap lay everywhere, trails of all the things Scarlet had us buy and then forgot about. I couldn't imagine how the janitors found their way around to empty the wastebaskets at night.

Our landlord hated us. All the other tenants were small austere offices made up of well-behaved lawyers. They hated us too. No one could keep track of who worked for Red City, or how many, not even us. People came and went, were hired and fired like we were a suburban strip club for amateurs. Only the really sick and the really sad stayed for long.

I was one of the sad ones. I saw now that Scarlet was a narcissist, and some sort of psychic vampire, and probably a bunch of other unsavory things. I saw that she controlled and manipulated and abused people. I saw every little detail that I had missed in the beginning, everything that I wished I didn't have to see now.

But I still didn't see why I had stuck around for it.

A normal person would have walked out the door months ago. A normal person would have backed away from Scarlet the first time she violated her word, their boundaries, or anything else from the basic code of ethics most people lived by. A normal person would have written her off as crazy, or an asshole, or just plain fucked up, and run for the hills. But I wasn't a normal person, and I knew now that some part of me had wanted this experience all along.

The hardest experiences brought the most wisdom, I had learned that lesson early on. And in the past few years all I had pursued were hard experiences. I'd taken this piece of knowledge and that one, following them like breadcrumbs out of a dark forest. But somewhere along the way I'd lost my perspective. At some point I'd become so focused on finding the next piece, taking the next little bit of wisdom, that I'd lost sight of the big picture. Just as when I had first landed in San Francisco and when I first quit drinking, I felt isolated and trapped. I had no idea how to pick the trail back up again, how to escape the dark forest.

All I knew was that it was up to me if I got out now. And I had to do it all on my own.

●●●

We needed another person, Scarlet announced. Someone to get the office in order. She had created a new position, a legal compliance officer, she said, and then hired someone the next day. His name was Artie Kim.

He was shaped like a box. Kind of like a refrigerator box, I thought. He was probably in his early 30s, wore wire-framed glasses that were boxy too, and was utterly forgettable. If some violent foreign mafia, like the Russians or the Chinese, the guys who torture you in zany and creative ways, had interrogated me on what Artie Kim looked like later, those glasses were possibly the only physical trait about him that I could have produced.

To get the office in order, he started with the files. He took out each file and punched holes into it, and then snapped in metal file clamps. He grunted each time he snapped one down and then sighed.

"What are you doing?" I asked, already exasperated with him.

"Fixing the files," Artie said. "Scarlet likes things neat."

I rolled my eyes and went back to my latest to-do list. My only solace was that I probably wouldn't have long to wait. Scarlet was sure to find some reason to fire Artie next week.

A couple days after that he gave up on the files and tried to work with Scarlet directly, but he met with absolutely no success. Every time he showed up at her office door Scarlet closed it in his face and bolted it quick, citing a last-minute confidential phone meeting she needed to have on legal matters. "But I'm the legal compliance officer," Artie whined to the door. He was whining to himself. Scarlet heard no sound except that of her own voice.

One day, after being shut out again, Artie shuffled down the hall to me. He collapsed in a stray chair parked across from my desk.

"This place is weird," he grumbled.

I lifted an eyebrow but didn't look over. His near proximity was already irritating me. Silently, I ordered him to go away. The seconds ticked by. He didn't move. Finally, I glanced up. He was looking at me.

"What?" I said curtly.

"Well, it is," he said.

"It is what?" I felt like an exhausted mother of toddlers.

"Weird," he repeated. "It's weird around here."

"Yeah, so?" I went back to typing.

"Well, I'm going to get to the bottom of it. Something strange is going on around here and I'm going to find out what it is," he said.

Artie could have found out everything if he'd only looked in the right place. He was too busy trying to make sense of the files in the cabinet when he should have been looking through the files in Scarlet's head. Artie would have found a file on Stephanie with one bright yellow paper inside marked in black capital letters: *Daddy Issues*. He would have seen similar signs in Una's file, in Benjie's file, in mine.

Low self-esteem.

Feels worthless.

BROKEN.

That's why we were all here, because she needed slaves. And we'd signed right up.

He started with interviews.

"If I can just sit everyone down, one-by-one," he said to me, a few days later, "I can get an honest assessment of where everyone's at. And then maybe I can get to the bottom of why this office seems to be so dysfunctional."

I glanced his way and took in the pictures of the Eiffel Tower that covered the walls, approximately 62 boxes of red paperclips stacked on top of the filing cabinet, and the six-foot-tall fake gold trophy shoved into the corner.

"Mm-hm," I murmured. "Maybe."

Over the next week I watched Artie interview most of the staff in the conference room, right across from my desk. He closed the doors so I couldn't hear anything above muffled conversational sounds. But the doors were glass and I saw everything that went on anyway.

First, he interviewed Benjie, whose mouth barely moved for every answer. His face was as stoic as a Chinese general going into battle. I doubted the KGB could crack Benjie, much less someone like Artie Kim.

Then Stephanie was up. She slouched heavily into the chair, her nostrils flared. In the last few months her pouty lips had curdled and hardened. She crossed her arms and waited for Artie to begin. When I heard her voice raised I looked up to see her bang the table with the flat of her hand. Artie leaned in close and I could tell he was pressing her with questions. *What is it? What?* His mouth formed. But all the air and fire, all the sputtering crackle went out of Stephanie as she slumped back into her chair, mutely shaking her head back and forth.

Interview over.

Artie might as well have interviewed Worthington and William together. It was like watching the same reel of film over again. Both of them smiled pleasantly, laughed appropriately, and answered reasonably to everything Artie asked of them. I could tell by the feeling coming through the glass that the sea was on an even keel in these two interviews, everyone agreed with each other and the world was just what it was supposed to be. Both Worthington and William kept their hands busy though, the entire time. Worthington shredded a napkin and William snapped apart his plastic coffee stirrer, breaking each bit into tiny little pieces.

Then it was my turn.

I shut the door and took my seat. The room was hot and there were no windows. Artie Kim glistened in front of me as he rustled through his papers.

"Okay, let's start with the basics," he said. "How long have you worked here?"

"Eight months."

"Did you know Scarlet before that? How did you come to be hired?"

"I was a writer at the Red City sessions over at the mansion. I volunteered and helped Una—still do—and she recommended me for the company."

"Okay." Artie frowned down at his papers. "How do you feel about the company now?"

"Um, great." I smiled wide at him. "Excellent."

"Okay, uh, how would you say other people on the staff feel? About the company? About Scarlet?"

"Great." I repeated. "Excellent."

"What about Stephanie?" Artie looked up at me. I shrugged.

"I don't know. Didn't you just interview her?"

"Yeah...but she—it's like—" Flustered, he set down his papers and looked at me. "It's like she won't tell me anything." He let out a frustrated breath and for a moment—just a flash—I had a vision of him in second grade, crying in an empty classroom because he'd been left out of something. I looked at him and didn't say anything. The corner of his mouth twitched.

"It was good here—at first," I relented. "It got really bad after Makiah left."

Artie instantly perked up. "After Makiah left? Okay, good, that's good. That's exactly what I'm looking for. Why would you say it got bad after Makiah left? What was different?"

"Well, the air just sort of went out of everyone," I tried to explain. "When the company first got started, when I first came on back in October, it was fun. It was really fun. I always thought that Scarlet, Makiah, and

Una were the three parts of the body of the company. Scarlet was the brain, Una was the heart...and Makiah was the soul."

"Okay, okay...brain, heart, soul..." Artie muttered to himself, scribbling down notes.

"Uh, well then—" I stopped.

"Yeah? Go on," Artie urged. I looked around furtively. The room was small and packed with junk, it would have been impossible for anyone to hide in it. But my reflex nowadays was to check under any table I was sitting at, even though I never did when I knew it could be noticed because I also knew how weird it would look.

Lately, I was beginning to understand how Vietnam War vets must feel.

"Are you going to show this to anyone, Artie?" I asked suddenly. "Like Scarlet? Are you going to show her what you find out?"

Artie blinked at me and sighed, dropping his papers again. "Truthfully? No. I doubt she'd even listen to me or care anyway. Honestly I..." He paused as if considering if I could be trusted. I knew the feeling exactly. "Honestly, I don't even know why she hired me," he finally said, and then it all spilled out of him in a flood of choked words. "She won't let me see anything, she keeps me locked out of her office all the time. She hired me to 'fix' this place, whatever that means, to 'get to the bottom of things,' like she said, of why everything in this office is so fucked up, but she won't tell me anything!" I listened and nodded.

"And neither will any of you guys," Artie's lower lip pooched out. Then he glanced my way and—rapidly deciding I might be his only ally—straightened up again.

"I just don't know what the hell's going on. And I have no idea how to find out."

I sighed. I felt sorry for Artie.

But I couldn't tell him the truth, he would never believe me. What would I say? That Scarlet's main energy source was the essence of others? That she was an extreme narcissist who had been slowly consumed by greed and lies and spiritual toxins until now she was just a shell of a person? That she wanted the absolute best and brightest juice to feed her batteries and so she had created a haven where highly creative people would flock to her without her having to work at hunting them down, one by one?

Maybe I could tell him that a long time ago she could have nourished herself on her own inner light, but she chose to become what she was now instead, and she exacted her revenge against her wasted destiny by drinking in the light of every artist she found with any sensitivity at all toward the intangible world behind our everyday reality, until she grew giant and swollen, like a sun which demanded that around it every planet must revolve, while the creative people she fed off grew dimmer, until they were like a dying fire, stars winking out until nothing was left but impenetrable darkness.

And how would I tell Artie I knew all this? That I had poked around in her head and the heads of anyone who came near her for the past eight months and I just *felt* it?

Yeah, right.

"Well, what have you noticed, Artie? Anything... uh... peculiar... about Scarlet?"

"Yeah," he chuckled. "She's a little crazy, I guess."

"But anything else, anything besides being a little crazy," I pressed. "I mean, look around, there's a lot of stuff in this office. Stuff we don't really need. I mean, uh, wouldn't you say she *consumes* a lot more than other people?"

"Sure, maybe. I don't know. I guess." He shrugged and looked uninterested. I decided to change tactics.

"Okay, well, how did the interviews go with everyone else? What did you get from them?"

"I already told you. Nothing," Artie grumbled. "No one will tell me anything."

"No, I mean, not what they said. But what did you *get*. What did you *feel* from them?" I had to watch myself. I sounded feverish, excited.

"Huh? What do you mean?" said Artie.

"I mean, what did you *feel* from each person? The stuff they didn't say but that you knew anyway. The stuff they didn't tell you but that you *felt*."

"Uh, I don't know." Artie looked confused. "Stephanie seemed pissed?"

I blew out a frustrated sigh and leaned back in my chair.

"Okay, let's go back to Scarlet. Don't you think she's kind of different from other people? Don't you think there's something that's just a little bit *off* about her?"

"Well, yeah, of course. I saw that the very day I got here," he said. I instantly brightened. "But she's a writer, what do you expect?" he finished abruptly. "You guys are all pretty much weirdos."

"Yeah," I whispered and lowered my eyes back down to the table. I couldn't even look at his big doughy stupid face anymore. "I guess you're right."

Without waiting for anything else I shoved my chair back and left the room.

Interview over.

●●●

That night I went home and told James about the interview with Artie Kim. He listened to me relay the whole story while he slowly rolled a joint, licking the edges expertly and carefully lighting it. Then he fired it up and passed it to me.

"I don't know what you expected to get out of telling this Artie guy about Scarlet."

"Because I want to know that someone else sees it! Someone else besides me."

"You know that already. You said Danica and Benjie and all of them see it. They know how she is."

"Yeah, but they're like me. I wanted someone normal to see it."

James took the joint from my hand and took a long drag. He had his thinking face on, the face that said he wanted to tell me something but he didn't want to hurt me with the honesty of it.

"What?" I prompted.

"This thing with Scarlet is something that's outside of normal people. They're never going to see what she is. They can't. It's enough that *you* see it. The problem isn't with this Artie guy and what he can or can't see. It's with you. Your thing with Scarlet is your deal."

For no reason at all I suddenly felt very close to crying. I looked down and became absorbed in chewing on my thumbnail.

"So what do I do?"

"I can't tell you what to do," James said, and then he took a long drag and exhaled a cloud of smoke. He stayed silent for a few seconds. "But...I can tell you this...you stopped drinking only to start working for Scarlet. Now she's your drug of choice. And no one can tell you to put it down before you decide you want to."

Abruptly, James squeezed the joint out between his fingers and dropped it in the ashtray sitting between us on the couch. Then, without looking at me, he got up and walked down the hall. A few seconds later I heard the front door latch shut when he left and closed it behind him.

I sat there afterward, staring at the floor and thinking, for a long time.

28

I had imagined what it would be like when I finished my book many times. I had pictured myself crowing the news to the whole office, calling family members I hadn't talked to in years, running breathlessly to Scarlet with the tattered manuscript—half written, half typed—to get her advice on how to proceed and what to do next. But now, sitting with Una and all the others that Wednesday night at the mansion and finally writing *The End*, I thought about those old daydreams and I shuddered to think of Scarlet ever seeing it.

The book was done. It was out of me and the birth was over. For that I could be thankful, and relieved. But what about the next one? It wasn't big yet, but I could feel the seed inside me already. How could I possibly write another one without Red City? And if I left Scarlet, would I ever write again?

Did I have what it took to practice magic on my own?

I honestly didn't know.

The conversation with James had stayed with me. He was right. Scarlet was now my drug of choice and only I could say when I would put her down. I had a feeling that my terror of not being able to write anymore if I gave up Scarlet was akin to my fear of not being able to live anymore if I gave up drinking. Well, I hadn't had a drink in over three years and I was still

272

here, alive and kicking. But, to quit drinking, I'd had to die in a way. I'd had to set fire to what I'd been and rise up out of the ashes of the mess I'd collapsed into on that long-ago day when I was lying flat on that cold bathroom floor.

Then, one morning in early June, I woke up and knew that today was the day. I wondered if this was what it was like to make the decision to commit suicide. I felt like I'd been set free, and also like I couldn't see anything past the next 24 hours. I knew one thing and one thing only, and that one thing drew me forward and gave me strength where I'd had none before.

I was leaving Scarlet.

"I'm going to kill myself today," I said out loud, just to see what the words felt like, and then I shook my head. I had no idea why I had said that.

When I got to the office I was as light as a feather, and simultaneously shook and trembled as if that same feather had been chucked onto an electric fence. Stephanie got there five minutes later.

"I'm quitting today," I said.

"What?" She whirled around, snapping at me. She almost looked like she was going to hit me. I didn't care. I was going to kill myself—or something like that— later.

"Yup. I'm out. Gone. Leaving. I'm telling Scarlet this morning." I liked the way that sounded, the way it echoed in my mind. *Gone. Leaving. I'm telling Scarlet this morning.*

Stephanie stalked off, shaking her head. I knew she didn't believe me.

Didn't matter. I was gone. I was leaving. I was telling Scarlet this morning.

When Scarlet got there, I smiled and greeted her as usual and then held my breath until I saw her walk all the way back to her office. I was nearly frozen to my seat with fear. A carousel of images revolved in my head—October sun, moving day, Benjie under a desk, Stephanie with her huge glasses, Danica kicking her feet up on a chair, Makiah spinning, dancing and laughing, Una spinning, drowning in lists, and then all of us, disintegrating.

I took a deep breath and stood up, forcing my legs and feet to move in the direction of Scarlet's office. I rapped lightly and then walked right in.

"Scarlet, can I talk to you?" I sat down without waiting for her to tell me to have a seat. She turned toward me, red-lipped, open and smiling like a piece of peeled fruit, her skin as white as the rind of an orange. Giving me her full attention for once, I observed ruefully.

"I'm giving my two-weeks' notice."

In a story there's always a few seconds' pause between the character receiving the news and then realizing exactly what the news means. They're always smiling like Scarlet was in that moment, and then the news really sinks in and two or three seconds later their face crumples and they hit the floor, devastated by the attack. It wasn't like that with Scarlet. I would've been lucky to have to deal with only two to three seconds of eerie ghost-faced denial. With Scarlet, it was a full 30 minutes.

Her smile didn't flicker, not for one moment.

First, she talked about money. It was what she always reverted to when things got sticky. But things were going to get more than sticky, I'd already slit both wrists with my last words. Now, slippery warm streams of blood coursed to my elbows. I kept my arms tented on the armrests, my hands clasped in front of me forming a triangle, in order not to disturb the perfect lines of those two red rivers.

After a few minutes, she gave up on the money angle and I knew that meant she'd had enough time to review her mental files on me. One of my secrets that most never knew, Scarlet had known from the start. Money didn't mean anything to me. Like an expert acrobat, she deftly switched gears in mid-air. I couldn't run out on the company, she said. People needed me. She needed me. How could there be any Red City if there wasn't any me?

I refrained from pointing out that I would actually still exist. I just wouldn't exist for her. Instead, I nodded calmly and adjusted my elbows so that the blood stopped dripping into my lap. Now it pooled on the floor in gentle little *plips*, a small rain shower just beneath me.

It was time off I needed, Scarlet went on. A good week of vacation. I was burned out. I'd come back better than ever. I adjusted my elbows again, rubbing my wrists together to make beautiful bright red smears. I smiled tightly and repeated myself.

"I'm leaving Scarlet. You have my two-weeks' notice."

Her 30 minutes were up. Scarlet's face started collapsing at the edges.

Then she started to cry. For real.

I'd never seen Scarlet cry before.

I won't lie, it scared me.

Not scared me like I was worried about her. Scared me like I was worried about *me*. Because now Scarlet was showing real weakness, those weren't

275

crocodile tears. I could feel the real in those tears. And that's why I was scared. Because I doubted she left anyone standing who saw her this way.

And then, I entered the ring as a toreador.

I wore tight black satin pants, a black vest, a white blouse, and a fringed black jacket, my mass of curly hair pushed up under a black cap. I held a red flag, rolled up tight in one fist. In the other I gripped a sword.

The crowd was going wild, but when I entered a hush fell over them. The air was dry, I could taste the dust. It landed on my tongue like dead moth wings, crumbling into dry particles that coated my throat. Somewhere faraway, in between Scarlet's office and this bullfighting ring, somewhere on a different plane, softly a Spanish guitar began to play. An opening strum. A warning. A gate swinging wide, letting other things in.

In the ring, Scarlet appeared.

Half woman, half bull, the female part of her was also a monstrous harpy, draped in blood red lace, with white and yellow mucous running from her eyes. The bull part sweated and shone, glistening along its heaving black flanks. It snorted wildly and then was still.

Sitting across from her in an ordinary San Francisco office on a sunny Wednesday morning, I listened to her begin.

"I can't believe you," she hissed. "Leaving the company? Are you out of your mind? Do you know how much you stand to lose? And where will you go? Onto some other little secretary job?" Her eyes narrowed. "Without me you'll be nowhere. Without me you'll never end up *anywhere*." Her lips pressed together, drained of every drop of ruby-red color. "Without me you'll end up poor. A poor penniless little old lady. You'll end up old, starving on the street, eating cat food—with nothing to show for it. With nothing to show for your *life*." A low growl crawled forth from the back of her throat, an echo of the beast in the ring.

I clasped my hands together tighter. The rivers of blood had clotted and stopped flowing. Faraway, I still heard the Spanish guitar. I looked Scarlet in the eyes. Locking her pupils with my own, I opened myself to her.

Come in Scarlet. Look around. Take what you want...you know you want to.

Outwardly, I smiled at her.

"Be that as it may," I said. "I'm leaving."

She flinched. In the ring, the harpy shivered and reeled, red lace trembled all around. I stepped forward and bowed. I took a small dancing step toward the monster, holding the sword that was too big for me in my left hand. It wobbled crazily to-and-fro but steadied itself when I got within range of the beast, holding itself thrumming and true, like a divining rod.

I plunged forward. The sword glanced off the bull's black, fur-matted shoulder. Blood spurted instantly, soaking a wide swath of red lace. The harpy's face contorted in fury, she shrieked and flew at me.

Scarlet grimaced and leaned forward, clasping her long pale hands in front of her.

"I trusted you, and now you're leaving me?" she pleaded. Her huge eyes filled with tears again, they spilled over the edges, down her face. "I need you here. You can't go," she insisted. "What kind of friend are you? What kind of person are you? To leave me like this. You were the one who was going to help me through. You were the one, the writer with me from the beginning. And now, now it's *inconvenient* for you—" Her eyes narrowed hatefully again. "Now it's too *hard*,

277

so you're out the door. I should have known. I should have known better. I should have known you didn't have it in you to see something like this through."

In the ring I danced closer. I brandished the sword over my head and the beast charged.

Quick as an ember flaring in the dark, I spun and flew and now I was behind the bull. The red flag lay twisted in the dirt. With my free hand I grasped its harpy head, long greasy tendrils of blonde hair wound between my knuckles. Holding on for dear life, I sunk the sword deep into the beast's back, in between its shoulder blades. The crowd clapped rhythmically, in time to the melody of the Spanish guitar.

I was on top of the beast now, and as it shuddered and lurched, I cocked my head. I recognized that song. And then I knew, it had come from me.

Deep down, it was all me. Everything that materialized in front of my eyes or rang in my ears or trembled and pulsed under my fingertips, it all came from me. The illusion I held that any of it came from the outside was a great big joke. I was me sitting there in Scarlet's office trying to out-mindfuck her, and I was Scarlet herself. I was the bull and I was the harpy. The blood running out of me in that office chair, in tracks down my arms and pools at my feet, was the blood of the bull, the essence of the beast, dying slowly, humiliated, in that ring.

The fact is, I hated myself. Scarlet was just an excuse.

The truth is, I knew exactly what I meant when I woke up that morning and said, "I'm going to kill myself today." I was doing it now.

The bull shuddered and rolled and I rocked back and forth on top of it and sweat and blood flew everywhere. Long gooey strings whipped across my eyes, the dust clouded up in suffocating whirlwinds from the stamp of the bull's sharp hooves. I stretched my fingers out before me. They tingled and throbbed, a white halo around each one. And then I saw: Inside of the girl sitting in the office watching herself astride a lurching, heaving beast, lancing it to death, another girl sat in a wide empty room watching them both, listening to it all.

It didn't matter if Scarlet was a half bull, half harpy creature, or an ordinary piece-of-shit person, or not real at all. The reality was me in the ring with a monster who wanted nothing less than my guts hanging from its horns. It didn't matter how I got here, what mattered was that I had to find a way out.

I swung myself off the bull, circling around to the front, panting hard. The beast roared in red hot fury, and then it lunged. At the very last second, I leapt. I plunged the sword deep into the beast's eye.

Then I saw that same empty room, and the girl who stood there all alone. She smiled at me, and nodded her head just once, as if conveying a secret signal that only I would get. And suddenly I knew that even if sometimes the girl sitting in the office across from Scarlet hated herself, the girl sitting in that empty room never did. The girl in that room could be so many different things, a writer, and a lioness, a magician, and sometimes, *sometimes* a demon, too. She could be so many things there was no room for hate.

I pulled my sword out of the beast and then stabbed again, and again, into its brain. The beast went insane. It jolted its head and blood erupted out of its eye like a spewing volcano. I stood back and the world went silent. The crowd was gone. The bull collapsed in slow motion, its crumpled hide a cracked mirror, spattered with blood.

Back at the office I walked out. I left Scarlet sitting at her desk.

I never saw her again. Not in that world, and not in this one.

Epilogue

Two months later I was cleaning out our apartment down by the beach, scrubbing the closets and wiping down the sun-washed walls, listening to Stevie Wonder sing hopeful melancholy songs about yesterday. It was the first week of August and James and I were packing up to head back to Seattle. After that hard conversation about Scarlet we'd had a few more hard conversations until finally he'd come clean with me. He still wanted to leave, he said. He'd never found his place in the City. As for me, well, I couldn't tell what I felt about San Francisco. Maybe I'd loved it and hated it along the way, but after meeting Scarlet it was all about her, all about Red City. I couldn't imagine staying anymore.

The writing sessions at the mansion dissolved soon after I quit. Scarlet abandoned the whole program and all the writers in it. No one had any idea why except for me and Una, and we weren't talking. Benjie quit right after I did and then so did Stephanie. Una and Danica weren't far behind. Kristy got fired for snooping and spying, her initial enthusiasm souring into rancid resentment as Scarlet sucked her, and her rich fiancé, dry. And then she fired William too, just for no reason I guess.

By the time I left for Seattle almost the entire original team was gone from Red City, and no one talked to Scarlet anymore. Not if they could help it.

We all met up for a barbecue about a week before James and I moved. Everyone looked happy, relieved to be free. Excited to start over, and start something new. We grilled hot dogs and played badminton. It was a good afternoon. Sunny and warm on the grass, cool under the trees in Dolores Park, the kind of day that's a really good day in San Francisco. Only once or twice did Scarlet's name even come up. When it did, shadows crossed everyone's face, and we changed the subject fast.

●●●

Months later, back in rainy Seattle again, I opened up a Christmas card from Stephanie. Tastefully chic as expected, I almost put it aside before the lines down at the bottom caught my eye:

I still have dreams sometimes...about her, and about that time. But I'm glad that we went through it all the same, together. Aren't you?

Yes, I was.

And I still am.

About the Author

Lauren Sapala is the author of *Between the Shadow and Lo* and *West Is San Francisco*, the first two books in *The West Coast Trilogy*. She is also the author of nonfiction books for writers, including *The INFJ Writer*, a guide for sensitive intuitive writers. She currently lives in San Francisco. To find out more visit laurensapala.com.